Praise for *All My Puny Sorrows*

#1 NATIONAL BESTSELLER

Winner of the Rogers Writers' Trust Fiction Prize
Finalist for the Scotiabank Giller Prize

A *New York Times Book Review* Editors' Choice
A *Globe and Mail* Best Book
A *Washington Post* Best Book

"In *All My Puny Sorrows* Miriam Toews manages to marry humour and grief so expertly that the most unbearable sadness is tempered by laughter and can therefore be borne. Yoli and Elf, the two sisters at the heart of the novel, are on opposite sides of a question about whether to live or die, but the love and compassion between them never falters. Toews, a dazzling literary alchemist who manages to summon all the joyous and heartbreaking humanity of her characters, has produced a work of astonishing depth. Reading it is an unforgettable experience."

Rogers Writers' Trust Fiction Prize jury citation

"I devoured Miriam Toews's latest novel, *All My Puny Sorrows*. . . . I loved the book. . . . [It] is irresistible. . . . The dialogue is realistic and funny, and somehow, almost magically, Toews gets away with having her characters discuss things like books and art and the meaning of life without seeming pretentious or precious; they're simply smart, decent and confused. . . . Its intelligence, its honesty and, above all, its compassion provide a kind of existential balm—a comfort not unlike the sort you might find by opening a bottle of wine and having a long conversation with (yes, really) a true friend."

Curtis Sittenfeld, *The New York Times*

"Bold, brash and big-hearted. . . . Toews writes from the point of view of Yoli, whose interior monologue reads like a cross between David Foster Wallace and Robin Williams if both were, in fact, a forty-something Mennonite woman with authority issues. She's a smart aleck with heart, a philosopher with a comic's timing."

The Dallas Morning News

"Although Miriam Toews is a practised storyteller and although her books have all been laced with honour and compassion, her new novel may be her best to date. It is a book to rival such earlier triumphs as *A Complicated Kindness* . . . *The Flying Troutmans* . . . and *Irma Voth*. *All My Puny Sorrows* is a variation on Toews's familiar themes, on the Manitoba writer's fine rendering not only of her Mennonite roots but on sibling relationships and on the after-shocks of sorrow. While the book is a nod to grief and frustration, it offers an even stronger nod to the pull of life in spite of its vicis-situdes. In *All My Puny Sorrows* she tackles, headlong and with empathy, the mental breakdown of a beloved sister. The book, poignant, heartbreaking, yet suffused with wit, is a stellar achieve-ment. . . . It is, as well, a superb offering from a writer of rare origi-nality and undisputed talent."   *The London Free Press*

"Rich with a tenderness born of acceptance. To write powerful fiction out of personal events of such magnitude is hard, surely almost unbearably so, but the result is a novel that reaches beyond the limits of itself."   *Financial Times*

"I can think of no precedent for the darkly fizzing tragicomic *jeu d'esprit* that is Miriam Toews's sixth novel. Its compulsive readabil-ity is all the more remarkable since the story issues from such a dark place in the author's heart. . . . As I read, I laughed aloud even as tears rose in my eyes."   Stevie Davies, *The Guardian*

"Miriam Toews's brilliant and desperately sad new novel . . . is one of the most moving and accurate representations of [the] compli-cated situation [of a sibling's suicide that] I have ever read. . . . Which sounds rather grim, when you spell it out. But it isn't, because this is a Miriam Toews novel, which are always delicate braids of sadness and humour. In this sense, and all others, for that matter, *All My Puny Sorrows* is her most accomplished novel yet. It's funny—often really funny. . . . But even in the many moments of lightness, there is a dangerous undercurrent of sadness. . . . The book's great gift [is] its reminder that feeling such things is normal. In a world where everyone has that sorrow in them—which is to say, a world like ours—we find permission to embrace that sadness, rather than a rallying cry to escape it.... In this devastating novel—as in life itself—tenderness and tragedy are, like siblings, forever bound." Jared Bland, *The Globe and Mail*

"Tender and bittersweet novel.... The prose throughout the book is lively and original and moves along at a steady clip.... The novel is a triumph in its depiction of the love the sisters share, as Yoli tries, just as when she was a page turner, to stay a few beats ahead." *Publishers Weekly* (starred review)

"Devastatingly heartbreaking—and hilarious." *Toronto Star*

"While each unhappy family is, as Tolstoy said, unhappy in its own way, the terrain of guilt, frustration, anger, despair and fear looks similar no matter where you stand and Toews has done a fine job of exploring that landscape.... This is a book well worth reading, brave and perceptive. The author set herself a heartbreakingly difficult task, and she should be proud of what she's accomplished." *National Post*

"Miriam Toews's riveting new book ... *All My Puny Sorrows*, is an unforgettable story that mingles laughter with heartbreak, and in the end, asks an impossible question: if the person you love doesn't want to live, is it kinder to let them go?" *Zoomer*

"It is quite rightly being hailed as one of the best, most powerful novels of the year." Matt Galloway, CBC Radio

"[Miriam Toews] is able to take the details of tragedies in her own life, fictionalize them and say something powerful about life, love and art. Her humour and humanity make sensitive issues approachable, taboo topics part of normal conversation.... It's engaging and beautiful—and her characters ... are believable and quirky." *Toronto Star*

"A heartbreaking illustration of unselfish love that transcends illness and death; it is also a critical commentary on the treatment of suicidal patients under psychiatric care. Toews offers a non-judgmental reflection on the choice some make to end their lives and asks, 'How could you understand what another person's suicide means?'"   *Quill & Quire* (starred review)

"It is a remarkable novel . . . funny, sad and, somehow, optimistic."
National Post

"This must have been an impossibly painful book to write but it is nothing but pure pleasure to read."   *Sunday Express*

"A powerful and enthralling book."   *The Independent*

"Unbelievably, despite the dark premise of the book, Toews fills *All My Puny Sorrows* with her trademark humour that springs from the depth and warmth of characters who are often painfully sympathetic."   *Calgary Herald*

"[Miriam Toews] is known for her masterful fusion of humour and heartbreak. Her latest book, *All My Puny Sorrows*, is a joyful story about sisterhood and compassion, but also a sombre meditation on suicidal thoughts."   CBC Radio

"Toews has this brilliant, organic way of relieving the grimness with humour. . . . What might have been a throat-cutting, nihilistic story is countered by Yolandi's voice."   *The Sydney Morning Herald*

"In *All My Puny Sorrows* [Toews] has pulled off another triumph. . . . Yoli's complex emotions are articulated so beautifully that the reader suffers right along with her."   *Prairie books NOW*

"Miriam Toews's latest [novel is] a tender, compassionate balancing act. . . . Like Carol Shields's *The Republic of Love* and Margaret Laurence's Manawaka books, place is so important in *All My Puny Sorrows*, and a genuine love of Winnipeg runs throughout the novel. . . . Toews convincingly distinguishes characters through their unique voices—certainly one of her many writerly strengths. . . . While death weighs heavy throughout *All My Puny Sorrows*, Toews effortlessly diffuses its gravity with humour as she sees fit, elsewhere forcing her characters to deal with grief, loss and depression head-on. . . . The book's title encapsulates both the diminutive, self-deprecating nature of growing up in a somewhat stifling Mennonite town as well as the genuine, solitary internal anguish of mental illness. . . . Given the [recent] dialogue . . . regarding assisted suicide, *All My Puny Sorrows* is timely. Regardless of where people stand on right-to-die issues, this novel tenderly grapples with decisions of the head and the heart with a deft hand. *All My Puny Sorrows* is a novel that balances humour and darkness, and it will stay with readers for a long time."

Winnipeg Free Press

"A story that is both personal and philosophical at the same time. This book is sure to raise discussions about mental illness, life and death, and the right to die. . . . A dark and daring work."

Prairie Daily Herald-Tribune

"In *All My Puny Sorrows*, Toews has found beauty and humour in one of society's most taboo topics, suicide. Her fans will not be disappointed."

Waterloo Region Record

"When you know about the real life of Miriam Toews, you sort of know her fiction because that life is right there on the page. As is the case with her new novel, *All My Puny Sorrows*. [This is a] poignant, powerful and ultimately uplifting book."

Ottawa Citizen

"Toews writes in a cool, deceptively simple voice that moves seamlessly between the memory of past joy and the sometimes surprising banality of present pain. This often edges towards poetry. . . . The novel [Toews] has written—so exquisitely that you'll want to savour every word—reads as if it has been wrenched from her heart."

The Sunday Times

ALL
MY
PUNY
SORROWS

MIRIAM
TOEWS

VINTAGE CANADA

First published in Canada by Vintage Canada, a division of Random House
of Canada Limited, a Penguin Random House Company, in 2015. Originally
published in hardcover in Canada by Alfred A. Knopf Canada, a division
of Penguin Random House Canada, in 2014. Distributed in Canada by
Penguin Random House of Canada Limited, Toronto.

Vintage Canada with colophon is a registered trademark.

www.penguinrandomhouse.ca

Library and Archives Canada Cataloguing in Publication data is available
upon request

ISBN 978-0-7352-7295-8

Text and cover design by Kelly Hill

Cover image: Rauf Aliyev/Shutterstock.com

Printed and bound in the United States of America

2 4 6 8 9 7 5 3 1

Penguin
Random
House

VINTAGE CANADA

For Erik

ONE

OUR HOUSE WAS TAKEN AWAY on the back of a truck one afternoon late in the summer of 1979. My parents and my older sister and I stood in the middle of the street and watched it disappear, a low-slung bungalow made of wood and brick and plaster slowly making its way down First Street, past the A&W and the Deluxe Bowling Lanes and out onto the number twelve highway, where we eventually lost sight of it. I can still see it, said my sister Elfrieda repeatedly, until finally she couldn't. I can still see it. I can still see it. I can still . . . Okay, nope, it's gone, she said.

My father had built it himself back when he had a new bride, both of them barely twenty years old, and a dream. My mother told Elfrieda and me that she and my father were so young and so exploding with energy that on hot evenings, just as soon as my father had finished teaching school for the day and my mother had finished the baking and everything else, they'd go running through the sprinkler in their new front yard, whooping and leaping, completely oblivious to the stares and consternation of their older neighbours, who thought it unbecoming of a newly married Mennonite couple to be cavorting, half dressed, in full view of the entire town. Years later, Elfrieda would describe the scene as my parents' *La Dolce Vita* moment, and the sprinkler as their Trevi Fountain.

Where's it going? I asked my father. We stood in the centre of the road. The house was gone. My father made a visor with his hand to block the sun's glare. I don't know, he said. He didn't want to know. Elfrieda and my mother and I got into our car and waited for my father to join us. He stood looking at emptiness for what seemed like an eternity to me. Elfrieda complained that the backs of her legs were burning up on the hot plastic seat. Finally my mother reached over and honked the horn, only slightly, not enough to startle my father, but to make him turn and look at us.

It was such a hot summer and we had a few days to kill before we could move into our new house, which was similar to our old house but not one that my father had built himself with loving attention to every detail such as a long covered porch to sit in and watch electrical storms while remaining dry, and so my parents decided we should go camping in the Badlands of South Dakota.

We spent the whole time, it seemed, setting everything up and then tearing it all down. My sister, Elfrieda, said it wasn't really life—it was like being in a mental hospital where everyone walked around with the sole purpose of surviving and conserving energy, it was like being in a refugee camp, it was a halfway house for recovering neurotics, it was this and that, she didn't like camping—and our mother said well, honey, it's meant to alter our perception of things. Paris would do that too, said Elf, or LSD, and our mother said c'mon, the point is we're all together, let's cook our wieners.

The propane stove had an oil leak and exploded into four-foot flames and charred the picnic table but while that was happening Elfrieda danced around the fire singing "Seasons in the Sun" by Terry Jacks, a song about a black sheep saying goodbye to everyone because he's dying, and our father swore for the first recorded time (What in the Sam Hills!) and stood close to the fire poised to do something but what, what, and our mother stood there shaking, laughing, unable to speak. I yelled at my family to move away from the fire, but nobody moved an inch as if they had been placed in their positions by a movie director and the fire was only fake and the scene would be ruined if they moved. Then I grabbed the half-empty Rainbow ice cream pail that was sitting on the picnic table and ran across the field to a communal tap and filled the pail with water and ran back and threw the water onto the flames, which leapt higher then, mingled with the scents of vanilla, chocolate and strawberry, towards the branches of an overhanging poplar tree. A branch sparked into fire but only briefly because by then the skies had darkened and suddenly rain and hail began their own swift assault, and we were finally safe, at least from fire.

That evening after the storm had passed and the faulty propane stove had been tossed into a giant cougar-proof garbage cage, my father and my sister decided to attend a lecture on what was once thought to be the extinct black-footed ferret. It was being held in the amphitheatre of the campground, and they said they might stick around for the second lecture as well, which was being given by an expert in astrophysics about the nature of dark matter. What is that? I asked my sister and she said she didn't know but she thought it constituted a large part of the universe. You can't see it, she said, but you can feel its effects, or something. Is it evil? I asked her. She laughed, and I remember perfectly or should I say I have a perfect memory of how she looked standing there in her hot pants and striped halter top with the shadowy eroded Badlands behind her, her head back, way back, her long thin neck and its white leather choker with the blue bead in the centre, her burst of laughter like a volley of warning shots, a challenge to the world to come and get her if it dared. She and my father walked off towards the amphitheatre, my mother calling out to them— make kissing sounds to ward off rattlesnakes!—and while they were gone and learning about invisible forces and extinction, my mother and I stayed beside the tent and played "What Time Is It, Mr. Wolf?" against the last remaining blotches of the setting sun.

On the way home from the campground we were quiet. We had driven for two and a half days in a strange direction that took us away from East Village until finally my father had said well, fair enough, I suppose we ought to return home now, as though he had been trying to work something out and then had simply given up. We sat in the car looking solemnly through open windows at the dark, jagged outcroppings of the great Canadian Shield. Unforgiving, said my father, almost imperceptibly, and when my mother asked him what he had said he pointed at the rock and she nodded, Ah, but without conviction as though she had hoped he'd meant something else, something they could defy, the two of them. What are you thinking about? I whispered to Elf. The wind whipped our hair into a frenzy, hers black, mine yellow. We were in the back seat stretched out lengthwise, our legs entangled, our backs against the doors. Elf was reading *Difficult Loves* by Italo Calvino. If you weren't reading right now what would you be thinking about? I asked again. A revolution, she said. I asked her what she meant and she said I'd see someday, she couldn't tell me now. A secret revolution? I asked her. Then she said in a loud voice so we could all hear her, let's not go back. Nobody responded. The wind blew. Nothing changed.

My father wanted to stop to see ancient Aboriginal ochre paintings on the rock escarpments that hugged Lake Superior. They had endured mysteriously against the harsh elements of sun and water and time. My father stopped the car and we walked down a narrow, rocky path towards the lake. There was a sign that said Danger! and in small letters explained that people had been known to be swept off these rocks by giant rogue waves and that we were responsible for our own safety. We passed several of these signs on our way to the water and with each dire warning the already deep furrow in my father's brow became deeper and deeper until my mother told him Jake, relax, you'll give yourself a stroke.

When we got to the rocky shore we realized that in order to see the "pictographs" one had to inch along slippery, wet granite that plunged several metres into the foamy water and then hang on to a thick rope that was secured with spikes driven into the rock and then lean way back over the lake almost to the point of being horizontal with your hair grazing the water. Well, said my father, we're not about to do that, are we? He read the plaque next to the trail, hoping that its contents would suffice. Ah, he said, the rock researcher who discovered these paintings called them "forgotten dreams." My father looked at my mother then. Did you hear that, Lottie? he asked. Forgotten dreams. He took a small notebook from his pocket and wrote down this detail. But Elf was completely enchanted with the idea of suspending her body on a rope over crashing water and before anybody could stop her she was gone. My parents called to her to come back, to be careful, to use some common sense, to behave herself, to get back now, and I stood silent and wide-eyed, watching in horror what I believed would be the watery end of my intrepid sister. She clung to the rope and gazed at the paintings, we couldn't see them from where we stood, and then she described to us what she was seeing which was mostly images of strange, spiny creatures and other cryptic symbols of a proud, prolific nation.

When we did, finally, all four of us, arrive back alive in our small town that lay just on the far western side of the rocky Shield in the middle of blue and yellow fields, we weren't relieved. We were in our new house now. My father could sit in his lawn chair in the front yard and see, through the trees across the highway to First Street, the empty spot where our old house had been. He hadn't wanted his house to be taken away. It wasn't his idea. But the owner of the car dealership next door wanted the property to expand his parking lot and made all sorts of voluble threats and exerted relentless pressure until finally my father couldn't take it anymore and he buckled one day and sold it to the car dealer for a song, as my mother put it. It's just business, Jake, said the car dealer to my father the next Sunday in church. It's nothing personal. East Village had originated as a godly refuge from the vices of the world but somehow these two, religion and commerce, had become inextricably linked and the wealthier the inhabitants of East Village became the more pious they also became as though religious devotion was believed to be rewarded with the growth of business and the accumulation of money, and the accumulation of money was believed to be blessed by God so that when my father objected to selling his home to the car dealer there was in the air a whiff of accusation, that perhaps by holding out my father wasn't being a good Christian. This was the implication. And above all, my father wanted to be a good Christian. My mother encouraged him to fight, to tell the car dealer to take a hike, and Elfrieda, being older than me and more aware of what was going on, tried to get a petition going amongst the villagers to keep businesses from expanding into people's homes but there was nothing that could be done to assuage my father's persistent guilt and the feeling that he'd be sinning if he were to fight for what was his in the first place. And besides, my father was thought to be an anomaly in East Village, an oddball, a quiet, depressive, studious guy who went for ten-mile walks in the countryside and believed that reading and writing and reason were the tickets to paradise. My mother would fight for him (although only up to a point because she was, after all, a loyal Mennonite wife and didn't want to upset the apple cart of domestic hierarchy) but she was a woman anyway, so very easily overlooked.

Now, in our new house, my mother was restless and dreamy, my father slammed things around in the garage, I spent my days building volcanoes in the backyard or roaming the outskirts of our town, stalking the perimeter like a caged chimp, and Elf began work on "increasing her visibility." She had been inspired by the ochre paintings on the rock, by their impermeability and their mixed message of hope, reverence, defiance and eternal aloneness. She decided she too would make her mark. She came up with a design that incorporated her initials E.V.R. (Elfrieda Von Riesen) and below those the initials A.M.P. Then, like a coiled snake, the letter *S* which covered, underlined *and* dissected the other letters. She showed me what it looked like, on a yellow legal notepad. Hmm, I said, I don't get it. Well, she told me, the initials of my name are obviously the initials of my name and the A.M.P. stands for All My Puny . . . then the big *S* stands for Sorrows which encloses all the other letters. She made a fist with her right hand and punched the open palm of her left hand. She had a habit then of punctuating all her stellar ideas with a punch from herself to herself.

Hmm, well that's . . . How'd you come up with it? I asked her. She told me that she'd gotten it from a poem by Samuel Coleridge who would definitely have been her boyfriend if she'd been born when she should have been born. Or if he had, I said.

She told me she was going to paint her symbol on various natural landmarks around our town.

What natural landmarks? I asked her.

Like the water tower, she said, and fences.

May I make a suggestion? I asked. She looked at me askance. We both knew there was nothing I could offer her in the way of making one's mark in the world—that would be like some acolyte of Jesus saying hey, you managed to feed only five thousand people with one fish and two loaves of bread? Well, check *this* out!—but she was feeling magnanimous just then, the excitement of her achievement, and she nodded enthusiastically.

Don't use your own initials, I said. Because everyone in town will know whose they are and then the fires of hell will raineth down on us, et cetera.

Our little Mennonite town was against overt symbols of hope and individual signature pieces. Our church pastor once accused Elf of luxuriating in the afflictions of her own wanton emotions to which she responded, bowing low with an extravagant sweep of her arm, *mea culpa* m'lord. Back then Elf was always starting campaigns. She conducted a door-to-door survey to see how many people in town would be interested in changing the name of it from East Village to Shangri-La and managed to get over a hundred signatures by telling people the name was from the Bible and meant a place of no pride.

Hmm, maybe, she said. I might just write *AMPS*, with a very large *S*. It'll be more mysterious, she said. More *je ne sais quoi*.

Um . . . precisely.

But don't you love it?

I do, I said. And your boyfriend Samuel Coleridge would be happy about it too.

She made a sudden karate-chop slice through the air and then stared into the distance as though she'd just heard the far-off rattle of enemy fire.

9

Yeah, she said, like objective sadness, which is something else.

Something else than what? I asked her.

Yoli, she said. Than subjective sadness obviously.

Oh, yeah, I said. I mean obviously.

There are still red spray-painted *AMPS*s in East Village today although they are fading. They are fading faster than the hearty Aboriginal ochre pictographs that inspired them.

Elfrieda has a fresh cut just above her left eyebrow. There are seven stitches holding her forehead together. The stitches are black and stiff and the ends poke out of her head like little antennae. I asked her how she got that cut and she told me that she fell in the washroom. Who knows if that's true or false. We are women in our forties now. Much has happened and not happened. Elf said that in order for her to open her packages of pills—the ones given to her by the nurses—she would need a pair of scissors. Fat lie. I told her that I knew she wasn't interested in taking the pills anyway, unless they were of such a volume that their combined effect would make her heart seize, so why would she need a pair of scissors to open the package? Also, she could use her hands to tear it open. But she won't risk injuring her hands.

Elfrieda's a concert pianist. When we were kids she would occasionally let me be her page-turner for the fast pieces that she hadn't memorized. Page turning is a particular art. I had to be just ahead of her in the music and move like a snake when I turned the page so there was no crinkling and no sticking and no thwapping. Her words. She made me practise over and over, her ear two inches from the page, listening. Heard it! she'd say. And I'd have to do it again until she was satisfied that I hadn't made the slightest sound. I liked the idea of being ahead of her in something. I took real pride in creating a seamless passage for her from one page to the next. There's a perfect moment for turning the page and if I was too early or too late Elfrieda would stop playing and howl. The last measure! she'd say. Only at the last measure! Then her arms and head would crash onto the keys and she'd hold her foot on the sustaining pedal so that her suffering would resonate eerily throughout the house.

Shortly after that camping incident and after Elf had gone around town with her red paint, making her mark, the bishop (the alpha Mennonite) came to our house for what he liked to call a visit. Sometimes he referred to himself as a cowboy and these encounters as "mending fences." But in reality it was more of a raid. He showed up on a Saturday in a convoy with his usual posse of elders, each in his own black, hard-topped car (they never carpool because it's not as effective in creating terror when thirteen or fourteen similarly dressed men tumble out of one car) and my father and I watched from the window as they parked in front of our house and got out of their cars and walked slowly towards us, one behind the other, like a tired conga line. My mother was in the kitchen washing dishes. She knew they were coming but was intentionally ignoring them, passing off their "visit" as a minor inconvenience that wouldn't interfere too much with her day. (It was the same bishop who had reprimanded my mother for wearing a wedding dress that was too full and billowy at the bottom. How am I to interpret this excess? he'd asked her.) My sister was somewhere in the house, probably working on her Black Panther look or re-piercing her ears with a potato and rubbing alcohol or staring down demons.

My father went to the door and ushered the men into our home. They all sat down in the living room and looked at the floor or occasionally at each other. My father stood alone with panicky eyes in the middle of the room, surrounded, like the sole remaining survivor of a strange game of dodge ball. My mother *should* have come out of the kitchen immediately, all bustle and warmth, and offered the men coffee or tea and some type of elaborate homemade pastry culled from *The Mennonite Treasury* cookbook, but instead she remained where she was, clanking dishes, whistling with a forced nonchalance, leaving my father to fight alone. They had argued about this before. Jake, she'd said, when they come here tell them it's not a convenient time. They have no right to march into our home willy-nilly. He said he couldn't do it, he just couldn't do it. So my mother had offered to do it and he had begged her not to until she agreed but said she wouldn't bounce around waiting on them hand and foot while they laid out plans for her family's crucifixion. This par-ticular visit was about Elf planning to go to university to study music. She was only fifteen but the authorities had heard from a local snitch that Elf had "expressed an indiscreet longing to leave the community" and they were apoplectically suspicious of higher learning—especially for girls. Public enemy number one for these men was a girl with a book.

She'll get ideas, said one of them to my father in our living room, to which he had no response but to nod in agreement and look longingly towards the kitchen where my mother was

staked out snapping her dishtowel at houseflies and pounding
baby veal into schnitzel. I sat silently beside my father on the
itchy davenport absorbing their "perfume of contempt" as my
mother described it. I heard my mother call my name. I went
into the kitchen and found her sitting on the counter, swinging
her legs and chugging apple juice straight from the plastic jug.
Where's Elf? she asked me. I shrugged. How should I know?
I hopped up on the counter next to her and she passed me
the jug of apple juice. We heard murmuring from the living
room, a combination of English and Plautdietsch, the vaguely
Dutch sounding and unwritten medieval language spoken by all
the old people in East Village. (I'm called "Jacob Von Riesen's
Yolandi" in Plautdietsch and when my mother introduces
herself in Plautdietsch she says "I am of Jacob Von Riesen.")
Then after a minute or two had passed we heard the opening
chords of Rachmaninoff's Prelude in G Minor, Opus 23. Elf
was in the spare bedroom next to the front door where the
piano was, where her life mostly took place in those days. The
men stopped talking. The music got louder. It was Elf's favourite piece, the soundtrack to her secret revolution perhaps.
She'd been working on it for two years non-stop with a teacher
from the conservatory in Winnipeg who drove to our house
twice a week to give her lessons and my parents and I were
familiar with every one of its nuances, its agony, its ecstasy,
its total respect for the importance of the chaotic ramblings
of an interior monologue. Elf had described it to us. Pianos
weren't even allowed in our town technically, too reminiscent
of saloons and speakeasies and unbridled joy, but my parents
snuck it into the house anyway because a doctor in the city had
suggested that Elf be given a "creative outlet" for her energies

to prevent her from becoming "wild" and that word had sinister implications. Wild was the worst thing you could become in a community rigged for compliance. After a few years of having a secret piano, hastily covered with sheets and gunny sacks when the elders came to visit, my parents grew to love Elf's playing and even made occasional requests along the way, like "Moon River" and "When Irish Eyes are Smiling." Eventually the elders did find out that we were harbouring a piano in our house and there was a long discussion about it, of course, and some talk of a three-month or six-month excommunication for my father who offered to take it like a man but when he appeared to go down so willingly they decided to let it go (meting out punishment isn't fun when the victim asks for it) as long as my parents oversaw that Elf was using the piano only as an instrument for the Lord.

My mother began to hum along, her body began to sway. The men in the living room remained silent, as though they were being reprimanded. Elf played louder, then quieter, then louder again. The birds stopped singing and the flies in the kitchen stopped slamming up against the windows. The air was still. She was at the centre of the spinning world. This was the moment Elf took control of her life. It was her debut as an adult woman and, although we didn't know it at the time, her debut also as a world-class pianist. I like to think that in that moment it became clear to the men in the living room that she wouldn't be able to stay, not after the expression of so much passion and tumult, and furthermore that to hold her there she would have to be burned at the stake or buried alive. It was the moment Elf left us. And it was the moment my father lost everything all at once: approval from the elders, his authority as head of the household, and his daughter, who was now free and therefore dangerous.

The opus came to an end and we heard the piano top slam shut over the keys and the piano bench scrape the linoleum floor in the spare bedroom. Elf came into the kitchen and I passed her the jug of apple juice and she drank it all, finished it off and chucked the container into the garbage can. She punched a fist into her palm and said finally nailed it. We three stood in the kitchen while the men in suits filed out of our house in the order they had filed in and we heard the front door close softly and the men's car engines start and the cars pull away from the curb and disappear. We waited for my father to join us in the kitchen but he had gone to his study. I'm still not sure whether or not Elf knew that the men were in the living room or even that the bishop and the elders had paid us a visit at all, or if it was just a coincidence that she chose that exact time to play the Rachmaninoff piece to fierce perfection.

But shortly after the visit from the bishop and his men Elf made a painting and put it in an old frame she'd found in the basement. She hung it in the middle of our living room wall right above the scratchy couch. It was a quote. It read:

"I know of a certainty, that a proud, haughty, avaricious, selfish, unchaste, lecherous, wrangling, envious, disobedient, idolatrous, false, lying, unfaithful, thievish, defaming, backbiting, blood-thirsty, unmerciful and revengeful man, whosoever he may be, is no Christian, even if he was baptized one hundred times and attended the Lord's Supper daily."

—Menno Simons.

Okay, but Elfie? said my mom.

No, said Elfie. It's staying right there. It's the words of Menno Simons! Aren't we supposed to be following them?

Elfie's new artwork hung in our living room for about a week until my father asked her: Well, kiddo, have you made your point? I'd really love to put mom's embroidered steamship back in that spot. And by then her righteous indignation had blown over like so many of her wild personal storms.

TWO

ELFRIEDA DOESN'T DO INTERVIEWS. One time she let me interview her for my cheesy class newspaper but that's it. I was eleven and she was leaving home again, this time for good. She was on her way to Norway for a recital and to study with an old man she referred to as the Wizard of Oslo. She was seventeen. She'd finished high school early, at Christmas. She'd got honours everything and six scholarships to study the piano and a prize from the Governor General of Canada for highest marks which sent the elders into paroxysms of rage and fear. One day at dinner, a few weeks before she was due to leave,

Elf casually mentioned that while she was in Europe she might as well go to Russia to explore her roots and my father almost stopped breathing. You will not! he said. Yeah, I might, said Elf. Why not?

My grandparents originally came from a tiny Mennonite village in Siberia in 1917, the year of the Bolshevik revolution. Terrible things happened to them there in the land of blood. Any hint of the place, the slightest mention of anything Russian, and my parents would start clawing the air.

Plautdietsch was the language of shame. Mennonites had learned to remain silent, to shoulder their pain. My grandfather's parents were murdered in a field beside their barn but their son, my father's father, survived by burying himself in a pile of manure. Then, a few days later, he was put in a cattle car and taken with thousands of other Mennonites to Moscow and from there sent off to Canada. When Elf was born, he told my parents: Don't teach your kids Plautdietsch if you want them to survive. When my mother went to university to become a therapist she learned that suffering, even though it may have happened a long time ago, is something that is passed from one generation to the next to the next, like flexibility or grace or dyslexia. My grandfather had big green eyes, and dimly lit scenes of slaughter, blood on snow, played out behind them all the time, even when he smiled.

Absurdities and lies, Yoli, said my mother. The worst thing you can do in life is be a bully.

My interview happened in the car on the way to the airport in Winnipeg. As usual, our parents were in the front seat, my dad was driving, and Elf and I were in the back. You're never coming back, are you? I whispered to her. She told me that was the stupidest thing she'd ever heard. We looked at fields and snow. She was wearing her white leather choker with the blue bead and an army jacket. We were driving over black ice.

Is that your question for the interview? she asked me.

Yeah, I said.

Yoli, she said. You should have prepared other questions.

Okay, I said, what's so hot about playing the piano?

She told me that the most important thing was to establish the tenderness right off the bat, or at least close to the top of the piece, just a hint of it, a whisper, but a deep whisper because the tension will mount, the excitement and the drama will build—I was writing it down as fast as I could—and when the action rises the audience might remember the earlier moment of tenderness, and remembering will make them long to return to infancy, to safety, to pure love, then you might move away from that, put the violence and agony of life into every note, building, building still, until there is an important decision to make: return to tenderness, even briefly, glancingly, or continue on with the truth, the violence, the pain, the tragedy, to the very end.

Okay, I said, that should do it, well thanks for sort of answering my question, Weirdo.

Both choices are valid, she said. It depends where you want to leave your audience, happy and content, innocent again, like babies, or wild and restless and yearning for something they've barely known. Both are good.

Got it, thanks, I said. Who's gonna be your page-turner now? Some Norwegian?

She took a book out of her army backpack—she was into military-issued everything like Patty Hearst and Che Guevara—and chucked it into my lap. When you're finished with that horse series, she said, your real life starts here. She tapped the book with her finger. She was referring to my obsession with *The Black Stallion*. Also, I had recently started horseback-riding lessons with my friend Julie and was on my way to becoming third-best barrel racer in the provincial Under Thirteen category, which contained only three members.

In a way I'm relieved that you're going to Oslo, I said.

It was either that or hitchhike barefoot to the west coast, she said.

The roads are icy, said my father. See that semi in the ditch? He wanted to change the subject. Elf's hitchhiking plan was a crazy idea he had buried. My mother had laughed and said hitch-hiking barefoot to the west coast is a reasonable idea, maybe, but not in January. She didn't believe in burying anything.

What is this? I was looking at the book Elf had given me.

Oh my god, Yolandi, she said. When you see the words "collected poems" on the cover of a book what do you think is inside the book?

Can you drive any faster? I asked my father. We don't want her to miss her plane. I was trying to act tough but I truly believed that I might die from heartbreak when my sister went away, to the extent that I had written a secret will, bequeath-ing my skateboard to Julie and my lifeless body to Elf, which I hoped would make her feel really guilty for leaving me to die alone. I had nothing else but my skateboard and my body to give to people but I attached a note of gratitude to my parents and a drawing of a motorcycle with the New Hampshire state motto: Live Free or Die.

And by the way, I said, I'm not reading those horse books anymore.

What are you reading then? my sister asked.

Adorno, I said.

She laughed. Oh, because you saw that I'm reading him? she asked.

Don't say "reading him," I said. You think you're so big.

Yoli, said Elf, don't say "you think you're so big." That's what everyone around here says when somebody purports to know about something. I could say tomorrow is Thursday and you'd say "oh, you think you're so big." Don't say it anymore. It's déclassé.

Our mother said, Elf, c'mon, enough advice on how to live like a dilettante. You'll be gone soon. We should be using this precious time to have fun! Elf sank back and explained that she was just trying to help me survive the world outside our hamlet. And also, she added, *dilettante* is the exact wrong word for you to have used in this situation. Okay, Elf, said my mom, but let's just speak English or sing or something like that. She'd had fifteen brothers and sisters so she knew about keeping the peace. Our father suggested we play I Spy.

Oh my god, Elf whispered into my ear. Are we six? Don't ever tell them I've had three different types of sex already, okay?

What do you mean, *three*?

Elf told me that after the poet Shelley drowned, his body was cremated right there on the beach but his heart didn't burn so his wife Mary kept it in a small silk bag in her desk. I asked her if it wouldn't have rotted and begun to smell but she said no, it had calcified, like a skull, and that really it was only the remains of his heart. I told her that I would do that for her too, keep her heart with me in my desk or in my gym bag or my pencil case, somewhere very safe, and she hugged me and laughed and told me I was sweet but that really it was a romantic thing for lovers to do.

Before she disappeared behind the frosted glass doors of airport security Elf and I had played one last game of Concentration and in the midst of all that leg slapping and hand clapping she said, Swivelhead (that was her nickname for me because I was very often looking around for solid clues to what was going on and never finding them) you better write me letters. I said yeah, I will, but they'll be boring. Nothing happens in my life. Nothing has to happen, she said, for it to be life. Well, I said, I'll try. No, Yoli, said Elf, better than that. She yanked on my arms. Please. You have to. I'm counting on you.

They were calling her flight and she released her grip, she was pulling away from me. Our parents stood stricken but acting brave, smiling big and dabbing at their eyes with tissues. So I said, I will, okay? Take a chill pill. All right, said Elf, I'm outta here . . . Also, don't say "chill pill." *Adieu, Arrividerci!* I know she was crying but she turned her head away at the very last second so I wouldn't notice and I thought I should include that in a letter to her under Observations of Things Meant to be Hidden. On the way home from the airport my mother drove and my father lay in the back seat with his eyes closed. I sat next to my mother in the front. It was snowing. We couldn't see anything except snowflakes in the headlights and a tiny bit of the road ahead. I thought the snowflakes looked like notes and signatures falling and swirling over the little stave of road we could see in front of us, one measure of music. My mother told me she would tap the brake slightly to see if it was still icy and before I could stop her we had spun out of control and landed upside down in the ditch.

———

Janice comes into the hospital room to talk with us. We know Janice from the other times. She's a psych nurse and during her time off she loves to tango because, she says, tango is about the embrace. She wears light pink track suits. She has a small furry stuffed animal chained to her belt loop. It's supposed to be something that makes the patients relax and smile. She comes into the room and gives Elf a hug and tells her that she's happy to see her but unhappy to see her here. Again.

I know, I know, says Elf. I'm sorry. She rakes her fingers through her hair and sighs.

My cellphone buzzes and I reach into my bag to turn it off.

Hey, says Janice. It's not about being sorry. Right? We don't say sorry. You haven't done anything bad or wrong. You've acted on a feeling. Right? You wanted to end your suffering. That's understandable and we want to help you end your suffering in different ways. In healthy ways. Right, Elfrieda? Constructive ways? We'll start again. She sits down on one of the orange chairs.

Okay, says Elf. Okay.

She's cringing because she feels like an idiot. These words, Janice's tone. But Janice is Mother Teresa compared with the other psych nurses and Elf is lucky not to have been thrown naked into the empty concrete room with the drain in the middle of the floor.

How are you, Yolandi? says Janice. She gives me a hug too. Good, fine, I say. Thank you. Worried. A bit.

Of course you are, says Janice. She looks pointedly at Elf who turns away.

Elfrieda? Janice really wants Elf to look at her. I clear my throat and Elf sighs and twists her head around slowly to make eye contact with Janice. Elf is deeply pissed off, mostly with herself for botching things, but she's trying really hard to be polite because "good form" is her mantra. It used to be "love" but the more she said it the more it sounded like something doomed, like a wax effigy, and that had made her panic and weep. Then stop saying it! I'd tell her. I know, Yoli, I know, she'd say, but still. Still what? I'd ask. Elf explained to me that she was exactly like this guy she'd read about in the paper, a guy who was blind from birth and then at the age of forty-something he had a corneal operation and could suddenly see, and although he was told that life would be amazing for him then, after the operation it was awful. The world depressed him, its flaws, its duplicity, its rot and grime and sadness, everything hideous now made manifest, everything drab and flaking. He sank into a depression and quickly died. That's me! Elf had said. I reminded her that she had her sight, she could see, she'd always been able to see but she told me she'd never adjusted to the light, she'd just never developed a tolerance for the world, her inoculation hadn't taken. Reality was a rusty leg trap. Look, I said, then just stop saying "love" over and over, okay? Just don't do it. But Yoli, you don't understand, she said. You can't understand. Which wasn't true, entirely. I understand that if you say a certain word over and over and it begins to make you feel bad then you should goddamn stop saying that word. Why do we keep having these exasperating conversations? I would ask. They're not conversations! she'd say. We're working things out. We're working things *out*.

Elfreida, Janice says, my brother saw you playing in Los Angeles and said he wept for two hours afterwards. Elf doesn't say anything. Gratitude or something like that is expected of her but she doesn't budge. The three of us are quiet in the room. Elf is examining the hem of her blanket and smoothing out its creases. I'm imagining two hours of weeping. Janice finally clears her throat loudly and both Elf and I are startled.

Do you have concerts coming up? asks Janice.

Yes, ostensibly . . . Elf says. She's whispering. I'm afraid she'll stop talking altogether.

She has a five-city tour actually, I say. Starting . . . when, Elf? Elf shrugs. Soon, I say, in a few weeks. Mozart. Elf. Is it Mozart?

Sometimes my sister stops talking. Our father did it too, once for a whole year. Then, after watching a vaudeville show in Moose Jaw, Saskatchewan, he started talking again as though he had never stopped. At first it scared me when Elf did it until I realized that her mood hadn't really changed, she'd just gone silent. She'd write notes to us.

But when Elf plays concerts she talks a lot afterwards about mundane things, earthly things, every little thing, she yabbers away talking for hours and hours like she's trying to ground herself, to stay, to come back from wherever it was the music took her.

Piano scales were the musical soundtrack to my youth. I could do anything to Elf when she practised her scales and she wouldn't notice. I could put raisins on the keys and she'd flick them off unperturbed as her fingers zoomed up and down the entire length of the piano. I could lie on top of the piano in a sexy pose and sing I am a V-A-M-P like Cher and she wouldn't miss a single note, her eyes never left the keys except when they

25

closed in rapturous ecstasy for a second or two and then the pace of the music would change and Elf would open her eyes wide and fling herself at the piano like a leopard onto a snake, a savage assault as though the piano were both her lover and most mortal enemy.

She did eventually come home again from Norway and a bunch of other places. She moved back home with my parents and stayed in bed and cried for hours at a time or stared at the wall. There were dark circles around her eyes and she was sombre, listless and then strangely exuberant and then despondent again. By that time I had moved away from East Village to Winnipeg and had two kids with two different guys . . . as a type of social experiment. Just kidding. As a type of social failure. And I was scrambling around trying to make money and to study and master (and fail at mastering) the art of being an adult.

I'd visit my parents and Elf, with my little kids in tow, Will was four and Nora was a baby, and I'd lie in the bed next to Elf and we'd look at each other and smile and hold each other while the kids crawled around on top of us. She wrote letters to me during that time. Long, funny letters about death, about strength, about Virginia Woolf and Sylvia Plath and the intricacy of despair on pink stationery in coloured felt-tipped markers. Then, after a few months, she slowly got her health back. She started playing the piano again and doing a few concerts and then she met a guy, Nic, who adored her and now they live together in Winnipeg, which means Muddy Waters, number one on the Exotic City Index—the coldest city in the world and yet the hottest, the farthest from the sun and yet the brightest, where two fierce, wild rivers meet to join forces and conquer man. Nic took piano lessons from Elf for a few months. That's how they met, but Nic admitted later that the only reason he took piano lessons from her was so that he could sit next to her on the little bench and have her gently place his fingers on the keys. He even bought her a new piano bench, although as soon as she saw it she commanded that he rip off its soft padding—What the heck is *that* doing there?—as if playing music is about comfort.

Nic loves Elf's odd requests, each one is like a holiday for him. Nic is a very precise guy. He believes in textbooks and manuals and recipes and hat and collar sizes. He can't stand the wonky looseness of "small," "medium" or "large." When Elf suggested he learn to play *around* the notes he almost lost his mind to bliss and the craziness of it all. And he's not a Mennonite, which is important—in a man—for Elf. Mennonite men have wasted too much of her time already, trying to harvest her soul and shackle her to shame. Nic is a medical scientist. I think he's trying to rid the world of stomach parasites but I'm not exactly sure. My mother tells her friends he's working on a cure for diarrhea. She's skeptical of cures. And Nic, she'll say, I *do* see dead people. And I converse with them. They're as alive to me as the living, perhaps more so. How does "your science" explain that? Nic and Elf always talk about living in Paris because there's some kind of lab there where he could work and because they both love to speak French and argue politics and wear scarves all year round and console themselves with old-world beauty, but so far they're still here in Muddy Waters, the Paris of the Northwest Passage.

Elf has beautiful hands, not ravaged by time or sun because she doesn't go out much. But the hospital has taken her rings. I don't know why. I guess you could choke on a ring if you decided to swallow it, or pound it against your head for several weeks non-stop until you did some damage. You could throw it into a fast river and dive for it.

How are you feeling right now? Janice is saying.

If I squint across the room at Elf I can change her eyes into dark forests and her lashes into tangled branches. Her green eyes are replicas of my father's, spooky and beautiful and unprotected from the raw bloodiness of the world.

Fine. She smiles feebly. Dick Riculous.

I'm sorry? says Janice.

She's quoting our mother, I say. She says things like that. Chuck you Farley. You know. She means ridiculous.

Elfrieda, you're not being ridiculed, okay? says Janice. Right? Yoli, are you ridiculing Elf?

No, I say, not at all.

And neither am I, says Janice. Okay?

Neither am I, says a voice unexpectedly from behind the curtain, her roommate.

Janice smiles patiently. Thanks, Melanie, she calls out.

Any time, says Melanie.

So we can safely say you are not ridiculous, Elfrieda.

Well, it's called self-ridicule, whispers Elf, but so quietly that Janice doesn't hear it.

Was it good seeing Nic and your mother? asks Janice. Elf nods obediently. And isn't it great to see Yolandi? You must miss her now that she's not in Winnipeg.

Janice turns to look at me with some kind of look, I don't know, and I feel the need to apologize. Nobody moves away from Winnipeg, especially to Toronto, and escapes condemnation. It's like the opposite of the Welcome Wagon. It's like leaving the Crips for the Bloods. Elf rolls her eyes and touches the stitches in her head with her finger, one after the other. She's counting them. Some clanking sounds are emanating from the hallway and a man is moaning. I want you to know that you're safe here, Elfrieda, says Janice. Elf nods and looks longingly at the slab of Plexiglas next to her bed, the window.

How about if I give the two of you some time to your-selves, says Janice.

She leaves and I smile at Elf and she says come here, Swiv, and I get up and walk two steps to her bed and I sit on the edge of it and flop on top of her and she smoothes my hair and sighs under the weight of my head. I go back and sit on my orange vinyl visitor chair and blow my nose and stare at her.

Yolandi, she says, I can't do it.

I know, I say. You've made that point.

I can't do the tour. There's no way I can do the tour.

I know, I say. It doesn't matter. Don't worry. None of it matters.

I really can't do the tour, she says.

You don't have to do anything, I reassure her again. Claudio will understand.

No, says Elf, he'll be upset.

Only because you're not . . . because you're here . . . He'll just want you to feel better. He knows about all this stuff. Friend first, agent second, that's what he always says, right? He's weath-ered your storms before, Elfie, he'll do it again.

And so will Maurice be angry, says Elf, he'll go crazy. He's been planning this for years.

Who's Maurice . . . ?

And remember Andras, the guy you met in Stockholm . . . when you saw me play?

Yeah, so?

I just can't do this tour, Yolandi, says Elf. He's coming all the way from Jerusalem.

Who is?

Isaak. And a bunch of other people.

So what? I say. All those guys will understand and if they don't it doesn't matter. It's not your fault. Remember what mom used to say? "Shred the guilt." Remember?

She asks me what that horrible sound is and I tell her I think it's dishes falling onto the concrete floor in the corridor, but she asks me if somebody is being shackled out there in the hallway and I say no, of course not and she begins to tell me that it happens, she's seen it, that she's terrified, have I heard of Bedlam, and she doesn't want to let anybody down. She says how sorry she is and I tell her nobody is angry, we want her to be okay, to live. She asks me how Will and Nora are, my kids, and I tell her fine, fine, and she covers her face with her hands. I tell her that she and I could mock life together, it's a joke anyway, agreed, okay? Agreed! But we don't have to die. We'll be soldiers together. We'll be like conjoined twins. All the time, even when we're in different cities. I'm desperate for words.

A chaplain comes into the room and asks Elfrieda if she is Elfrieda Von Riesen and Elf says no. The chaplain peers at her in wonderment and then tells me he could have sworn that Elf was Elfrieda Von Riesen, the pianist.

No, I say. Wrong person. The chaplain apologizes for bothering us and leaves.

Who would do that? I ask.

Do what? says Elf.

Just ask another person in a hospital if she's who they think she is. Aren't chaplains supposed to be more discreet?

I don't know, says Elf. It's normal.

I don't think it is, I say. I think it's totally unprofessional.

Things are always bad for you if they're unprofessional. You always say oh, that's so unprofessional as though there's some definition of professional that's also a moral imperative for how to behave. I don't even know what professional is anymore.

You know what I mean, I say.

Just stop lying to me about what life is, Elf says.

Fine, Elf, I'll stop lying to you if you stop trying to kill yourself.

Then Elf tells me that she has a glass piano inside her. She's terrified that it will break. She can't let it break. She tells me that it's squeezed right up against the lower right side of her stomach, that sometimes she can feel the hard edges of it pushing at her skin, that she's afraid it will push through and she'll bleed to death. But mostly she's terrified that it will break inside her. I ask her what kind of piano it is and she tells me that it's an old upright Heintzman that used to be a player piano but that the player mechanism has been removed and the whole thing has been turned into glass, even the keys. Everything. When she hears bottles being thrown into the back of a garbage truck or wind chimes or even a certain type of bird singing she immediately thinks it's the piano breaking.

A child laughed this morning, she says, a little girl here visiting her father, but I didn't know it was laughter, I thought it was the sound of glass shattering and I clutched my stomach thinking oh no, this is it.

I nod and smile and tell her that I'd be terrified of breakage too if I had a glass piano inside me.

So you understand? she asks.

I do, I say. I honestly, honestly do. I mean, what would happen if it broke?

Thank you, Yoli.

Hey, are you hungry? I ask her. Is there anything I can do for you?

She smiles, no, nothing.

THREE

ELFRIEDA IS SO THIN, her face so pale, that when she opens her eyes it is like a surprise attack, like one of those air raids that turns night to day. I ask her if she remembers that time she and I sang a really slow aching version of "Wild Horses" for a group of elderly Mennonite nursing home residents. Our mother had asked us to participate in the seventy-fifth wedding celebration of the town's oldest married couple and we had thought the song was killer cool and entirely appropriate for the occasion. Elf played it on the piano and I sat next to her and we both sang our hearts out to our bewildered audience who sat around in wheelchairs or stood leaning hard on canes and walkers.

I thought the memory would make her laugh but it makes her ask me to leave. She realized before I even did that I was spinning out this anecdote because it represented something else and more than the sum of its parts. Yoli, she says, I know what you're doing.

I promise I won't talk about the past if it causes her pain. I won't talk about anything if she doesn't want me to, as long as I can stay.

Please go now, she says.

I tell her I could read to her the way she used to read to me when I was sick. She would read Shelley and Blake, her poet lovers she called them, mimicking their voices, male and British, clearing her throat . . . "Stanzas Written in Dejection, near Naples." *The sun is warm, the sky is clear, the waves are dancing fast and bright.* How about I sing? Or I could dance. Like a wave. I could whistle. I could do impersonations. I could stand on my head. I could read Heidegger's *Being and Time* to her. In German. Anything! What's that thing again, that word?

Dasein, whispers Elf. She half smiles. Being there.

Yeah, that! Please! I sit down and then stand up again. C'mon, I say. You like books with *being* in the title, don't you? Please. I sit down next to her again and then put my head on her stomach. What was that quote on your wall? I ask.

What quote? she says.

On your bedroom wall, when we were kids.

You put the fist in pacifist?

No, no . . . that other one, about time. Something about the horizon of being.

Be careful, she says.

The piano?

Yes. She puts her hands gently on my head and keeps them there as though she is resting them on a pregnant belly. I can feel their heat. I hear her stomach rumble. I smell the Ivory Snow scent of her T-shirt that she has on inside out. She massages my temples and then pushes me off her. She says she doesn't remember the quote. She tells me that time is a force and we must allow it to do its work, must respect its power. I consider arguing that she herself is disrespecting that power by attempting to sidestep it but then realize she might already have made note of that and is talking to herself as much as she is talking to me. There is nothing to add. I hear her whisper yet another apology and I begin to hum a Beatles song about love and need.

Remember Caitlin Thomas? I say.

Elf says nothing.

And remember how she barged drunkenly into Dylan's hospital room at St. Vincent's in New York City where he was dying of alcohol poisoning and threw herself on top of his beleaguered body begging him to stay, goading him to fight, to be a man, to love her, to speak, to stand, to stop dying for god's sake. My sister says she appreciates being compared to Dylan Thomas but apologizes and asks me again to leave, she needs to think. I tell her all right, I'll leave but I'll be back tomorrow. She says isn't it funny how every second, every minute, every day, month, year, is accounted for, capable of being named—when time, or life, is so unwieldy, so intangible and slippery? This makes her feel compassion towards the people who invented the concept of "telling time." How hopeful, she says. How beautifully futile. How perfectly human.

But Elf, I say, just because you have no use for the systems that help us measure our lives doesn't mean that our lives don't need measuring.

Maybe, she says, but not according to some bourgeois notion of time compartments. That's a fascistic arrangement of a thing—time—that's naturally and importantly outside the realm of categorization or even definition.

Actually, I am okay with leaving right now after all, I say. Sorry to have to leave class early, Professor Pinhead, but I'm running out of time on my meter. I bought two hours and I think they're up. Speaking of time.

I knew I could get you to leave, she says. And we hug and I begin to tell her that I love her before words become impossible and we simply breathe together in each other's arms for a minute, before I go. Before I have to be elsewhere.

I check my messages while I descend the hospital stairs two by two to the exit. A text from Nora, my fourteen-year-old: *How's Elf??????????????????????? Will broke the front door.* And another from Will, my eighteen-year-old son who's in his first year at NYU but whom I've commandeered to stay with Nora for a few days in Toronto while I am back in Muddy Waters: *Nora told me her curfew is four am. True? Give Elf a hug from me! The shower drain is plugged from N's hair.* And a text from my oldest friend, Julie, who is expecting to see me later that evening: *Red or white? Give my love to Elfie. xo*

The last time my sister tried to kill herself was by slowly evaporating into space. It was a furtive attempt to disappear by starving herself to death. My mom phoned me in Toronto and told me that Elf wasn't eating and she was begging her and Nic not to call a doctor. They were desperate. Would I come? I went directly from the airport to Elf's bedroom and knelt by her side. She asked me what I was doing there. I told her I was there to call a doctor. Mom might have made a promise not to call a doctor but I hadn't. Our mother stayed in the dining room. She had her back to us. She couldn't support one daughter's idea over the other daughter's idea, like any good mother, so she removed herself from the proceedings. I'm calling, I said. I'm sorry. Elf pleaded with me not to. She implored me. She put her hands together in supplication and begged. She promised to eat. Our mother stayed sitting at the dining room table. I told Elf the ambulance was on its way. The screen door was open and we could smell the lilacs. I won't go, said Elf. You have to, I said. She called to our mom. Please tell her I won't go. Our mother said nothing. She didn't turn around. Please, said Elf. Please! She used what little strength she had left to give me the finger as the paramedics loaded her into the back of the ambulance.

That was the first time I met Janice. I had been standing next to Elf's stretcher in the emergency room. Her broken backpack hung on the IV unit next to her. I was sliding my hands back and forth on the steel railing that held her in and I was crying. Elf took my hand, weakly, like an old dying person, and looked deeply into my eyes.

Yoli, she said, I hate you.

I bent to kiss her and whispered that I knew that, I was aware of it. I hate you too, I said.

It was the first time that we had sort of articulated our major problem. She wanted to die and I wanted her to live and we were enemies who loved each other. We held each other tenderly, awkwardly, because she was in a bed attached to things.

Janice—she had that furry creature hanging from her belt loop even then—tapped me on the shoulder and asked if she could talk to me for a minute. I told Elf I'd be right back and Janice and I walked over to a little beige family room and she passed me a box of Kleenex and told me that I had done the right thing by calling the ambulance and that Elf didn't really hate me. That feeling can be broken down, she said. Right? Let's consider the components. She hates that you saved her life. I know, I said, but thanks. Janice hugged me. A close, hard hug from a stranger is a potent thing. She left me alone in the beige room. I tore away at my fingernails and cuticles until I bled.

When I went back to Elf she was still in Emergency. She told me she'd just overheard a great line, just great. What was it? I asked her. She quoted: We are very much amazed at what little intelligence there is to be found in Ms. Von R. Who said that? I asked her. She pointed at a doctor who was scribbling something at the circular desk in the middle of all the dying people. He was dressed like a ten-year-old in skater shorts and an oversized T-shirt like he'd just come from an audition for *Degrassi High*. Who the hell did he say that to? I asked. That other nurse, said Elf. He figures that because I'm not grateful for having my life saved I must be stupid. Asshole, I said, did he talk to you? Yeah, sort of, said Elf, it was more of an interrogation. C'mon Yolandi, you know how they are.

Equating intelligence with the desire to live?

Yeah, she said, or decency.

———

This time her method wasn't starving, it was pills. Elf had left a note, ripped from the same type of lined yellow legal pad she had used years ago to design her exceptional signature AMPS, expressing her hope that God would receive her, no time left for making one's mark, and a list of names of all the people she loved. My mother read out the names to me over the phone. She told me that Elf had written them with a green marker. We were all there on the list. Please understand, she'd also written. Please let me go. I love you all. My mother told me there was some quote on the page as well, but she couldn't make it out. Somebody named David Hume? she said. But she said it like *whom* which didn't make any difference anyway. Wait, I thought, so Elf does believe in God?

Where did she get all those pills? I asked my mom.

Nobody knows, said my mom. Maybe she called 1-800-PILL. Who knows.

My mother had found her unconscious at home in her bed and by the time Elf came to in the hospital I had already flown from Toronto and was standing next to her when she opened her eyes. She smiled slowly, fully, like a child comprehending the structure of a joke for the first time in her life. You're here, she said, and told me we had to stop meeting like this. She introduced me in a formal way, like we were at a consulate dinner, to the nurses in the emergency ward and to the woman hired to sit beside her bed on a chair and watch her every move.

This, she said, thrusting her chin out at me because her hands were tied down with cotton ribbons, is my younger sister, Yoyo.

It's Yolandi, I said. Hi. I shook the woman's hand.

She told me I looked like the older one. That happened all the time because Elf has curiously escaped the erosional side effects of living. Then Elf told me that she and the woman hired to watch her were having a discussion about Thomas Aquinas. Weren't we? my sister said, smiling at the woman, who smiled grimly at me and shrugged. She wasn't hired to make small talk about saints with suicide patients. Why Thomas Aquinas? I said, sitting down in the chair near to the woman. Elf strained to make eye contact with her, the guard, in the chair. There was still a lot of medication in her system, said the woman.

But not quite enough, said Elf. I began to protest. I'm kidding, Swiv, she said. Good grief.

When Elf fell asleep, I went out into the waiting room to find my mom. She was sitting next to a man with a black eye and reading a whodunit. I told her that Elf had been talking about Thomas Aquinas.

Yes, said my mom, she was talking about him to me too. In her delirium she asked me if I'd "Thomas Aquinas her" and later I thought about it and I decided that she must have meant would I forgive her.

And will you? I asked.

That's not the point, said my mom. She doesn't need forgiving. It's not a sin.

But fifty billion people would disagree with you, I said.

Let them, said my mom.

That was three days ago. Since then my mother has shipped off to the Caribbean because Nic and I forced her to. All she had in her tiny suitcase were heart pills and whodunits. She keeps phoning from the ship to find out how Elf is. Yesterday she told me that a bartender on the ship had prayed for our family in Spanish. *Dios, te proteja*. She told me to tell Elf that she had bought a CD for her from a guy on the street. A Colombian pianist. It might be a fake, I said. She told me she'd had a conversation with the captain of the ship about burials at sea. She told me she had been tossed out of bed on a stormy night but it hadn't woken her up, that's how tired she was. In the morning she woke up to discover that she had fallen and rolled all the way over to the balcony of her little cabin. I asked her if she could conceivably have rolled right off the balcony into the sea and she said no, even if she had wanted to the railings would have stopped her. And if the railings hadn't stopped her she would only have fallen into one of the lifeboats hanging on the side of the ship. My mother was so confident of being rescued in life, one way or another or another.

On my way out of the hospital I stopped at the front desk and asked Janice if it was true that Elf had fallen in the washroom that morning and Janice said that yes, she had. This was after she'd been moved from the emergency ward to the psych ward. They'd found her lying on the floor bleeding from her head and clutching her toothbrush in her fist the way you'd hold a paring knife if you were just about to plunge it into someone's throat. Just then Janice had to go running off to restrain a patient who was using a pool cue to smash the television set in the activity room. Another nurse peered at Elf's file. The nurse said that Elfrieda needed to start eating and then she'd have the strength not to fall down, and that she needed to be somewhat more aware of her surroundings.

I wanted to go back to Elf's room and tell her this last thing the nurse had said in some attempt to get her to roll her eyes with me, to forge a small bond of mutual disdain at least. I also wanted to tell her that there was a guy in the ward who hated TV as much as she did and maybe she could be friends with him. But she had asked me to leave and I wanted her to know that some of her requests were reasonable and that they could be granted, that I respected her wishes (sort of) and that in spite of being a psychiatric patient with her name misspelled and scribbled messily on a white board behind the nurses' desk, she was still my wise albeit alarming older sister and I would listen. I walked away and crashed into a stainless steel trolley full of plastic trays of food. I apologized to two people shuffling past me in housecoats.

That shit's inedible anyway, man, one of them said. I'd kick the tray over too if I was more coordinated.

Yeah, said the other guy. Yeah!

I said inedible, said the first guy.

I know, man. I heard you the first time.

Over all the other voices?

Ha, yeah, funny.

That's what put you in the nuthouse?

No, it was stabbing that guy who broke into my shed.

Not the actual stabbing but the voices telling you to, though, right?

Yeah, you got it. The knife was real, though.

Yeah, that's too bad. That's the unfortunate piece of the story.

I liked these shuffling men. I really liked "unfortunate piece of the story." I wanted to introduce these guys to Elf. I started to pick up the trays but the nurse said I shouldn't. She'd get somebody, an orderly, to do it. I joked with the nurse that perhaps my sister's lack of awareness of her surroundings was a genetic thing I shared with her, ha, but I received no laugh, no smile, remembered the description I had once read of an angry woman's mouth resembling a pencil with two sharpened ends, and left. As I took the stairs down, two, four, six, eight, who do we appreciate, I silently apologized to Elf for leaving her there on her own and made a mental list of the things I'd bring the next day: dark chocolate, egg salad sandwich, Heidegger's *On Time and Being* (we do not say time is and being is, we say there is time and there is being), fingernail clippers, clean panties, not scissors or gutting knives, amusing anecdotes.

I drove away in my mother's beater Chevy, careening down Pembina Highway, a bleak section of asphalt and derelict strip malls, blasting towards nothing, really, other than *le foutoir,* as Elf put it, of my life. She loved to use elegant-sounding French words to describe the detritus, a way to balance things out maybe, to polish up the agony until it shines like Polaris, her guiding light and possibly her true home.

I saw a bedding store with a sale sign all lit up in the window and pulled into the parking lot. I stood for ten minutes staring at pillows—down-filled pillows, synthetic fibre–filled pillows and other pillows. I took a few from the shelves and squeezed them, held them against the wall and tried to rest my head on them, feel them out. The salesperson told me I could test them on the testing bed. She laid a protective piece of fabric over the pillow and I lay down and rested my head for a minute. The salesperson told me she'd be back after I'd had time to test the others thoroughly. I thanked her and closed my eyes. I had a short power nap. When I woke up, the sales clerk was standing next to me, smiling, and for a second I remembered childhood and a certain peace that had accompanied it.

I bought Elf a shiny purple pillow the size of a rolled-up sleeping bag with silver dragonflies embroidered into the satin. I got back into my mom's car and drove to the drive-through beer vendor at the Grant Park Inn and bought a two-four of Extra Old Stock, then stopped at a 7-Eleven and bought a pack of cigarettes, Player's Extra Light. Whatever *extra* thing I could buy, I would. I bought an extra-big Oh Henry! bar too and drove to my mother's high-rise apartment overlooking the Assiniboine River where I hunkered down with my supplies all ready to wait it out. It was spring breakup time when the ice on the river begins to thaw and crack and large frozen slabs grind and scrape against each other and make a horrible screaming noise as they're dragged downstream by the current. Spring does not come easily to this city.

I stood on my mother's balcony clutching the purple pillow with the silver dragonflies, shivering and smoking, plotting, thinking, trying to crack Elf's secret code, the meaning of life, her life, the universe, time, being and drinking beer. I walked around the apartment looking at things belonging to my mother. I examined a photograph of my father taken two months before he died. He was watching Will play baseball in a park. Little League. He had on his big glasses. He looked relaxed. His arms were crossed and he was smiling. There was a photo of my mom with Nora when she was a baby, a newborn. They were looking deeply into one another's eyes as though they were passing important secrets back and forth telepathically. I looked at a photograph stuck to the fridge of Elf performing in Milan. She was wearing a long black dress hemmed with staples. Her shoulder blades poked through the fabric. Her hair was really glossy. It was flopping down around her face as she bent over the keys. Sometimes when Elf plays, her ass lifts right off the bench, just an inch or two. She called me after that gig from a hotel, sobbing, telling me how cold she was, how lonely. But you're in Italy, I'd said. Your favourite place in the world. She told me her loneliness was visceral, a sack of rocks she carried from one room to the next, city to city.

I dialed my mom's cellphone to see if she could get service on her ship. Nothing.

There was a note on the dining room table. It was my mother telling me to please return her DVDs when I got a chance. I knew she was totally burned out from trying to keep Elf alive. The day before she flew to Fort Lauderdale to get on that ship she was bitten by a Rottweiler belonging to the crazy neighbour down the hall and she hadn't even noticed until the blood began to seep through her winter coat and she had to get stitches and a tetanus shot. At night it was all she could do to collapse in front of her TV and watch every episode of every season of *The Wire*, methodically, like a zombie, one after the other after the other, the volume cranked because she was half deaf, falling asleep while a messed-up kid from Baltimore spoke to her from the TV set, comforted her in his way and told her what she already knew, that a boy's gotta make his own way in this motherfuckin' world.

The morning she left for the airport my mother acciden-tally pulled down the shower rod and curtain, the whole works. She showered anyway and when she came out she was smiling, her game face on, shiny and new and ready for an adventure. I asked her how it had worked without a curtain, wasn't it . . . and she said no, no, it worked well, no problem at all. When I went into the bathroom there was an inch of water on the floor and everything, the toilet paper, the toiletries and makeup on the counter, all the clean towels, the artwork done by my kids, everything, was soaked. I realized that the idea of "working well" was a relative one for us and that in the context of our present lives my mother was right, it was absolutely fine, no problem. Elf was actually now safe, sort of, safer anyway while she was in the hospital than at home where she was alone most of the days while Nic was at work, so it was a good time for my mother to disappear for a couple of weeks and get some rest.

I stood on my mom's balcony and listened to the ice breaking up. It sounded like gunfire, a mob scene playing out over a track of roaring animals. The moon was full and hanging low like a pregnant cat. I could see lights in the houses across the river. I saw people dancing. I could make them invisible with the tip of my finger and one eye closed. I phoned the hospital and asked to speak to Elf. I paced outside on the balcony while I waited for the hospital's main switchboard to connect me to psych. I made the dancing couple appear. Disappear. Appear.

Hello?

Hello.

May I speak to Elfrieda?

Is this her sister?

Yes.

She appreciates the call.

Oh, great. But can I talk to her?

She'd prefer not to.

She'd prefer not to?

Yes.

Can you bring the phone to her?

We'd rather not.

Well, but.

Why don't you try again later.

Can I speak to Janice please?

Janice is not available at the moment.

Oh. Do you have an idea of when she will be?

I don't have that information.

What do you mean?

I don't have access to that information.

I'm just asking you when it would be a good time to call in order to speak to Janice.

And I'm just telling you that I don't have that information.

It's not information, it's just an answer.

I'm sorry but I'm not authorized to answer that question.

About when Janice will be available? What do you mean not authorized?

You'll have to call back later, I'm sorry.

But don't you have a system or something for finding Janice?

I'm afraid there's nothing I can do.

Can you page her?

Have a good day.

Wait, wait.

I'm afraid there's nothing I can do.

You could make an exception.

I'm sorry? (She couldn't hear me over the ice.)

I just want to hear my sister's voice.

I thought you wanted to talk with Janice.

I know, but you said that—

I'd really recommend that you try again later.

Why doesn't my sister want to talk to me?

I didn't say she didn't want to talk to you. I said she'd prefer not to come to the common room to answer the call. If I had to bring the phone to patients every time they got a call I wouldn't have time for anything else. And we'd rather have patients make an effort to connect with family rather than the other way around.

Oh.

I'd really recommend that you try again later.

I agreed, sure, why not.

I hung up and threw the phone into the river. I didn't throw the phone into the river. I stopped myself at the last second and muffled something like an already muffled scream. I decided I'd rather set the hospital on fire. I'd prefer not to have my soul crushed. Bartleby the Scrivener preferred not to until he preferred not to work, not to eat, not to do anything, and died under a tree. Robert Walser also died under a tree. James Joyce and Carl Jung died in Zurich. Our father died beside trees on iron rails. The police gave my mother a bag of his belongings afterwards, the things he'd had on him when he died. Somehow his glasses didn't break, maybe they flew off his face into soft clover, or maybe he had carefully removed them and put them down on the ground, but when she took them out of the plastic bag they crumbled in her hands. His watch too. Time. Smash it. His wedding rings were bashed and nearly all of his two hundred and six bones broken.

He had seventy-seven dollars on him at the time and we used the money for Thai takeout because, as my friend Julie says about times like this: You still have to eat.

FOUR

NIC WAS GOING TO SEE ELF in the evening after he got home from work and afterwards he and I would meet for a beer, we would stare at each other, embattled and bewildered, and talk about our next move. We were trying to assemble a team of caregivers who would work with Elf when she was released from the hospital.

Nic had very gently suggested to Elf that an element of co-operation was a key factor in her journey towards health. She wasn't into the idea. Obviously. She said the only thing she saw when she heard the word *team* was four runaway horses. There's

no *I* in *team*, is there Yoli? She was quoting our high school basketball coach and she said that expression had always terrified
her. What would this team do with her? she asked. What would
Elf do with the team? Make lists? Set goals? Embrace life? Start
a journal? Turn that frown upside down? She kept unearthing
huge fundamental problems with the whole concept. Oh my
god, Nicolas, she'd said. Journey? Health? Listen to yourself.
I had also been listening to Nic and thought it sounded pretty
good but Elf was up in arms, gnashing her teeth against the
smarmy self-help racket that existed only to sell books and
anaesthetize the vulnerable and allow the so-called "helping"
profession to bask in self-congratulation for having done what
they could. They'd make lists! They'd set goals! They'd encourage their patients to do one "fun" thing a day! (Oh you should
have heard the derision in Elf's voice when she said the word
fun like she'd just spit out the word *Eichmann* or *Mengele*.)

The experts involved had the hardest time understanding
our family's extreme hostility to the entire health network. *We*
had the hardest time understanding our family's extreme hostility to the entire health network. When my mother had her lawn
mower accident and was lying there in the grass next to two of
her toes and the paramedics leapt out of their ambulance and
ran over to her she looked at them and said what on earth are
you guys doing here? When the doctor told my mother that I'd
need a tonsillectomy she told him, yeah we can probably do that
ourselves at home but thanks.

Mostly we just didn't want Elf to be left alone. Nic would
have to get back to his work eradicating the runs and I would
eventually have to return home to Toronto to relieve Will of
his babysitting duties so that he could get back to his classes

on overthrowing the one percent. In the Mohawk language, Toronto is spelled *Tkaronto* and means "trees standing in water." (I appreciate that our Canadian cities were named after things like mud and trees and water, especially when they are now given such monikers by overachievers as the Financial Hub or the Technology Centre or the Publishing Capital or the Most Cosmopolitan City in the World.) But in the meantime, this evening, I was going to share a bottle of wine with Julie, on the front porch of her rickety house in Wolseley, an inner-city neighbourhood where massive elm trees create a cathedral ceiling of speckled shade, while her kids watched a video inside.

Julie and I grew up together in East Village. We're second cousins and our mothers are also best friends. (For that matter, Elf and I are also cousins, and sisters, but to understand this you have to know that only eighteen or so initiative-taking Mennonites came to Canada from Russia to get away from the Anarchist army, so . . . you know.) Julie and I bathed together as children, invented a game called Hide the Soap and experimented touching tongues with each other when it slowly became horrifyingly clear to us that it would be a thing we'd have to do a lot of in the future if we were to have normal lives with boys and men.

Julie's a letter carrier, a hard-core postie who walks fifteen miles a day with two twenty-pound bags of mail on each of her shoulders. When it rains she opens one of those green mailboxes you see on corners with a key from a giant metal ring and sits inside it, smoking and listening to BBC News podcasts on her headphones. She's been reprimanded several times by her supervisor for that and countless other acts of insubordination, like rolling up the waistband of her Canada Post–issued "skort" to make it sexier. Sometimes she gets a one-day or a two-day or a three-day suspension, depending on the severity of her crime, and that's fine with her because then she can hang out with her kids before they go to school rather than having to wake them in the dark and shuffle them over to her neighbour's house in their pyjamas. She recently split up with her husband, a very tall sculptor and painter working in oils, and so takes advantage of the Canada Post health plan that pays for her to see a therapist. Nothing is awful in her life, she's quite happy, she just likes the luxury of being able to talk about herself, her feelings, her goals, her hopes, her disappointments. Who wouldn't? Her therapist, a Jungian, had told her that she was the most optimistic person he'd ever encountered in all his years of practising therapy and that Julie's dreamless sleeps were a constant challenge for him.

We sat on her porch and drank cheap red wine and ate cheese and crackers and talked about everything other than Elf, who was a subject like time in that I couldn't grasp it but it had a mighty hold on *me*. Julie's two kids are a boy and a girl ages eight and nine, who still love to hug people and sit on their laps. They were indoors watching *Shrek* and every five or ten minutes would come out onto the porch (every time that happened Julie would fling her lit cigarette into the grass so they wouldn't see her smoking and then retrieve it later) and say oh my god, okay, guys? You have to see this. It's like, it's like . . . And then they'd argue with each other for a minute or two about what it was like, truly, and Julie and I would nod in utter amazement, Julie occasionally glancing at her dwindling cigarette in the front yard. Then suddenly with no warning they'd vanish like meadowlarks, darting back into the house to assume their positions on the couch.

They think smoking causes AIDS, said Julie, retrieving her smouldering cigarette. We talked about how it didn't matter how old or young they were, we obsessed over their well-being and suffered wildly, exquisitely, and blamed ourselves for every single nanosecond of unhappiness they experienced. We would sooner self-immolate than see our children's eyes fill slowly with tears ever again. We talked about our ex-husbands and our old boyfriends and our fear of never being desired sexually ever, ever again and of dying alone and unloved in our own shit, with bedsores so deep they exposed our crumbly bones, and had we done anything right in our lives?

Probably, we concluded. We had maintained our friendship, we would always be there for each other, and one day when all our children had grown up and left us to wallow in regret and melancholy and decrepitude and our parents had died from the accumulative grief and exhaustion of living and our husbands and lovers had all flown the coop or been banished from our doorsteps we would buy a house together in some beautiful countryside somewhere and chop wood, pump water, fish, play the piano, sing together from the soundtracks of *Jesus Christ Superstar* and *Les Misérables*, reimagine our pasts and wait out the end of the world.

Deal?

Deal.

We high-fived and rolled a joint. We were getting cold out there on the porch. We sat listening to the river break down and crack up a block away, and I wondered if those slabs of ice could fly, could ever be released and lifted right up from all that roiling pressure and what it would be like to see a giant slab of ice winging its way over Portage Avenue on its way back home to the north. We stared up at the night, April crisp and clear, no stars. We watched as lights went out up and down the street and we peeked at Julie's kids through the window, asleep on the sofa in flannel pyjamas, clutching remote controls to a thousand modern devices.

So why isn't Dan looking after Nora? asked Julie. (Dan is Nora's father. He's rambunctious and sentimental. We're in the throes of a divorce.) It's not like this isn't an emergency. Didn't he tell you you could always count on him in an emergency? Have you told him about Elf?

He's in Borneo or something, I said. With an aerialist.

Must be nice. But I thought he was living in Toronto.

Yeah, he is . . . to be closer to Nora, he says, except he's in Borneo at the moment.

Indefinitely? said Julie.

No, not forever. I don't know. Nora did tell him about Elf.

And Barry's putting Will through university in New York? asked Julie. (Barry is Will's father. He's loaded because he spends his time creating stochastic local volatility models for a bank and has a mysterious demeanour. We hardly talk.)

Yeah . . . so far.

How's Nora liking dance? (Dance was the main reason we moved to Toronto. So Nora would be able to go to a certain ballet school, thanks to her scholarship since I wouldn't have been able to pay for it otherwise.)

She loves it but thinks she's too fat.

God, said Julie. When will that shit ever end.

I caught her smoking.

She's smoking so she doesn't eat?

I guess so, I said. All the dancers are. I talked to her about it but . . .

And Will loves New York? she asked.

He really does, I said. And he's a Marxist now, I think. He just says *Kapital*, doesn't even use the *Das*.

Cool.

Yeah.

Eventually I helped Julie manoeuvre her kids up to bed, half walking, half carrying, and said good night. She hadn't received any type of suspension for insubordination unfortunately, so had to get up early to work the next morning. She put out her Canada Post–issued spiked boots and prepared the kids' lunches. The spiked boots were useful for walking on ice. One winter during an ice storm, I found myself stranded on the slippery fishbowl bank of the Assiniboine. I had walked across the frozen river and had planned to climb up the bank to the sidewalk near the Osborne Street Bridge. It would have been a shortcut on my way downtown but instead I got stuck on the icy bank with smooth-soled shoes and was completely unable to get enough of a grip to climb up the steep embankment. I tried grabbing at the thin branches of trees that hung over the bank but inevitably they'd snap off and I'd slide back down to where I had started. I lay on my back on the ice wondering what to do, munching on a granola bar I'd found in my bag, and then I remembered Julie's special shoes with spikes. I called her from my cellphone and she told me that she was actually nearby on her mail route and would come and rescue me. She showed up a few minutes later and took off her spiked shoes and threw them down to me so that I could put them on and finally climb up the bank. She stood on her mailbag so her feet wouldn't get wet and smoked a cigarette while I clomped up the riverbank like Sir Edmund Hillary in her spiked shoes. Then we went for a coffee and a Boston cream doughnut. Rescue missions are occasionally very straightforward.

I said goodbye to Julie and drove around the city for a while wanting and not wanting to drive past the old house on Warsaw Avenue, trying and not trying to remember those years of marital happiness.

Dan, my second ex, the father of Nora, raised Will as his own while Will's biological father, my first ex, was in the States embracing volatility, and we both really felt like we'd gotten things right this time around after crappy first marriages, that at long last we'd resolved the agonies of unfulfilled romantic yearnings and were finished with bad decisions. Now we're engaged in a war of attrition but mostly, like modern lovers, through texts and e-mails. We have very brief truce-like moments at times when we're either too tired to fight or somehow simultaneously feeling nostalgic and full of goodwill. Sometimes he sends me links to songs he thinks I'll like or essays about waves or whatever, the universe, or apologies for a million things and sometimes he gets drunk and writes long scathing diatribes, litanies of my failures—which are legion.

The words "nothing bad has happened yet," a lyric from a Loudon Wainwright song, knocked around in my head while I cruised past the house on Warsaw Avenue. This was the house where I started writing my teen rodeo novels which did okay for a while, well enough to help with the mortgage payments and buy groceries. There are nine of them so far. The Rodeo Rhonda series. But it's time for Rhonda's world to change, according to my publisher. More teenagers live in cities now and can't relate to barrel racers and broncobusters. My editor is being very patient with me these days while I work on my "literary book." She said she's quite happy to wait for Rodeo Rhonda number ten while I "expand my oeuvre." The new owner was in the process of painting a thick layer of austere white over the original red and yellow that Dan and I had painted it years ago on a goofy whim when we were broke but happy and fearless and oh so confident in our love, our future, the kingdom of our newly minted family and our unshakable footing in the world. The fence hadn't been repainted yet, it glowed a cheerful yellow in the dusky light, and I could still make out the decals that Nora had stamped all over it, sweet images of frogs and cars and half moons and blazing suns with happy faces. A little metal sign we'd bought on some family road trip that said Beware: Peculiar Dog Lives Here was still screwed to the gate. Sometimes people say at this point: I don't know what happened. I don't know where we went wrong.

I went to Nic and Elf's house and parked in their driveway. It was finally dark. I watched Nic through the window for a minute as he sat, also in darkness, staring at his barely glowing computer. It was time for us to talk about Elfrieda, our nightly conference that would leave us no closer to a solution but would at least reinforce our solidarity in the cause of keeping her alive. We sat in the living room among piles of music books and Mandarin novels, Nic's latest fascination, sipping herbal tea from the last of their clean cups, and exchanged thoughts like: She seemed slightly more upbeat today, more willing to engage in conversation, didn't you think? Well, yeah, maybe . . . What about that fresh cut? That fall? Do you know, is she taking her meds? She says she is but . . . The nurse told me today that we weren't supposed to bring her food from the outside, that if she was hungry she was supposed to get out of bed and walk to the communal eating area at regular mealtimes. Yeah . . . but she won't. She'll just starve. Well, they won't let her do that. No, you're sure? Hmmm . . .

We still hadn't heard back from the "team" of psychiatric home care workers and were beginning to wonder if it actually existed. We wanted to know how often the team would be able to visit or how much it would cost. We agreed that the cost didn't matter and Nic said he'd call the contact person again the next morning from work and I offered to try once again to meet with Elf's psychiatrist, which was like trying to meet with the head of the Gambino family. I wasn't even sure if he existed. Or at least, I said, I would talk to one of the senior nurses who was familiar with Elf's case history, and basically beg anyone who would listen not to let her go home until we had this other plan in place or until she really, seriously had turned a corner, as they say.

And what about the tour? I said.

Fuck the tour, said Nic.

Yeah, I said. I agree with you. But we've got to deal with it. She's worried about letting everyone down.

I know. Nic stood up and grabbed a piece of paper off the piano. Messages for Elfrieda, he said. Jean-Louis, Felix, Theodor, Hans, Andrea, I don't know half these people.

Have you told Claudio?

No. No . . . He's been leaving messages though. The Free Press wants to do a profile for a music anthology, and *BBC Music Magazine* wants to do something as well. Ha!

Nic returned to the table and leaned his chin on folded hands. His eyes were bloodshot. His whole face seemed kind of bloodshot. He smiled, because he was brave.

Tired? I asked.

Epically, he said.

He got up to put on a record, vinyl was his thing now. He liked the step-by-stepness of it, the process. He held the record the way people hold records, not with his fingers but with his palms. He blew on it. The music was a soft whisper, one acoustic guitar, no voices. When he came back to the table he asked me to look at his eyes.

They're seeping, he said. Like I have an infection or something.

Pink eye? I asked.

I don't know, he said. They always seem to be running, just clear liquid, not pus. I lie in bed and all this liquid dribbles out the sides. Maybe I should see a doctor, or optometrist or something.

You're crying, Nic.

No . . .

Yes. That's what they call crying.

But all the time? he asked. I'm not even conscious of it then.

It's a new kind of crying, I said. For new times. I leaned over and put my hands on his shoulders and then on the sides of his face in the same way that he'd held his record.

We sat quietly for a while then Nic told me Elf was supposed to be doing a run-through in three weeks, two days before the opening. I said there was no way she would be ready and he agreed because all she talks about is not being able to do the tour, and the sooner concerned parties got the news the better. Then I told him to just call Claudio, he would deal with it, the way he's always dealt with it.

I'll phone Claudio if you want, I said.

Well, maybe we should hold off a bit.

I think he needs to know now.

Listen, I know what Claudio will say, said Nic. He'll say, let's wait and see. He'll think she can come out of it again, like she did last time. He'll say performing saved her life and that's what it will do again.

Maybe.

And maybe he's right and she should be pushed a little bit and she'll be okay.

Yeah, I said.

But . . . she obviously doesn't have to do the tour if she doesn't want to do the tour, said Nic. It doesn't matter in the big picture. I'm just saying that she might suddenly decide she really wants to do it and then . . .

Yeah, so we shouldn't cancel now, I said.

Nic's head fell to the table, slowly, like a snowflake. His arm was stretched out beneath it, his empty palm in the shape of a little cup.

Nic, I said. Hey Nic, you should go to bed.

We did then what we always did at the end of our talks. We sighed, rubbed our faces, grimaced, smiled, shrugged, and then we talked about a few other things, like the kayak that Nic is building from scratch in his basement, and his plan to finish it soon and in springtime carry it on his head down to the river which is only a block away and paddle upstream to somewhere, that will be the hard part, and then drift downstream all the way home again.

I left him sitting at his computer, his face lit up like Boris Karloff in the ghostly funnel of the monitor's light. I wondered what he was looking at. What sorts of things do you google when your favourite person in the world is determined to leave it? I got into my mother's car and checked my phone. A text from Nora in Toronto: *How's Elf? I need your permission to get my belly button pierced. Pleeeze???? Love you!* Another one from Radek inviting me over. He's a sad-eyed Czech violinist that I met when I was walking with Julie on her delivery route the last time I visited Winnipeg. (He was actually the reason *why* I accompanied her on her route. She had mentioned that she delivered mail to a really handsome European guy who also seemed lonely and desperate. Like you, Yoli, she'd said.) He had come to Winnipeg to write a libretto. But who hasn't? It's a dark and fecund corner of the world, this confluence of muddy waters, one that begs the question of hey, how *do* we set words to life's tragic score? Radek and I don't speak the same language, not really, but he listens to me patiently, comprehending, well, I don't really know what—that if he sits tight for an hour or two listening to me ramble on about my failings in a language he doesn't really understand he'll eventually, inshallah, get laid?

Just now I'm worried that "get laid" is a term no longer used but I'm too ashamed to ask Nora for an update. I'm at an age where I'm stuck between two generations, one using the term "getting laid" and the other "hooking up," so what are you supposed to call it? I sat in the little kitchen of the attic apartment Radek is renting on Academy Road and talked to him about Elf, about her despair, her numbness, her "hour of lead" as Emily Dickinson puts it, and my house-of-cards plan to make her want to live, and about futility and rage and the seas on the moon named Serenity and Cleverness and which one would he prefer to live next to (Serenity) and did he know there was a glacier somewhere in Canada called Disappointment and that it feeds into Disappointment River and that the Disappointment River empties into the Disappointment Basin but that there is no Disappointment stopper in the basin? And Radek nodded and poured me wine and made me food and when he walked past me on his way to the kitchen to stir the pasta or the rice he kissed me on the back of my neck. He is very pale with black wiry hair that covers his entire body. He jokes in broken English that he is not quite fully evolved and I tell him that I admire him for not burning it or ripping it all away like North Americans who are terrified of hair and fur in general. Body hair is the final frontier in the fight for the liberation of women, Radek. I'm so *exhausted*. He nodded, ah, yes?

When he gently placed the pasta on the table, he said, I have seen your sister play.

What? I said. You have? You never told me that.

In Prague, he said. And I am not surprised.

Surprised by what? I asked him.

By her suffering, he said. When I listened to her play I felt I should not be there in the same room with her. There were hundreds of people but nobody left. It was a private pain. By private I mean to say unknowable. Only the music knew and it held secrets so that her playing was a puzzle, a whisper, and people afterwards stood in the bar and drank and said nothing because they were complicit. There were no words.

I thought about his words for a while, his old European charm, and the way he talked. Maybe we could fall in love and move together with Will and Nora to Prague, and my life would become less like my life and more like Franz Kafka's. Will and Nora could study tennis and gymnastics and Radek and I could go to operas and ballets non-stop and become intense and poetic and revolutionary.

I would put her in the same category as Ivo Pogorelich, or perhaps Evgeny Kissin, he said. She understands that the piano is the perfection of the human voice.

She has a glass piano inside of her that she worries will break, I said.

Yes, he said. Maybe it already has. And she's barely holding the pieces in place before it shatters. I think I fell in love with her just suddenly that evening. I wanted to protect her.

Oh, great, you're hot for my sister? He laughed and said no, of course not but I figured he was lying. So much for my Prague fantasy. Well, I thought, Prague obviously hadn't been a barrel of laughs for Franz Kafka anyway, so never mind, never mind!

Do you want more wine? he asked. What was she like as a child?

All she did was play the piano, I said. And petition for things.

Ah well, if there is one thing you're going to do in life it may as well be playing the piano, said Radek. But you must have other memories, no?

She learned French when she was really young, I said, and sometimes that's all she spoke and sometimes she'd stop talking for long periods of time like our father. She had different nicknames for me: Swivelhead, Mayhem. She tried to pretend that our Mennonite town was an Italian village in Tuscany or something by renaming everything and everyone. All the streets, everything. She became obsessed with Italy. When our old Mennonite relatives came over she'd address them as *signor* and *signora* and offer them espressos and grappa. People made fun of her. It was a bit embarrassing for me too.

Ah, but she was only creating excitement, said Radek, yes? Being funny and sophisticated!

Yeah, I can see that now, I told him, but at the time . . . you know. A town like ours is not the best place to work on your comedy routine. Our house was once shot at.

What? said Radek. Because of Elfrieda?

I don't know, I said. We never found out. A lot of people made fun of our dad too for riding his bike all the time and wearing a suit every single day and reading books. That made Elf cry. She would get really angry. She would fight with people, mostly with words, trying to defend him. When she went away to Oslo to study music she sent me tapes of herself talking about her life in the city, and then she was studying with some guy in Amsterdam and after that a woman in Helsinki. I listened to the tapes over and over in the dark and pretended she was there with me. I had them memorized, every inflection, every breath, and I talked along with her, over her, even her little chuckles. I had memorized it all.

Radek poured us each another glass of wine and said he was thinking of something Northrop Frye had said about the energy it takes to get out of a place and how you must then move forward on that momentum to keep creating, to keep reinventing. Would I agree?

I would agree, yes, I said. Is it even *legal* to disagree with Northrop Frye?

Of course, said Radek, perhaps you—

I know, I know, I was just kidding. But I do agree.

You missed your sister, said Radek succinctly.

Yeah, but it was more than that. I didn't really want her to come back. I don't know if I was conscious of that at the time but I knew, somehow, that she had to stay away. And yet at the same time I felt I needed her in order to survive that place, so I was really busy and anxious trying to figure out for myself how to be brave when she was gone. She played tennis a lot with me when she came back to visit. We played in the dark. Blind Tennis. It was fun but we lost a lot of balls. She told me I had to listen very carefully when we played Blind Tennis, that was the thing. We laughed our heads off in the dark and screamed when we got hit with the ball. When she played the piano I could tell what her mood was. She got all the top scholarships in school, she was even on some TV quiz show, but a lot of things made her mad. People not trying hard enough made her so mad. Bad form made her crazy. When the pastor and his old guys from our church came to our house to tell our parents they shouldn't let Elf go away to study because she'd get big ideas, she lit his revival tent on fire that night and the cops came to our house . . .

Oh my, said Radek.

But first, when the church guys were at our house she played Rachmaninoff in the other room. My mom and I were hiding in the kitchen. And it was like the more pressure they applied to my dad, the deeper she screamed. Well, screamed with the piano. She drove them away with her brilliance and her rage, like Jesus with the money changers or you know like Dustin Hoffman in *Straw Dogs* . . .

Like sunlight to vampires, said Radek.

They were such simple, brutish men, it was like playing for an audience of mastodons . . . She didn't—

Which piece was it? asked Radek.

G Minor, Opus 23.

What happened when the police came to your house?

My parents wouldn't let them put her into juvenile detention or send her away to the Christian reprogramming camp in the woods, I think it was just a threat anyway, but we all went on a long road trip to Fresno, California, to get away from the police and when we came back they'd forgotten about it. Elf convinced a boy in Fresno to be her boyfriend while we were there and he tried to hide in the trunk of our car on the day we were leaving but our father felt the extra weight when we drove off and stopped to get rid of him. Elf and this boy started making out like crazy after my dad hauled him out of the trunk and my dad couldn't deal with it so my mom had to get out of the car and tell Elf we had to go. I remember her tugging on Elf's arm while she was still kissing the boy. And then Elf finally got into the car sobbing her eyes out and the boy ran behind us for as long as he could like the farm dogs around East Village.

Radek laughed. Do you have a photo of her? he asked. I took one out of my wallet and showed it to him. She was all huge green eyes and shiny black hair. She looks like an alien, doesn't she?

He said, She is beautiful.

———

The first time I ate at Radek's table I told him that I had been faithful to my husband and had raised children with him, and Radek smiled sweetly, nodding, as though he liked that woman, preferred her even, but you know, here *we* were. I'm so tired these days that often I put my head down on his table and fall asleep while he cleans up the dishes and then he picks me up and carries me to his bed and removes my clothing carefully, draping my jeans over his chair so that my lip balm doesn't fall out of the pocket and roll under his bed into the dust, and he places my shirt over his lamp to cast an interesting aura, and he makes love to me very gently, like a gentle gentleman. Those are the words my grandmother used to describe my grandfather when I asked her what he'd been like as a husband. Gentle. It's all I can think of too to describe Radek. When he comes he says something softly in Czech, one word. I like to play with the tips of his fingers, feeling the hard ridges and grooves that are formed from pushing down on his violin strings for five or six hours a day.

He told me that once I barked like a dog in my sleep. I had a very vague recollection of doing it, of a dream I was having where everything I was feeling and everything I wanted to say about everything I was feeling came out, finally, as one lousy inchoate bark. Sometimes I think that I'm coming a little closer, at least in my dreams, to understanding Elf's silences. When I was living alone in Montreal, heartbroken over a lost love, she sent me a quote from Paul Valéry. One word per letter, though, so it took me months to figure out. *Breath, dreams, silence, invincible calm . . . you will triumph.*

FIVE

IT'S THE MORNING NOW and I'm hungover. My eyes are ringed with purple bags and smudged black mascara and there's a thin crusty line of red wine on my lips. My hands are shaking. I'm drinking takeout coffee from Tim Hortons. Double double double double. My mother is on a ship. Nic is drowning in equations having to do with tapeworms. I brought Elf the things she asked for, the dark chocolate, the egg salad sandwich, the clean panties and the nail clippers. She was sleeping when I arrived. I knew she was alive because her glasses were resting on her chest and bobbing up and down like a tiny stranded lifeboat. I put the purple dragonfly pillow next to her head and sat in the orange vinyl chair near the window and waited for her to wake up. I could see my mother's beater Chevy way down below in the parking lot and I pushed the green button on her automatic starter to see how far away I could be from something to make it come to life. Nothing happened, no lights came on.

I checked my BlackBerry. There were two messages from Dan. The first one contained an outline of my shortcomings as a wife and mother and the second an apology for the first. Alcohol, sadness, impulsive, regrettable behaviour. Those were his reasons. The staples of discord. I understood. Sometimes he sends me e-mails that are so formal they seem to have been drafted by a phalanx of lawyers and sometimes he sends me e-mails that are sort of a continuation of our conversations over the years, a kind of intimate banter about nothing as though this whole divorce thing is just a game. All the recriminations and apologies and attempts at understanding and attacks . . . I was guilty of these things too. Dan wanted me to stay. I wanted Elf to stay. Everyone in the whole world was fighting with somebody to stay. When Richard Bach wrote "If you love someone, set them free" he can't have been directing his advice at human beings.

I went into the washroom Elf shares with her roommate when she has one (Melanie has gone home for a visit with her family) and looked around for signs of self-destruction. Nothing. Good. Even the cap on the toothpaste had been replaced and who, let alone a person wanting to die, would bother with that? I rubbed the wine line off my lips and brushed my teeth with my finger. I tried to wash away my smudged mascara and made it worse, ghoulish.

I willed my hands to stop trembling and ruffled my hair a bit and prayed to a God I only half believed in. Why are we always told that God will answer our prayers if we believe in Him? Why can't He ever make the first move? I prayed for wisdom. Grant me wisdom, God, I said, the way my father used to say *grant* when he was praying instead of *give* because it's less demanding. Meek. I wondered if my father has inherited the earth because according to Scripture he should be running the entire show down here right now.

Elf opened her eyes and smiled wearily, resigned to have woken once again but obviously disappointed. I heard her thinking: What fresh hell is this? Our favourite Dorothy Parker quote and one that makes us laugh every time we say it except this time. Really, it was only once that it made us laugh, the first time we heard it.

She closed her eyes again and I said no! No, no, no, please keep them open. I asked her if she remembered Stockholm. The embassy, Elf? Remember? She'd invited me to hang out with her in Sweden for a week when I was pregnant with Will and we'd had a tragicomic experience at the Canadian embassy, where she'd been invited for lunch the day of her opening at the Stockholm Concert Hall. I went with her, dressed in some kind of enormous shimmering maternity dress I'd bought at Kmart or something, and spent most of the meal trying not to embarrass the Von Riesen family. We sat at a long white table in a white room with the ambassador and VIPs (who were also white) with names like Dahlberg and Gyllenborg and Lagerqvist. Elf was gorgeous, stunning in some simple European black thing, and a total pro at these fancy gigs. Everything about her was so sharp. So crisp and defined. I looked like one of those recently discovered giant squids next to her, oozing around in slow motion and dropping food on myself. Elf chatted in German with an exquisitely handsome, well-dressed couple, about piano playing probably, while the ambassador's aide asked me what I did in Canada. I'm trying to write rodeo books, I said, and you know (pointing at my stomach) having a baby. I was too emotional most of the time and had been vomiting up herring in Stockholm's perfect streets and sweating in my polyester dress and I was nervous and doing stupid things like knocking over the ambassador's wine with my huge stomach when I reached for a roll, and wrapping myself in the Manitoba flag so that Elfie could take my picture, and then pulling the flagpole over. I didn't know how to answer the questions I was being asked, questions like: Have you also been blessed with the musical gene? What is it like being sister to a prodigy?

Remember the egg? I said to Elf. She hadn't opened her eyes. We'd been served some kind of egg, not a chicken egg. Something else. A small, white, slimy eyeball thing, an embryo bobbing in green brine, and as soon as I saw it I made a break for the washroom. When I came back to the table Elf could tell that I'd been crying again and she immediately went to work trying to make me feel better the way she had always done from the time she quoted her poet lovers to me, like it was her profession. She turned me into a hero. She started telling stories about me when I was a kid and how I was the brave, adventurous one and how they should all see me on a horse—had they heard of barrel racing?—that I was the toughest girl in town, and that nobody made her laugh harder and that all her piano performances, really, were inspired by my life, by the wild, free rhythm of my life, combined with its delicacy, its defiance (which I knew was shorthand for being messed up but unable to admit it), or something like that. That she tried to play her piano the way I lived my life: freely, joyfully, honestly (shorthand for: like a cheerful halfwit with no social skills). She told all these people that the baby tucked away inside me was going to be the most richly blessed kid in the universe for having me as its mother and that I wrote beautiful rodeo books and that I was her best friend. All lies, except for maybe the very, very last part.

Elfrieda! Do you remember that day? She opened her eyes, finally, and nodded. I told her she had always looked out for me in situations like that one. She smiled, a big open smile. I pointed to the dragonfly pillow next to her head and told her that I'd brought her a gift. She seemed so inordinately happy about it. For me? Thank you! It's beautiful! She held it close to her body and thanked me again, more than she should have. It's just a pillow, I said. She asked me what I had in the plastic Safeway bag that I'd been dragging around with me all over town, and I told her it was my novel, a bunch of marked-up pages held together with an elastic band.

A new Rodeo book?

No, the book book. The real book.

You've finally written it? That's great! She asked me if I'd read to her from it and I said no. Just a paragraph? No. A sentence? No. Half a sentence! One word? No. A letter? I said okay, that I would read the first letter of the novel. She smiled and closed her eyes and sort of burrowed into her bed like she was preparing herself for a delicious treat. I asked her if she was ready and she nodded, still smiling, eyes closed. I stood and cleared my throat and paused and then began to read.

L.

She sighed and lifted her chin to the ceiling, opened her eyes and told me it was beautiful, BEAUTIFUL, and true, the best thing I'd written yet. I thanked her and shoved the page back into the plastic Safeway bag.

She asked me well, can you at least tell me what it's about, in a word? I told her yeah, sisters. And I glared at her and then I began to cry, inconsolable, for a good twenty minutes curled up in that torn vinyl chair by the window and she reached out and touched my foot, my calf, she stroked my leg, the part of it she could reach from the bed, and told me she was so sorry. I asked her what she was sorry for but she didn't say anything. I asked her again, my voice sounded harsh and vindictive, what was she sorry for? I slapped my hand against the reinforced window, quadruple paned to prevent jumpers from crashing through it, and it startled her. But again she answered me with silence and those huge green eyes fringed with ridiculously long lashes, dusky, haunted like my father's with pupils sunken ships in all that green.

I didn't give her the satisfaction of hearing me tell her I understand, that it's okay, that I forgive her, that she doesn't need to be forgiven, that I'll always love her, that I'll keep her heart in my pencil case. I looked away and calmly took out my BlackBerry to check for more important messages. Will had texted: *Nora is completely unreasonable. When are you back? How's Elf? Do you know where my basketball needle is?* I texted back: *Yes. Not sure. Alive. Try the junk drawer. Love you.* I googled "suicide gene" but cancelled the search at the last second. I didn't want to know. Plus, I already knew.

——

People ask: but how does this happen? To think that even with all the security measures we employ these days to keep things out—fences and motion detectors and cameras and sunscreen and vitamins and deadbolts and chains and bike helmets and spinning classes and guards and gates—we can have secret killers lurking *within* us? That we can turn on our happy selves the way tumours invade healthy, wholesome organs, the way "normal" moms suddenly throw their infants off the balcony is . . . who wants to *think* about that shit?

When my sister was born my father planted a Russian olive shrub in the backyard. When I was born he planted a mountain ash. When we were kids Elf explained to me that the Russian olive was a tough shrub with four-inch thorns that managed to thrive in places where everything else died. She told me that the mountain ash was called a rowan in Europe and that it was used to ward off witches. So, she said. We're protected from everything. Well, I said, you mean witches. We're only protected from witches.

I left the room and wandered around the hallways and nodded at the nurses at the nurses' station and walked into a linen closet by accident thinking it was a bathroom and out again, knocking over mops and cleaning products and muttering apologies, and back into Elf's room, fresh smile, tears rubbed away, my face by now a lurid mess of colours and grime, and I'm trying to comfort myself. I'm singing, not really singing, the Boss (because he's authoritative). "Thunder Road" . . . The anthemic tune that lit a fire in our plain girl hearts back in the eighties—serenading our own reflections with hairbrush microphones or belting it into the wind from the backs of half-ton trucks or the tops of towering hay bales—and that I'm calling on to give me hope once again.

I collapsed back into the orange chair and asked Elf to tell me about something. She wanted to know about what and I said anything, just tell me about something. Tell me about your secret lovers. She told me that lovers are secret for the reason that they're not spoken about and I nodded in agreement, that's true, that's intractable, I could take a page out of her book, but tell me anyway. Tell me about that guy, what was his name? Huge Boil. Elf grimaced and moaned and said Hugh Boyle was not a lover, he was a friend and I said so tell me about him, what was he like in bed? We didn't go to bed, said Elf, and I said okay, no problem, where'd you do it? On the floor? The fire escape? She shook her head. Okay, what about that other guy, Penis Breath? Ah, now she smiled. Denis Brecht, she said, was lovely but is ancient history. I'm a married woman now. You are? I asked. When did you get married? Okay, she said, you know what I mean. I told her that I am actually a married woman but have no husband. You, I told her, are not a married woman but have a husband. Whatever, Yoli, she said. She yawned. It was sweet of you to come back but I'm the one who needs to apologize. No, no, c'mon, I said. You must meet so many suave men with exciting accents and encyclopedic knowledge of European civilization, I said. Are you being sarcastic? she wondered.

She asked me about the hotshit lawyer guy in Toronto and I shook my head.

What's his name again? she said.

Finbar.

What? Oh my god, that's right. Finbar! I can't believe you're sleeping with a lawyer, first of all, and then with a lawyer named Finbar.

What's wrong with sleeping with a lawyer? I asked.

Well, nothing, she said, in theory. Just that you are, or were, is funny. She asked me if I was still seeing him and I told her I don't know and then I spilled all the details of my shambolic existence, that Finbar is not the only guy and she said Yolandi! How many? And I said only two but I'm so tired and overwhelmed and ashamed that I honestly can't remember if that's true or not. And one of them is in love with you, actually, and is only sleeping with me by proxy. She asked me if Finbar knows about the other guy and who is he and again I just shook my head no, yes, I don't think I told him. And besides he wouldn't care, and I told her okay, I know, this isn't my proudest moment or anything, it's some weird animal reaction to sixteen years of monogamy with Dan, so okay I've become a two-bit whore, whatever, burn me to death and she pointed to herself and then held her arms out to the psych ward spilling out around her to indicate where she was, empathy and a joke, my big sister, I love her, and we laughed a bit. A tiny bit. Not laughing, really, at all. And she said she hopes I'm using protection and this struck me as hilarious, coming from her.

I remembered the sex talk she gave me when I was twelve or thirteen. She asked me if I knew what a hard-on was and I said yes and she said great! That was it, the extent of it, my terse navigational guide to the biggest minefield confronting humankind. I remembered the four of us, our family, when we were all young and sane and alive, when we didn't have stitches in our heads and trembling hands, driving around in Winnipeg on some big night out in the city, maybe checking out the Christmas lights or something, and I was just learning how to read and was reading every sign out loud, practising, and when I saw Cockburn Avenue I said Cock Burn Avenue and then asked what's that? And Elf, she must have been eleven or twelve, said that's from too much sex and my mother said shhhh from the front passenger seat and we didn't dare look over at my dad who clutched the wheel and peered out the windshield like a sniper tracking his target. There were two things he didn't ever want to talk about and they were sex and Russia.

It was the first time I'd heard the word spoken, *sex*, and I had only a very vague notion of what it meant, that it had to do with hospitals. But more importantly, I remembered the look on Elf's face in the car. She was proud of herself, she smiled and hummed, stared out the window at the world she hoped to conquer one day, she had shaken things up in the bomb shelter of our tiny Mennonite microcosm and rattled the cages a bit. She had been shushed by our mother, which had never, ever happened before. That day I became acutely aware of her new powers and I wanted to be her. From then on I'd walk her bike solemnly up and down the sidewalk from one end of First Street to the other. I could barely reach the handlebars. I didn't even know how to ride a bike. I carried her textbooks up and down First Street too, shifting them wearily from one arm to the other, so great was my academic burden. I dabbed paint splotches on my dorky homemade jeans to look like her real ones and I practised looking soulful by pulling my bangs in front of my eyes and letting my lips go slack. I stood in front of the bathroom mirror and practised shooting myself in the head with an imaginary revolver, the way Elf did whenever she sarcastically felt she couldn't take it anymore. I thought it was brilliant. The timing, the quick beat between pulling the trigger and impact, and then jerking my head to the side. After a lot of practising I finally demonstrated to her that I'd mastered her very own signature move and she laughed and applauded and said well done, but that one's over now. This is the new one. And she showed me some elaborate mime involving an imaginary noose, a snapping neck, a lolling head. By then I'd lost interest in the idea itself and let her have it.

Yes, I told her, I'm using protection. She told me I could still get pregnant if I wasn't careful, that I wasn't too old, and I told her yeah, then she could be an aunt again.

When Will and Nora were little she babysat them a lot, reading to them, drawing with them, riding the bus with them, turning them into heroes and helping them create cool, fun worlds where anything was possible while I lurched about from part-time job to university class trying simultaneously to "set my sights high" and "lower my expectations." She still writes them letters and cards, or did until very recently, in different colours of ink, pink and green and orange, her distinct handwriting that reminded me of horses racing to the finish line, encouraging them to be brave, to enjoy life, to know how proud she is of them and how much she loves them.

I asked her if she would like it if I got pregnant, a ridiculous question implying that I'd do it, would immediately, that instant, get myself knocked up and have a baby if it would make her want to live. She answered with a sad smile, that gaze, the inconceivability of it all.

I asked her if she had had a nice visit with Nic last night, if she had eaten, if she had showered, if she had joined the others in the common room, if she had answered the call to breakfast or engaged with any other individual in the ward that day. She begged me not to interrogate her and I apologized, and she reminded me that we were going to chuck the apologies for a while. Yeah but apologies are what keep us civilized, I said and she said no, not at all, apologies allow for all sorts of brutality. Think about the Catholic notion of confession and how it allows for entire slates of indiscretion to be wiped clean and—

Okay, I said.

Do you know what Nellie McClung said? she asked me.

I'm afraid not, I said, but do tell.

Never explain, never retract, never apologize. Just get the thing done and let them howl.

I like that, I said, but isn't she talking about getting the vote for women? I just don't get the reference in this context. I was apologizing for *nagging* you.

Yoli, she said, I'm just saying that apologies aren't the bedrock of civilized society. All right! I said. I agree. But what *is* the bedrock of civilized society? Libraries, said Elf.

I thought about the fierce current of pride coursing through her veins, inherited from our father, buffeting or destroying, I didn't know which, and then of Pavese's last diary entry berating himself for not having the guts to kill himself. Even weak women (oh, go fly a kite, Pavese, as my mother would say) can do it, he writes, or something like that, and he concludes that the act requires humility, not pride.

Libraries, I said. Are you reading anything these days?

No. It's too hard to think.

And yet thinking is all you're doing.

I had started a book called *Am I a Redundant Human Being?*

Oh, Elf, I said. C'mon, man.

Do you think all we are is what we remember? she said.

No, I don't.

But Yoli, seriously . . . you answered so quickly, as if you just don't want me to ask that kind of question, but can't we at least consider it for a minute or two?

What do you mean? I don't know what you're asking me. I don't remember what I am. I am what I dream. I am what I hope for. I am what I don't remember. I am what other people want me to be. I am what my kids want me to be. I am what Mom wants me to be. I am what you want me to be. What do you want me to be? Don't we need to stick around to find out what we are? What do you want me to be?

Oh I don't know, said Elf. Tell me about your life in Toronto.

Well, I said, I write. I shop for food. I pay parking tickets. I watch Nora dance. Many times a day I ask myself questions. I walk around a lot. I often try to start conversations with people but it hardly ever works. People think I'm crazy. I came across a man playing his guitar in the park the other day and a lot of people, just people who happened to be in the park, were singing softly with him, so beautifully. I stopped to listen for a while.

What was the song? asked Elf.

I don't know, I said. One line I remember was we all have holes in our hearts. Or maybe he said lives. We all have holes in our lives. And this impromptu choir of park people singing along with him, repeating the line we all have holes in our lives . . . we all have holes in our lives . . .

I took Elf's hand and kissed it like a gentleman.

And then I thought that people like to talk about their pain and loneliness but in disguised ways. Or in ways that are sort of organized but not really. I realized that when I try to start conversations with people, just strangers on the street or in the grocery store, they think I'm exposing my pain or loneliness in the wrong way and they get nervous. But then I saw the impromptu choir repeating the line about everyone having holes in their lives, and so beautifully, so gently and with such acceptance and even joy, just acknowledging it, and I realized that there are ways to do it, just not the ones that I'd been trying.

So now you're going to stop talking to random strangers? asked Elf.

I guess so, I said. That's why you're so lucky to have your piano.

Elf laughed. Don't stop talking to strangers. You love talking to strangers. You're just like dad. Remember when we'd be in restaurants or whatever and he'd be looking at people and wondering hey, what's their story and then he'd go over and start talking?

Well, yeah, I said, but now that you mention it I was always a little bit embarrassed by it. I remember pulling dad away from strangers sometimes saying no, dad, it's okay, you don't have to talk to them. Nora and Will are probably mortified by me now.

Not probably, said Elf. They're teenagers. What else? Tell me more about Toronto.

Well, I said, the other day when I was walking down a back lane near my place I saw this old couple trying to reach something that was near the top of their garage door. I got closer and saw that they were trying to erase some graffiti but I didn't know what it was. And then I saw that the man was standing on a really low stool, it was only six or seven inches off the ground, and the woman was standing behind him, like spotting him, holding on to his hips so he wouldn't fall. I just wanted to cry. They were so old. And so concerned for each other, and just wanting to have a nice, clean garage. They were helping each other like that and the stool was only half a foot off the ground but it would have been a disaster if he'd fallen.

That's beautiful, said Elf. Her eyes were closed. I hope their garage stays clean forever.

It won't, I said. It'll be covered in graffiti again soon.

Hmmm, said Elf.

But what's so moving about this couple is that they keep trying to get rid of it. I guess they've been doing it all their lives, hoping against all odds that for once it'll stay clean.

Yoli, said Elf, have you embedded some type of parable within this story? Something you hope I'll *take away*?

You mean something about not giving up? I said.

That's what I mean, said Elf.

Nope, I said. In fact, now that I think about it, the lesson one could take *away* from this particular anecdote is to stop risking your life in order to have a pristine garage.

Elf sighed heavily and held her hands out like a father welcoming a prodigal son, like *we don't have to talk about this and the past is the past*. My cellphone rang and it was Elf's agent, Claudio. She'd been with him since she was seventeen and studying in Oslo. He appeared at a concert of hers in Rome and afterwards, when she was out back behind the concert hall smoking and crying and trembling as she often did following performances, he walked up to her and held out his hand and told her it was an honour to finally meet her. He had heard so much about her. He told her he would like to "represent" her and Elf said you mean you will pretend to be me? Claudio patiently explained the arrangement and asked Elf if perhaps he should be in contact with her parents. He asked her if she was all right, if he could call a cab for her, if she needed to eat. She was wearing her military jacket over her black concert dress and had kicked off her shoes and was sitting on the ground, crushing her cigarette into the asphalt, recovering, listening to this calm, debonair Italian man tell her she had an amazing future. I loved hearing Elf tell the story. And you decided right then to let him be your agent? I asked. No, she said, he insisted on flying to Manitoba first to meet mom and dad to ask their permission. Total class. I think he was the first real Italian ever to set foot in our town. Afterwards he said that some woman down the block, probably Mrs. Goosen, had gone over to mom and dad's just to stare at him. She told him she had never been out of the town. She gazed at him and told him that she just couldn't believe that she was standing in the same room as an Eye-talian! One small step for man, one giant leap for mankind. Elf didn't know anything about Claudio's personal life except that he visited his sick dad in Amalfi once a month and loved to swim long distances. He swims across straits and narrows and channels. Often his face is swollen from jellyfish bites. He's bailed Elf out in a million different ways.

I went out into the hallway. He apologized for phoning me but said that neither Elf nor Nic were answering their phones or e-mails and he had to go over the details of the tour with Elf and there was still a contract to be signed.

Do you know where she is? he asked.

Not exactly, I said. Hey, aren't you in Europe?

Yes, Paris. Listen, Yolandi, is it because she is doing her four-day meditation or is she on a kayaking trip with Nic?

I think, yeah, maybe . . .

The meditation thing?

Yeah.

Yolandi, please tell me everything is all right. I know Elf is unsteady as performance approaches. Is she well? Is she keeping it together? You know you can talk to me.

Um, maybe, I said. I'm not entirely sure.

You're not sure? he said. Well, does Nic know how she is? Yolandi, this tour is months in the making. She has to be ready in less than three weeks.

Probably Nic knows, yeah, I said. A nurse came up to me and told me that cellphones were not allowed on the ward. I motioned to her that I'd be off the phone in a second, sorry, sorry.

Are you in Toronto? said Claudio. Elf said you'd moved.

Well, yeah, I did, I said. It was for Nora, so she could dance.

Ah, beautiful! Are you liking it?

It's okay.

And Will? Where did you tell me he was studying?

New York.

Incredible! said Claudio. Please give them my regards.

Will do, I said. Thank you. I think I have to go though, I'm so sorry.

Not at all. Elf's scheduled for Toronto on the eighth I think, said Claudio. She'll probably have time for dinner.

Oh, that would be really great! I said. Yeah, I'll see her then. The nurse glared at me from her desk and I turned my back to her. Hey listen, Claudio, I'll find out where Elf is and get her to call you. My mom will know. Probably.

Yes, please do, Yolandi. I really must talk to her. I apologize for seeking reassurances from you.

No, no . . . don't apologize.

You know what's happened in the past, he said. I am sensitive to Elfrieda's *nervosa* . . .

Yeah, we appreciate that, thanks.

Do not thank me, he said. Oh and don't forget that there's the rehearsal two days before the opening . . .

The nurse was beating a path over to me now. Got it, I said. Where are you again?

Paris, said Claudio.

Paris, I said. For a second I stood dreaming of love.

I hung up and went back into Elf's room.

Booty call? she said.

Ha, yeah . . . I said. Hey, so are you missing your piano at all?

Elf looked out the window. Nic is dealing with that. I've already told you I can't—

You have almost three weeks. Maybe . . .

Yolandi, why are you . . .

I'm not doing anything, Elfrieda.

The cellphone-hating nurse came into Elf's room and said okay, two things: One, no phones on the ward. I've told you before. And two: No outside food. I noticed you brought her a sandwich. We want Elfrieda to eat with the other patients in the dining room.

Elf and I stared at her.

Elfrieda, said the nurse, can I get you to promise me that you'll come to the dining room for dinner this evening?

Uh, well, said Elf, I mean I can . . . I'll try. I'm not sure about you getting me to promise, though. She laughed.

I see, said the nurse. Is that a challenge?

What? No, said Elf. Not at all. I was just . . .

She was just joking around, I said.

Okay, that's great, said the nurse. We like jokes. Jokes are a good indication that you're feeling better, right?

Neither Elf nor I spoke. We couldn't look at each other.

If you're well enough to make a joke then I think you're well enough to join the others for dinner, right? said the nurse. Isn't that how it works?

I, uh . . . said Elf. Perhaps?

I guess so, I said.

I'm not sure, said Elf. I fail to understand the correlation between—

Yeah, yeah, I said. Dinner. I glanced at Elf.

Indeed, said the nurse. So, no cellphones? She was looking at me. No outside food?

Righto, I said. I gave her two thumbs up and smiled broadly.

The nurse left and Elf and I followed her with imaginary gunfire, blasting away with M-16s the way we did when we were girls and the burgermeister came to our house to tell our parents what Jezebels we were. We stopped firing and looked at each other.

Do you remember when you rescued me in my bedroom? I said. When I was naked and wedged between my bed and dresser?

Elf nodded. You were practising somersaults.

Do you remember when we went skateboarding in the hospital tunnel and those asshole boys locked me in the morgue and I was missing for like six hours and you were the one to find me all curled up on that stainless steel thing where they do autopsies?

Elf smiled and said oh no, don't talk about those days.

Why? I like to remember them, Elf. I like thinking about you rescuing me.

Yoli, moaned Elf. Talk about now. Keep talking to me about Toronto, she said. She had tears in her eyes.

I told her that I was in the process of having my tattoo removed. Dan and I have the same one. We had them done by a biker in Winnipeg's north end in our early days. And that having it removed now hurt more than I thought it would, but under the circumstances I was enjoying the pain and welcomed it. It felt like atonement of some kind. The biker who gave us the tattoos was a member of the Manitoba Warriors and lived in a house with a reinforced steel door that only opened from the inside. But wait, she said, then how did he get in? I don't know, I said.

I told her that I'd paid him twenty bucks and a bag of weed to get the tattoo and that I had to pay a thousand dollars to have it removed, and that it would take at least a year and a half because you only got a tiny bit of it removed at each session so that it wouldn't leave a big crater in your flesh. I told her the laser felt like an elastic band being snapped hard against my back about a hundred times. I had to wear goggles. Afterwards they put Polysporin on it and a bandage and gave me a mint and told me not to shower or exercise for two days and to continue putting Polysporin and fresh bandages on it twice a day for a week. I didn't bother with any of that.

I turned around in my chair and lifted my shirt so that Elf could see the fading imprint of my tattoo. It was a jester, an old-fashioned harlequin. As I recall, it had meant, I think, that Dan and I together would slay hypocrisy and the duplicity of the world with jokes and magic. She smiled again and closed her eyes. She said it made her sad. I said it made me sad too, but happy. I went on about Toronto, about the kids, each anecdote taking on the shape of a circus tent in my mind. I talked about my hapless love life, about the e-mail I'd received from Finbar the hotshit lawyer telling me that he was calling it off, my life was too intense, too troubled, my family was nuts, I was too emotional. He was bailing, or pulling the plug, or cutting me loose, something watery like that. Throwing me back like one of those fish caught for sport alone and not for keeping.

Then out of the blue, like that volcano in Pompeii, Elf asked me if I'd take her to Switzerland.

SIX

"THERE WAS SOMETHING, I suppose, like a wild waterfall in the headlong, broken, plunging quality of Mary's life. I stood and gazed at it roaring through the streets of Paris, visible only to me."

Which is what Richard Holmes says about Mary Wollstonecraft when she's in Paris "covering" the French Revolution. It's in his book *Footsteps*, in which he follows difficult artistic people through their lives—though long after their deaths—and tries to figure them out, and therefore himself. I'm currently reading it desperately as though somewhere in its pages are contained the directions to hell's only exit. It was my father and my sister who constantly beseeched my mother and me to read more, to find succour for life in books, to soothe our aches and pains with words and more words. Write it all down, my father would say when I went to him in tears about god knows what little injustice and here, read this, my sister would say chucking some tome at me when I asked her questions like, Is life a joke?

Well, Elf, no. I won't take you to Switzerland.

Please, Yoli, I'm asking you to do this one last thing for me. In fact, I'm begging you.

No. And don't say *one last thing*. That's so morbid.

Do you love me?

Yes! Which is why!

No, but Yo, if you truly love me . . .

Does it work that way? Don't you have to have a terminal illness?

I do.

You don't.

I do.

Well, no, you don't.

Yolandi.

Elfrieda! You are asking me to take you to Switzerland to be killed. Are you out of your fucking mind?

Yoli, said Elf. She was whispering. She mouthed the word *please* and I looked away.

Did Elf have a terminal illness? Was she cursed genetically from day one to want to die? Was every seemingly happy moment from her past, every smile, every song, every heartfelt hug and laugh and exuberant fist-pump and triumph, just a temporary detour from her innate longing for release and oblivion?

I remembered something I'd read, after my father's suicide, in Al Alvarez's book *The Savage God*. It had to do with some of the writers and artists who lived, and killed themselves, under Russia's totalitarian regime: "And, as we bow in homage to their gifts and to their bright memory, we should bow compassionately before their suffering."

I asked Elf if she was thinking at all of reasons to stay alive or if she was only trying to figure out an exit. She didn't answer the question. I asked her if those forces were constantly battling it out in her mind and she said if they were then it was a lopsided fight like Rodney King versus the LAPD. I asked her if she had any idea how much I would miss her. She looked at me. Her eyes filled up with tears. I shook my head. She didn't speak. I left the room. Then she called my name and I stopped and said, What.

You're not a slut, she said. There's no such thing. Didn't I teach you anything?

I went to the nurses' station and asked to speak to Janice. She came out of a little office holding tubes of paint and rolls of paper. Art therapy, she said. People love it. Yeah? I said. It's easier for a lot of our patients to express themselves with these—she waved the tubes around—than with language.

She took me into a little room with a gurney in it and a calendar and a chair that wasn't ripped. She pointed to the chair and I sat in it and she came over and put her hand on my shoulder. I took big breaths. She asked me how I was doing. I shook my head for such a long time. Just sat there with my index finger pressed to my lips, locking in the words, the way my father used to, staring at the calendar that was still in March when it should have been April and shaking my head. I wondered if she'd offer me a tube of paint and a piece of paper. She didn't move her hand from my shoulder. Finally I asked Janice about the pills. I asked her what was in them. What was the active ingredient? Do they give her the impression that there is meaning to life or do they flatten her to the point where she doesn't care if there is or isn't? Or do they enhance what is already in her mind and make it all right so that Elf could conceivably jump out of bed some morning and say hooray, it's true, there is no meaning to life but it's okay and now that I really know it and have had it confirmed and can stop searching for it I can go on living!

Janice told me that she didn't really know. She told me that it also didn't make much difference because Elf was refusing to take them anyway. Yeah, I said, she either takes an awful lot of pills at once or none at all. Janice was trying to make me feel better now too, so she patted me on the shoulder and then told me to go home and sleep.

I said I'd go say goodbye to Elf first but she told me just to go and that she'd tell Elf I'd be back soon. I was staring at the calendar and Janice followed my gaze and then walked over to it and flipped the page so it was showing the right month.

She said well, we've taken care of that now and I said, Yes, thank you.

I took the stairs to the basement by accident—two, four, six, eight—and ended up locked in a tunnel. I walked for a while and pushed on several doors but none of them would open. I wondered how long it would take before I was found. I checked my BlackBerry but couldn't get a signal. I saw footprints painted on the concrete floor. I followed them. They brought me to another locked door. I sat down in the tunnel and held my plastic Safeway bag in my lap. I looked up at the large pipes hanging from the ceiling of the tunnel. Then I took out my manuscript and held it in my hands for a while. I snapped the elastic holding it together a few times and put it back into the bag. I wondered if I would starve to death in the tunnel. Irony. Elf would feel bad, no? Jealous? A taste of her own medicine?

I got up again and walked in the opposite direction to the footprints and found another door. It was locked too. I went back to where I'd been sitting, following the footprints again, and then beyond that to a fork in the tunnels. I turned right and walked a while until I came to another door and I pushed on it and it opened. I was in an industrial kitchen or maybe I was in the morgue. Everything was made of stainless steel and the whole room hummed and shone. I walked through this room and through another door and straight into the emergency ward waiting room. A cop stood guarding something, I'm not sure what it was, but he told me to wash my hands. I told him they weren't dirty and he said that he had to ask everyone to wash their hands. He pointed at a makeshift handwashing stand. I asked him if he could hold my bag then for a minute while I washed my hands and he nodded and took it. I washed my hands very slowly, very thoroughly, and while I was washing I looked at the cop holding my manuscript in his hand. It felt safe there. I wanted to leave it with him but I dried my hands and took the bag and thanked him for holding it and walked out to the wrong parking lot in search of my mother's car.

———

Occasionally I sit in my mother's car and grip the steering wheel as hard as I can until my knuckles go white and I breathe out the word *Elllllfffff*. I'd punch a hole through the windshield if I didn't think I'd break my hand. And if it wouldn't create a big insurance nightmare, and a wicked draft in the winter. As a kid I used to go out to my bike and sit on it while it was in its stand going nowhere and I'd try out new swear words. I'd mutter them quietly under my breath, over and over, until they lost their sting and became ridiculous like Elf's one-time mantra of love. This car thing is similar to that. It feels like a controlled experiment. My own mobile laboratory of rage. If I can say things over and over they'll eventually lose their meaning and my anger will disappear. Elf, what are you fucking doing? I feel safe in the car, alone and protected. I can see people milling about in the parking lot but they can't see me. Well, they can but they think I'm insane so they look away which is the same as being invisible.

I met Nic for a beer on his way home from work. He told me he'd had no luck getting a hold of any of the care-team members except for one social worker who said that she wasn't sure there was still funding for that sort of thing. Nic had told her that he would pay for it himself, this team of bodyguards. The social worker wasn't sure it worked that way and Nic had asked her then in which way does it work? He talked to me about his kayak, its progress. He needed to have certain bolts mailed to him from Minneapolis. He was quite sure that he'd be in the river by May. But maybe it's just futile, I told him. To have her watched every second of the day. He agreed but what else were we supposed to do?

We drank our beer. He told me that Elf's book had arrived in the mail. It was *Final Exit*, the book on how to kill yourself with plastic bags and whatnot. I said oh my god, throw it away! But he said he couldn't do that because it would be an invasion of her privacy and an attack on her personal rights and freedoms. You don't just throw out someone else's mail. I argued with him for a while and he said maybe he could hide it away in a closet until she stopped being suicidal. And then what? I said. Haul it out and give it to her as a birthday surprise? Just throw the goddamn thing in the garbage. I can't throw a book, any book, in the garbage, he said. I said okay, then mail it back to Amazon or wherever it came from. But it's not mine, he said. All right, let me throw it out, I said. He said he can't let me do that, it's still not right.

Oh my god, Nic and I are having a fight. We don't want to have a fight. Or maybe we do if it makes us feel like we're doing something, getting somewhere, solving problems. Nic and I are approaching the task of caring for Elf from two entirely different angles, from a sterile laboratory and from the dark side of the moon. He is pragmatic, scientific, and believes in prescriptions, in doctors' orders and in their omnipotence.

One of my latest ideas for saving Elf's life is to have her parachuted into a strange and brutal place like Mogadishu or North Korea where she'd be forced to survive on her own in ways like never before. It was a risky plan. She could throw herself on the mercy of a child soldier and just get herself shot and that would be that or she could be jolted into a completely new notion of what it means to be alive and what is required to stay alive. Her adrenal gland would begin to work overtime and she'd be lifted up, energized, hunted, and desperate to outwit her attacker and survive. She would be utterly alone in this violent setting—though I would somehow have attached a live webcam to the side of her head or something like that so that I could track and monitor her progress. When I was convinced that she had established new parameters to living, found a new life strategy, as my father put it a couple of days before he ended it altogether, that she had come to thrive on the challenge, on the game of living, when she had come to the point of realizing that, like a normal person, lo and behold, she really didn't want to die, I'd have her helicoptered out and we could go on like before, laughing, walking, breathing, getting pedicures, making plans for next week and Christmas and the spring and old age. But Nic prefers the idea of medication and regular exercise and he's her primary caretaker, her husband, her immediate next of kin, so Elf won't be jumping out of a plane into downtown Mogadishu with nothing but the shirt on her back and a camera strapped to her head any time soon.

Nic and I stare off at the red booths of the restaurant and sip our beer and wonder and think. We have stopped arguing. I tell Nic that Claudio called me at the hospital, that he suspects something isn't right. I tell him that one of us definitely has to call him back. Nic sighs and says yeah, he knows, but what if she changes her mind and I remind him of how many millions of times she's said she can't do the tour and Nic says yeah, she always says that and then she does the thing and she's on top of the world. But only because she's survived it, I say. But then it doesn't take long before she realizes that she hadn't wanted to be rescued in the first place. I think that when she feels like she can't play anymore then her life is over.

Yeah, says Nic. Well, he's been calling me too. I don't answer. But I feel guilty about it.

It is so quiet in this restaurant. I ask Nic if he is also feeling the earth rotate on its axis. He reminds me that we're in a revolving restaurant at the top of Fort Garry Place in Winnipeg, Manitoba, Canada, and that the day is such and such. I thank him. I apologize for giving him a hard time about the phone call and the book and he waves it away and says no, no. I want to hug him. I want to thank him for loving my sister and her rights and freedoms. I ask him if the waiter will stop this thing, the building, to let us off and he says yeah, there's gotta be a switch somewhere. Or we could wave our arms in the air and yell faster, I say. We play a little tug of war with the check. I'll get this. No, I'll get this. We walk out into a tornado, it seems—it's a prairie wind—and Nic tells me that in the days and weeks after I left for Toronto Elf had adopted a new mantra.

What was it? I ask him.

Yolandi, he says.

Me? You mean my name?

She joked that maybe she'd be able to will you back into existence.

I was only in Toronto, I say, not dead. Besides, she told me that her mantras inevitably dissolve into meaninglessness and then begin to terrify her. And I'm fighting tears again. And apologizing to Nic for something. He tells me that Elf feels the same way about days, about the days constantly coming around, over and over, the sun rises, birds begin to sing, there is a moment of possibility, of excruciating hope, and then it's over, things darken, the day is simply another tease. There is no delivery from the torment of the days. It's the repetition of things that kills her? I ask. Nic sighs. He doesn't know. I trip over the uneven sidewalk and swear. He catches my elbow. Two boys walk past us with a canoe on their heads. We think they're boys but all we can see are hairy calves and beat-up sneakers, oversized basketball shorts and bare backs. No heads or arms. By the amount of hair and muscle on their calves and their narrow waists I'd say they're about fourteen or fifteen years old.

I wouldn't put that in the river right now, Nic calls out to them. It's too dangerous.

The boys stop and awkwardly turn themselves around, canoe and all, to listen.

We're not, one of them says. Four brown legs and a canoe on their heads for a surface, they are a designer table, strange and beautiful.

Seriously, says Nic, the river is crazy right now. It's moving at 380 cubic metres a second and it still has some ice on it.

The boys say nothing but the canoe shifts slightly and then we hear them softly mumbling to each other under the boat.

Don't do it, says Nic. Maybe in a week or so. Then suddenly in one beautiful, fluid motion the boys lift the canoe off their heads, flip it over like a pancake and lay it down on the grassy boulevard next to the sidewalk.

Oh, hi, says Nic. I wave hello and smile. The boys are grim, young and tired.

What about downstream? says one of them, and Nic shakes his head vigorously.

No, no, not in any direction. Just stay out of the river for the time being. What's the rush?

The boys tell us they're trying to get to Roseau River Reserve.

That's miles away, says Nic. That's near the U.S. border, isn't it?

We know, says one of the boys. We're from there.

The boys tell us that they want to get home, back to their real mom. They're foster kids in the city and they hate it and their foster parents beat them up and starve them, and the Warriors are trying to recruit them for operations and they're going home, that's it.

Now we have a situation, as the cops would call it. Neither Nic nor I know what to say or do. The boys shrug and mumble more things to themselves and bend to pick up the canoe, tipping it up and onto their shoulders.

You don't have life jackets, I say. The boys ignore me.

Yeah, he says. Listen. Hang on. The boys have already begun to walk away. They stop walking again, but they don't put the canoe back onto the ground. Nic and I walk over to where the boys are and stand next to them with the canoe acting as a barrier between us like a confessional booth.

You guys can't do this, says Nic to the front, the bow, of the boat. His voice is low and stern, *mano a mano*. Nothing happens. The boys breathe in silence and the canoe gently bobs up and down a bit on top of them. Nic asks the boys if they have somebody waiting for them in Roseau River.

Yeah, everyone— I think it is the smaller one's voice. We live there.

Okay, so how about this, says Nic. I'll give you money for two bus tickets to Roseau River and you leave the canoe with me. I'll bungee it to my car and keep it for you at my place and you can pick it up whenever it suits you, when you're back in the city, or whatever. I'll write down my address for you. How much are bus tickets to Roseau River? he asks.

There's no response from under the canoe.

Tell you what, says Nic. I'm going to get my car now and drive it back here, so just hang on. Yoli, can you write down my address for these guys.

Probably around twenty bucks, says one of the boys. Twenty bucks each. Nic leaves to get his car and the boys fling the canoe down onto the grass again and sit down on top of it, waiting.

So what's Roseau River like? I say. The boys shrug and stare off in the direction of the river. I am writing Nic's address on a scrap of paper as he pulls up and parks. He hands the boys some money, enough cash for the bus tickets to Roseau River.

How about we drive you to the bus depot? he asks. The smaller boy says okay but the other boy says nah, we'll get there ourselves. He leans over to take the cash from Nic, and the two begin to walk away towards Portage and Main, away from the river.

Hey, hang on, I call, you'll need his address. I run after them and hand one of the boys the scrap of paper. He looks at it for a few seconds and puts it into his pocket and says c'mon to the other kid and they're off, on their way to something they remember as being better than where they are.

Do you think they'll buy bus tickets? I ask Nic. We're driving back to his house with the canoe on the roof of the car.

Who knows, says Nic, but there was no way they were putting this thing into the river.

Do you think they'll come back for the canoe?

Probably not, says Nic, but I hope so. It might be a borrowed canoe, if you get my drift.

You saved their lives, I say, and Nic waves it all away like he'd done earlier with the check from the restaurant, like he does with all falsely inflated proclamations that can't be proven in a lab. My phone goes off and I read a text from Nora: *I've been banned for like a lifetime from Winners for having a testers war with Mercedes. Will ripped the screen breaking in. No key. Xxxxoooo*

I am talking to a police officer. I've been stopped on Sherbrook Street for texting while driving. I'm on my way over to Julie's for a quick coffee before I have to pick up my mother at the airport. Somebody worth risking your life and your pocketbook for, I presume? says the cop. Pocketbook? I repeat. Well yes, I say, it's my daughter. I just had to send her a quick message. But okay, sorry, the law and everything. How much is it?

Well, says the cop, one of the main things we hope the driver takes away from this particular lesson is the severity of the crime. The cost is administrative, minimal, but the offence itself is egregious, potentially.

That's true, I say, um . . . How much is it?

He asks to see my car registration and when I show it to him—it's my mother's car—he slaps the roof and says no way! I play Scrabble with Lottie down at the Waverley Club. You're her daughter? I smile too and say yep, one of them. Upshot of it all (that's an archery term, by the way, meaning the last shot of the competition) is that the cop spends ten minutes telling me how crazy he is about Lottie—she kicks my ass, man, she kicks my ass every time! Are you aware of her vocabulary?—and then pulls out his pad to write me a ticket.

Just doing my job, he says You know, you, my friend, are an asshole, I say. That's seven letters, incidentally, a-s-s-h-o-l-e, a good bingo word.

The cop leans into the car. You're not really supposed to call cops assholes. He sounds apologetic. We finally agree that he'll give me a warning only and I promise to pull over next time I want to send someone a text and I won't tell my mom that he's been a bit of a jerk.

I sense she's already slightly contemptuous of me being a cop, he says. She really hates authority, man, have you noticed?

I'll pick my mother up at the airport later that evening. She will have taken a boat, a train, a plane, a cab and another plane and a car to get home. I picture it all in my mind, all the various legs of her journey, and am comforted by this effort of hers to come back to us.

Julie and I sit on her back steps and are quietly amused by the sweet antics of Shadow, the family dog she has joint custody of along with her kids. She has made us smoothies with mint from her garden and we eat the perogies and salad she's managed to whip up magically in her chaotic kitchen that has bicycles and guitars in it. She used to play bass guitar in a band called Sons and Lovers. She has just bought this house and is in the process of fixing it up. She shows me a dildo she found wedged behind a cabinet in the bathroom.

I'm going to smoke a cigar, she says. Don't tell Judson. Judson is a guy she's been seeing on and off since splitting up with her husband. He says it's a condition of our relationship that I don't smoke, she says.

We laugh. We are tired. Too tired to confront conditions.

Shadow the dog is too old and arthritic to run but is still very excited by the idea of running so Julie plays a game she calls Run for Shadow and it involves her saying things like *shed* or *fence* and then running there herself while Shadow sits still in the yard and barks excitedly. When Julie has exhausted herself playing Run for Shadow she plops down beside me on the back steps and finishes her cigar.

Do you think you're still suffering from your grandparents being massacred in Russia? I ask her.

Am I suffering? she asks. It was just my grandmother. She couldn't run because she was nine months pregnant. My grandfather made it with the other kids.

Do you think that all that stuff can still affect us even now? She shrugs and takes a big haul off her illicit cigar.

SEVEN

LONG HUGS AT THE AIRPORT. We have missed each other. One of us is slightly tanned and smells like coconut and is wearing a T-shirt with a Scrabble tile on it with the letter *P*. We don't know about tomorrow. I smell fear and realize that it's coming from me. It feels like I don't have quite enough skin, that parts of me that should be covered are exposed. And we hold on to each other for longer than usual. On the way home we stop in on Nic, it's too late to go to the hospital to see Elf, and my mother tells us of her latest adventure at sea and we laugh a lot, too much, and Nic sits on Elf's piano bench while we talk, occasionally turning around to plunk on the keys tunelessly, and then we all head home to our beds. But strange things happen in the night. I have a dream about Elf. She's been discharged but nobody can find her. She's not at home. We can't reach her. Then I dream that grass is growing everywhere inside my house, it's tall, silky grass. It's coming up through the stairs. I don't know how to get rid of it and I'm worried. Then, in my dream, the solution comes to me: do nothing. And in an instant my anxiety is gone and I'm at peace. I also have a dream that I have a stone angel like Margaret Laurence's, the same one, and I have to take care of it, keep it safe and warm. In my dream the stone angel lies beside me in my bed, the blanket pulled up to her chin, her eyes perpetually staring up at the ceiling.

I wake up and call the nurses' station at the hospital and ask if Elf is still there. They tell me she is. I lie in bed for a while listening to the ice breaking up, and hear my mother moving around in the living room. I get up to see if she is okay. When she sees me she tells me she has a bit of jet lag from the trip and can't sleep. She is sitting at the dining room table playing online Scrabble with a stranger in Scotland. I tell her I met her cop friend and she frowns. He's ambitious, she says. To be ambitious, in her opinion, is the lowest a person can sink. I hear a trumpet sound the beginning of a new game. The Holy Bible, King James Version, is sitting on the table beside her computer. I ask her if she's been reading the Bible and she says yeah, well, you know with all of this . . . She makes a dismissive gesture. This life, I think she means. She tells me she has decided to read Psalms One but hasn't liked it. She doesn't like the way it talks about the ungodly as being like chaff in the wind, blown about, lost, so she reads Proverbs One instead but she doesn't like that one much either. She doesn't like the way it orders us to seek out knowledge and wisdom because . . . obviously!

She tells me the only reason she is reading the Bible right now is that she's been communing with her dead sister Mary who has somehow indicated to her, from the grave, that she should read the Bible more often. I nod and tell my mother to say hi to Aunt Mary from me next time they talk. I wonder if that's the real reason she's reading the Bible or if this evening she needs hope and solace and is looking to that oldest of friends, her faith.

I ask her if she wants to play a few rounds of Dutch Blitz, the only Mennonite-sanctioned card game, because instead of sinful-connoting things like clubs and hearts and diamonds and spades on the cards it has ploughs and buckets and wagons and pumps and because it's a game based on speed and concentration, not sneakiness, and the small room glows when she smiles.

My mother sits in the torn orange chair and I sit perched on the edge of Elf's bed. Elf lies smiling, her stitches have dissolved, and she has washed her face and brushed her hair. There's been a change according to Janice. She tells us that she had a long conversation with Elf that morning and that she is showing signs of improvement. My mother asks what improvement means and Janice says it means that Elf has eaten her breakfast and taken her pills. In the past my mother would have rejoiced at these tiny victories but today she nods and says hmm, so she's doing what she's told to do. I know that this doesn't please my mother. She believes in the fight, in sparks and pugilism, not meek subservience. On the other hand, she wants my sister to eat and take her medication. But wants Elf to want it herself.

I don't know exactly what happened, Elf tells us, but I woke up feeling like a different person. I think I'm ready to do the tour. I'm going to call Claudio. I want to play tennis again. And maybe Nic and I will move to Paris.

If ever there was a delayed reaction for the ages this is it, a vast, forlorn space like the Badlands, a no man's land, universes between her words and my mother's and my response. My mother and my sister smile at each other like it's a contest and I freeze. Rearguard action, I think. I stare out of the window and reflect on the similarity between writing and saving a life and the inevitable failure of one's imagination and one's goals and ambitions to create a character or a life worth saving. In life as in writing as in any type of creation that sets off to be a success, knowable and inspiring.

Really? I say. Paris? That's so great, Elfie. I can't believe it.

Her roommate, Melanie, says me neither from behind the curtain.

Elf turns to the curtain and says can I ask you to please mind your own business and Melanie tells her that she's not here on business.

I leave them and go into the hallway and shuffle like a chain gang over to the little alcove that is fast becoming my favourite nook where I can sit alone and gaze down at the parking lot and out to the fields beyond it. We have a choice, I think to myself. We can take her at face value, as they say, and hope. Or we can assemble that elusive team now and I mean right now because she's going home. I know it. She shall be released. I know that if she follows the rules and tells the nurses and the doctors that she's feeling good, positive, not suicidal, not at all—are you kidding me? and be forced to say goodbye to the majesty of all of this?—that she will be home in time for dinner today.

I call Nic and he doesn't answer. I go to the nurses' station and am told that Janice is on her break. I ask if Elf is going to be discharged today and the nurse says who's Elf and I say Elfrieda Von Riesen and the nurse says she doesn't know and hasn't heard.

I go back to Elf's room and discover my mother singing a song to her in Plautdietsch. It's called "Du." Which means You. Elf is holding her hand. It's a song about loving forever, even with the pain caused by loving so hard, a song she sang to us when we were kids.

Then things happen quickly. Janice comes back into Elf's room. She's smiling and she says hello all and tells us that Elf will probably be going home today just as soon as she's seen the doctor and he gives her the green light. I imagine the doctor as Ben Kenobi passing Elf a sabre. My mother and I together say wow, that's great, fantastic. Elf smiles at Janice and looks grateful.

Janice sits next to her on her bed and asks her if she's really feeling well enough to go back home. We all know what she means. Elf says yes, definitely, she wants to get back to Nic and her real life. She's combing her hair with her fingers. She's willing to take the medication and will book follow-up appointments with her shrink. She's ready. And she appreciates everything that's been done for her while she's been a patient here. She sounds like she's giving a rehearsed speech at the Oscars.

I give her a kiss on her cheek and say whew, that's so great. That's so great. My mother is sitting quietly with her hand on her heart, her eyes wide.

I'm panicking and confused. Janice says she'll leave us alone for a bit while Elf gets her things together and I follow her out into the hallway. I ask her if it's really a good idea that Elf goes home and she says she thinks it is and that she has no choice. She's been admitted voluntarily, not against her will, so she can leave when she feels like it too. I ask her if it isn't too soon and Janice says that it's very important for the patient to feel empowered by being allowed to make big decisions.

Well, I said, a very big decision would be the decision to kill herself and nobody wants to let her make that one, right? Janice agrees and gets my point but says her hands are tied. And they really need the bed. And let's give her the benefit of the doubt. Let's just see what happens, she says. And adds that she has a good feeling about it. She tells me that Elf wants to play tennis with me as soon as it warms up a bit and I don't know how to respond to that.

I try calling Nic on the phone and this time he answers. I tell him that Elf is coming home today and he's surprised. This was the first he'd heard of it. So what do we do? I say and he says he'll call that person about the team immediately. He says he'll leave work early and pick up groceries and meet us all back at the house later in the afternoon.

I go back into Elf's room and find her up and out of bed, looking for her clothes. I help her put some of her things into a plastic bag and then realize that I've misplaced my own plastic bag, the one with my manuscript in it, but I am strangely calm, and I think fine, okay, all right.

But then my mother says hey Yoli, is this yours? She's been sitting on it. She peeks inside and says oh, is this the new thing? I say yeah and she asks me how many words I have. For some reason this question makes me laugh. I shake my head. Elf tells her the first letter is amazing. My mother waits, smiling, for an answer. I don't have an answer. She guides me out into the hallway, her hand on the small of my back. She's so short and she smells so good, like coconut milk. She hugs me in the hallway and tells me everything will be all right. I love that she tells me this again and again but I wonder sometimes if she thinks I'm an idiot. Regardless, she's my mother and that's what mothers say. Bob Marley says it too but he says every *little* thing gonna be all right and that strikes me as an appropriate qualifier even if all he was doing was getting enough syllables to match the music. I remember humming that refrain over and over, singing myself to sleep with those lyrics in the days before my father kneeled in the path of a fast-moving train.

That evening we celebrate Elf's homecoming with spicy Indian food and good wine and Nic's special stash of Armagnac that my mother gave him for Christmas two years ago. Elf is smiling, a little shy, beautiful and serene, as though she alone holds the answer to the riddle of the Sphinx. Her hands shake only slightly and she's wearing a pale pink scarf around her throat. She's put a bit of makeup on the scar above her eye. Her pants are too big on her now but Nic has fashioned some kind of funky rope belt for her to wear. Nic is thrilled to have her home. He is calling her my love and my darling. My mom calls her honeybunch. I would like to give Elf a note right now that says we promised but I don't have a Sharpie thick enough to make my point. Nic is talking about Chinese literature and learning Mandarin and Elf is thumbing through a novel he's taken out of the library for her to read. There's no mention of Paris or tennis.

Listen! I want to shout at her. If anyone's gonna kill themselves it should be me. I'm a terrible mother for leaving my kids' father and other father. I'm a terrible wife for sleeping with another man. Men. I'm floundering in a dying non-career. Look at this beautiful home that you have and this loving man loving you in it! Every major city in the world happily throws thousands of dollars at you to play the piano and every man who ever meets you falls hard in love with you and becomes obsessed with you for life. Maybe it's because you've perfected life that you are now ready to leave it behind. What else is there left to do? But I'm finding it hard to make eye contact with Elfrieda. She's not looking at me. She barely lifts her head from the novel Nic has given her.

My mother is tired from her trip and basically from all time since Anno Domini but also refreshed and happy just to see Elf at home. Apparently she got stranded out at sea again this time. It happens to her every time she goes to an ocean. She just bobs along on her back enjoying the sun and the undulating waves and then gets too far out and can't get back and has to be rescued. She doesn't panic at all, just sort of slowly drifts away from the shore and waits to be noticed or missed. Her big thing is going out beyond the wake where it's calm and she can bob in the moonlight far out at sea. That's her biggest pleasure. Our family is trying to escape everything all at once, even gravity, even the shoreline. We don't even know what we're running away from. Maybe we're just restless people. Maybe we're adventurers. Maybe we're terrified. Maybe we're crazy. Maybe Planet Earth is not our real home. In Jamaica, my mom had to be dragged, laughing her head off, back to shore by three shirtless fishermen after she went flying off a banana boat and couldn't manage to climb back onto it.

Nic goes into the kitchen to get more drinks and I follow him and whisper what about the team, is it happening? He and I go downstairs on the pretence of getting more beer from the basement fridge and he tells me that this team is more mythical than anything. Apparently, with budget cuts and changes in policy and . . . He's speaking but my mind drifts as I stare at the spine of *The Rise and Fall of the Roman Empire*, a book lying all by itself randomly on the concrete basement floor as if it has been thrown down in a hurry . . . It's not really an option but he'll continue to pursue other possibilities. I go to the book and pick it up and hand it to Nic. But possibilities of what? I ask him. What are we talking about? He takes the book, says I know, really, and breathes out heavily. In the meantime he's made arrangements with Margaret, a friend of theirs, to stay with Elf for a few hours every day and my mother too will obviously visit every day. I know, I say, but Elf's supposedly going on a five-city tour in two weeks. Look at her, do you honestly think she can tour? Have you talked to Claudio?

God, he says. He hasn't talked to Claudio. He doesn't know, all he knows is that touring terrifies her before she goes and then makes her feel exhilarated when she's actually doing it. I tell him I have to go back to Toronto quickly. Will has to get back to New York for his exams and Dan is still in Borneo and I can't leave Nora by herself, unsupervised, for longer than a day or two. As soon as her classes end I'll come back here with her and we can spend the summer. I'll see Elf every day if she's not on tour. He understands and says he's got everything under control and there are airplanes, right? And telephones.

We go back upstairs and my mother is telling Elf about her Scrabble ratings. She's got an average of thirteen hundred and something and Elf is nodding, impressed, pretending she hasn't heard it before. My mother tells Elf she made the word *cunt* the other day at the club. It's a valid word! she says. Were you challenged? asks Elf. Nah, says my mom, the young guy I was playing with was so embarrassed he couldn't even look at me, this old grandma laying down a dirty word. Elf smiles. She's not saying much, though. But what is there to say? How is she feeling? Is this impromptu gathering a grotesque, fake sideshow in her opinion? Does she wonder what exactly we're celebrating? Her failure to properly execute her plan to die? Or is she genuinely happy and relieved to be here?

C'mon, Elf! I think. Stop your hands from shaking and say something. Address your nation and let us know there's reason to have faith in the future. Yes, there are airplanes and telephones.

I want to ask Elf if she's afraid. I'm short of breath again. I'm smiling and trying to cover up my panic and discreetly suck oxygen into my lungs. I'd like to take Elf with me back to Toronto. I'd like for us all, my mother, my sister, my kids, Nic, Julie, her kids—even Dan and Finbar and Radek—to live in a tiny isolated community in a remote part of the world where all we have to look at is each other and we are only ever a few metres apart. It would be like an old Mennonite community in Siberia but with happiness.

———

Eventually we all leave. Elf is sitting at the piano, her hands moving soundlessly across the keys. When she gets up from the bench to say goodbye to my mom and me there are tears on her face. My mother lives only a few blocks away and decides to walk. She says she needs the exercise. Elf and I watch her cross the street safely, like a kid, and we all wave.

I tell Elf I love her, that I will miss her, but that I'll be back in Winnipeg soon. Can I see her in Toronto when she's there playing? Maybe, she says. But she'll only be there for sixteen hours. She'll rehearse, sleep, eat, perform, go back to the hotel, sleep, get up early to fly away. Rosamund, Claudio's assistant, will be travelling with her this time. She tells me she loves me too. That she wants to know more about Toronto, my life there, and she asks me to write her letters, not e-mails but old-fashioned letters that will come to her in the mail in envelopes with stamps on them. I tell her I will, definitely, and will she write me back? She says she will, absolutely. Rock-solid.

I'm holding her wrists, my fingers encircle her tiny bones, and I squeeze hard until she says ouch and I apologize and let go. We don't talk about the meaning of life, about scars, about stitches, or the number of words that we have or promises that we've made in the faraway past.

Then I drive around the perimeter of the city like a dog marking its territory, over bridges and under bridges, the way I used to stalk the edges of my small hometown. This is mine. Nothing bad will happen here if I patrol the streets like a crazed vigilante. Welcome to Winnipeg, the population will not change. I drop in on Julie and tell her I'm leaving early the next morning now, and I agree to call her as soon as I'm back in Toronto and I stop in at Radek's and say goodbye and I thank him for the food and for the shelter from the storm and when he scratches his head and says yeah but . . . I shrug and shrug and smile and back away and continue to thank him for his sweetness, for his grace, for his time.

I drive my mother's car like it's a Panzer and the streets are my enemy, and I'm feeling bad and stupid and mean. I think about setting up an appointment with a therapist when I get back to Toronto but tell myself I can't afford it. I'll work harder, that's all. Besides, what would I talk about with a therapist? When my father killed himself I went to see one and he suggested I write my father a letter. It wasn't clear what I was supposed to say in the letter. I thanked the therapist and left thinking but my father is dead now. He won't receive this letter. What's the point? Can I just have my one hundred and fifty-five dollars back to buy some Chardonnay and a bag of weed?

When I get back to my mother's apartment she is sleeping, snoring very loudly, and season something of *The Wire* is blaring on her TV set and a small space heater is making noise too and the ice is still tearing itself apart on the river that runs beneath her. I stand next to her bed and look at her for a while wondering if her sleep is peaceful, if it's the only relief she knows. I go into the spare bedroom and lie down in my clothes on top of the covers. It seems futile now to undress and go to bed in a serious way because I have to get up soon and go to the airport. I fall asleep and then wake up to a commotion in the living room. My mother is up and talking to a man.

The story is: My mom woke up and went out onto the balcony for a look at the night sky and while she was doing that she happened to see this man, Shelby, parking his truck in the parking lot. She suddenly had a plan. She called down to Shelby to see if he'd be interested in hauling her old electric organ over to Julie's house for her kids to practise on. She really needed someone with a truck. She would pay him. He said sure. They had a conversation in the middle of the night with her standing in her nightgown on the balcony like Juliet's nursemaid. Now Shelby was in the apartment measuring the organ and wondering how he'd carry it down to the truck.

My mother said oh good, Yoyo, you're up.

So Shelby and I carried the organ to his truck and my mother held the apartment doors open with her nightgown flapping wildly in the wind. It started to rain. Soon it was pouring. My mother ran upstairs to get a garbage bag to cover the organ while it was in the truck being driven to Julie's house in the middle of the night. I asked my mother if Julie was expecting this delivery at this time and she said no, but we would deal with that when we got there.

Shelby and my mother and I squeezed into the cab of his truck and delivered the organ to Julie's house. She and her kids were fast asleep and not answering the door, so we carried it into the shed in the yard and put a sign on her door telling her that we had brought an organ to her house and that it was in the shed. We drove back to my mother's apartment block and she gave Shelby fifty dollars for his help. We said good night to Shelby and stood in her apartment dripping water all over the kitchen floor. There was also water all over the bathroom floor, and the river was forecast to spill its banks and lightning continued to rent the air.

Well, said my mother, that's done at least.

I understood her need to accomplish something, however strange, something with clear rising action and a successful ending. She said she would try to get a little sleep before I had to leave but to wake her up first. I was wide awake so I went downstairs to the apartment building's exercise room and stood on the treadmill. I pushed the start button and began to run. I was wearing chunky boots and tight jeans and my hair was spraying water all over the treadmill and onto the floor. I saw the empty swimming pool outside the glass patio doors and the list of Pool Rules written in cursive, and a thin red line against the horizon. I ran until I was drenched with sweat, gasping for air, until I pushed a button that said Cool Down, and I walked slowly on the machine, gripping the handlebars.

EIGHT

Dear Elf,

A handwritten letter, as commanded, as promised. We have an ant infestation. This happened while I was in Winnipeg. Our landlord believes it has something to do with the degree of filth in our apartment but I suspect it has more to do with the degree of natural decay in the universe. We're not that filthy anyway, just messy. I've put little white plastic trays filled with poison all over the apartment. Will has gone back to New York. He can't wait to see you and Nic this summer. He managed to keep

Nora alive but the place is a disaster. Apparently mess doesn't "scan" for either one of them. Nora has a boyfriend now, apparently, a guy in one of her classes who is also here on a scholarship, from Sweden. When I got home a boy was cooking an omelette in the kitchen. There were bags from Whole Foods all over the place. Whole Foods is an expensive healthy grocery store that I never shop at. I go to a place called No Frills. This stranger in my kitchen couldn't speak English so I had no idea what he was doing there and I had to wait until later that evening, when Nora showed up, to find out. In the meantime I went out for several long walks and in between smiled at him and pointed at a few things, nodding, etc.

I have a little room off my bedroom where I had planned to sit and work but I never go in there, it's too cold. So I write at the dining room table or in bed. I like to listen to the mourning doves when I wake up early. They make me sad and happy and nostalgic I guess for my childhood, our childhood, and the prairies and that feeling of waking up with nothing to do but play. Do you know I used to wake up singing for a while there when I was about nine and ten? When you were in that bedroom with the wooden walls and that Mikhail Baryshnikov poster called When Push Comes to Shove. Where is that guy these days anyway? And was it his dancing you loved so much, or his body, or the fact that he left everything behind in Russia with no hope of ever returning, just for his art? Anyway, apparently mourning doves are being shot and eaten these days. Can you believe it? When I heard about it I felt the same way I did when I heard that Joe Strummer had died. The music of my youth. When you're fifteen and you wake up in the morning to mourning doves singing *and* The Clash you know you're in Heaven. Anyway, Joe Strummer is dead and mourning doves are being eaten. What does that say about one's childhood? Who is left to lead us out of the wilderness?

I don't know a lot of people here. The only call I ever get is from a recorded voice saying Hello! Has your debt become uncontrollable? The last time it happened I whispered yes, yes, it has, and then quickly hung up like a hostage sending a cryptic message to my would-be rescuers. I've cashed in that RRSP thing that dad gave us a million years ago and have already spent my half of the house sale on rent in this city and yesterday my landlord told me it's going up to some number I've never even heard of.

Finbar, the lawyer, is texting again. He says he's worked through some stuff and thinks it's okay if he and I get together again in spite of my peripatetic lifestyle. He admires my hamstrings. I have a sixth toe now. Okay, it's a bunion. Sometimes, if I'm doing a lot of walking, it throbs like a little penis on the side of my foot. I also have some weird golf ball–sized thing growing on the back of my heel which I think is called Haglund's deformity. Our dog had one of those once, remember, and Uncle Ray gave her one of his horse tranquilizers and then hacked it off with that gutting knife? I just remember you carrying her around for a couple of weeks because she couldn't walk afterwards. Or you put her in that little wagon and

pulled her everywhere. Would you do that for me if my
deformity gets out of hand? Also, I was in a little accident the other day, did I tell you about that? Just a tiny
fender-bender but with insurance here in Ontario being
very expensive and blah blah and still having Manitoba
insurance (whoops) I'm not sure that I'll be covered and I
might have to pay a million dollars to the woman for her
totally unscathed BMW SUV. She actually got out of her
car and took a picture of her absolutely pristine bumper
with her cellphone while I stood there (in my cut-offs and
green windbreaker, holding a six of Heinekens) saying
c'mon, you are NOT serious.

Nora and I are conducting a bit of an experiment.
We're attempting to make eye contact with Torontonians.
It's frustrating. People are startled when we look at them
and quickly look away or somehow will themselves not
to even look in the first place. We've noticed that some
people visibly will turn their heads away from us and even
their shoulders so they're not tempted to look. Today
Nora and I went for a quick walk in our neighbourhood
(Little Malta) and of the sixty-eight people we passed on
the sidewalk only seven of them returned our gaze and of
those seven only one smiled and it might not have been
a real smile but a grimace due to gas. Nora and I pretend
to be indifferent to it, but it hurts! We've wondered if it's
because of how we dress or if we emit some kind of vibe
that makes people not want to have any contact at all with
us or if we seem desperate or dangerous or weird. Well, I
have to run to pick up Nora from a rehearsal and get her
to a dentist appointment on time. In the meantime, I'll be

thinking of you and missing you and . . . floating on the wings of nothingness.

Your humble and obedient servant, Y (see? I have read the letters of your poet lovers).

Elf is not answering the phone. I call my mother and she says yes, that's true, she's not. Well, sometimes she does, well, actually, no, I guess she doesn't. Well, sometimes, yes, sometimes but mostly not. Really not at all. Once in a blue moon, but basically no, she doesn't.

I can't bear to hear my mother waffle like this between hope and despair. My mother tells me that if she's there, at Elf's place, when the phone rings she does encourage Elf to answer it but even then it's a struggle and mostly Elf wins and the phone goes unanswered.

I can hear the trumpets sounding on her laptop indicating that another Scrabble game is about to begin.

Dear Elf,
Today I went for a long walk and ended up watching ducks dive headfirst into Grenadier Pond in High Park. I wondered for how long they could hold their breath and I counted seventy-eight seconds before one came up for air. What is it for humans? A minute? Today I heard a pretty good conversation on the streetcar. This guy got on and he was swearing his head off, really foul stuff like that fucking bitch can suck my cock if she fucking thinks . . . and the streetcar driver said hey, whoah, you can't swear

like that on the streetcar and the guy stopped and looked at him and then he said he was really sorry, really sorry, he understood, and he got off at the next stop and started swearing again as soon as he'd stepped off the streetcar.

I miss you. Nora and I went up to the top of the CN Tower yesterday. We're trying to understand our new city from a bird's-eye view. We put a loonie into a powerful set of binoculars but we still couldn't see you. We went up to the rooftop bar at the Park Hyatt and I had a glass of twelve-dollar wine and we shared some olives and almonds. We gazed off a little despondently in a westerly direction. *We* miss you. Nora asked me if I regretted having children which shocked me and made me feel like a terrible mother, like I'd been giving her the impression that she was slowly crushing the life right out of me. But then she went on to say that she was thinking of never getting pregnant because she couldn't bear the thought of her body housing an alien and ballooning into some grotesque caricature of womanhood. I hope she doesn't have an eating disorder. I've read that eating disorders are often the fault of overbearing mothers, but I'm so underbearing it's not even funny. Maybe she's imagined an overbearing mother to compensate for my lack of bearing and it's this imaginary pushy mother that's caused her to have an eating disorder. She doesn't have an eating disorder, not really. I shouldn't try to blame something that doesn't even exist on an imagined imaginary mother. I try to remember how skinny you were when you were her age. You still are!

So while we were out there on the rooftop bar an elderly suntanned man with a World Series ring, wearing white leather shoes and no socks, told Nora she was beautiful. He asked me if I was her sister. Ha ha, oh the oft-told jokes of stale old men on the make. He said Nora should be a model. I said well isn't that flattering but no, she's a dancer—with the words back off you transparent creep radiating unspoken from my assassin eyes. We walked all the way home singing mash-ups of old songs that both of us knew. It's so cute when she says things like, what! You know "Torn Between Two Lovers"? She even let me hold her hand for a minute or two. She told me that I was surprisingly attractive considering my features, which made me want to break down and bawl with gratitude. Like any fourteen-year-old, she's not exactly wildly indiscriminate with her compliments. Her feet are ravaged from dancing. They look like Grandpa Werner's. Remember when he did puppet shows with them and made us scream? I massage them for her and afterwards my own hands are calloused and raw from scraping them against her thorny feet. I asked her about her little Swedish boyfriend (to which she took exception, his name is Anders and he's apparently ripped) and if they were able to communicate in any language. She said no, dreamily, like it was perfect that way. I wanted to ask her if she was having sex with him but I didn't have the nerve. She's not even fifteen. I couldn't handle the answer. I'm a useless mother, my god.

So I called Will in New York last night and he told me he had rats in his apartment. He asked me how you were. He misses you too! Speaking of rats, I think, on top of the ants, we have mice, which I guess is comparatively speaking a relief. In Toronto they say that if you have mice you don't have rats and vice versa because rats eat mice. I wonder if rats eat mourning doves. Lately I've been having a recurring dream where a rat gets stuck under my shirt and I can't get it out of there and I have to pound away on my chest until the thing drops dead and bloodied onto the floor and I'm exhausted. The power keeps going out. I miss you like crazy.

Beyond all doubt, if you are not as happy as it is possible to be, you are more beloved than anyone who has ever lived, Y.

(That's what Madame de Staël wrote at the end of a letter to some Chevalier guy, but now it's what I've written to my Elfrieda.)

Write me back, Amps!

p.s. or pick up your goddamn phone.

p.p.s. Was talking to mom the other day. She says that you're listening non-stop to Górecki's Symphony Number Three? What is that one about?

Answering or not answering the phone has become symbolic of Elf's ability to cope with life. Elf has told my mother that the sound of a ringing phone has, for her, Hitchcockian implications and we both say ah, yeah, right, hmmmm . . . over the phone. I spoke to my mother this afternoon. She bore news. She told me that her sister Tina is on her way to Winnipeg for a visit and to spend time with Elf. She's driving her van across the country from Vancouver to help my mother who is exhausted, I can tell, but not admitting to it. I asked her but why, is it that bad? She said it's not that bad but it's also not that good. I asked her how exactly Elf was doing and she said well, you know, the same really.

Somewhere in between not bad and not good, I said.

That's about the long and the short of it, she said. She's not doing the tour.

What? Really?

That's what she says today.

I asked her if Elf was getting my letters and she said she didn't know, she'd ask. I phoned Nic at work and left a message for him to call me back. I phoned Will in Brooklyn and asked him how he was doing and he whispered fine, fine, yeah. He was in the library. He is always in a library or occupying Wall Street when I call him. He asked how things were. I told him great, good. He whispered how's Elf? And I whispered back pretty good, fine, yeah.

Someone has been sawing off all the branches of the tree outside my dining room window. I like to sit in my T-shirt and panties at the dining room table first thing in the morning and listen to the un-eaten mourning doves and write. The branches covered virtually the entire window and prevented the neighbours from seeing me sitting here in my underwear. But now the branches are coming away one by one and revealing me to my neighbours slowly like a puzzle taking shape.

Dear Elf,
When will you write me back? One thing I've noticed about men is that they become uncomfortable and a bit angry when, after having sex with them, you cry your eyes out for a few hours and refuse to tell them why you're upset.

Finbar and I are so incompatible. I only sleep with
him because he wants to and he's good-looking—
I'm pathetic, I know. Louche. And I'm a horrible role
model—a mother to a soon-to-be or already sexually
active daughter. Seriously, who wants a mother who buys
flavoured condoms from the machine at the Rivoli? (I was
caught off guard and that's all they had.) Although Nora
doesn't actually know about Finbar because I make sure
that all our sad outings are brief and furtive and spaced
far apart like eclipses. Just now, this second, telling you
about this stuff makes me want to cry my eyes out. I think
I might just do that. I'd like to fall in love again. I wish
Dan and I didn't fight so much—he's a good dad to Nora
when he's not in Borneo. You're so lucky to have Nic!
He's so lucky to have you! Say hi to him by the way. How's
his kayak?

Anders (N's little Swedish boyfriend) just told me he'd
blocked up the toilet, and that he'd messed up the washing
machine when he tried to wash all his clothes in one go—
why is he doing his laundry here???—so now his clothes
are locked in the machine, and the machine is leaking
water into the towels he used to cover the floor. He indicated all of this with charades and drawings because of
our language barrier.

It's evening now. Nora and Anders have gone to a
birthday party. Before they left I forced them to show me
some dance moves, something they were working on at
school, and they were reluctant at first but finally agreed
to do a quick one and oh my god, it was amazing. They're
just kids but suddenly they were these world-weary

though incredibly agile lovers swooning, then dying, then being reunited. They were so grave, so measured and yet free at the same time in all their movements. You have to come here to see them dance! When they were finished, bent and twisted into some kind of expressive shape which they held for an impossibly long time before standing up and bowing sweetly, I burst into applause—I was trying not to cry—and they were instantly transformed back into ordinary, awkward teens, shuffling out the door, bumping into each other, saying sorry, laughing nervously, holding hands shyly when a second ago it seemed like they were the original inventors of passion and grace. We've lost our power.

I was trying to edit my stupid novel with the lights off but the only key I can hit in the dark without missing is the delete key. Maybe it's a sign. By the way, I checked Wikipedia to see what it said about Górecki's Third Symphony. It's also called *The Symphony of Sorrowful Songs* and it's about the ties between a mother and a child. Have you seen her lately? Did she tell you that she finally found her lost hearing aid in the dryer?

I should go now and make my rounds, as the Hiebert kids (remember their station wagon and the garbage bags of pot plants?) used to say when they were selling drugs. I've unblocked the toilet but I still have to figure out how to fix the washing machine so it doesn't flood the basement and wash us all into Lake Ontario.

I will now have done with the ball, and I will moreover go and dress for dinner (to quote Jane Austen in a letter to her sister Cassandra). Yoli.

p.s. There's a hill in Toronto, which is exciting. You have
to walk up it if you're going north and down it if you're
going south. The shore of Lake Ontario used to come up
far higher. It would have been lapping at this third floor
window of mine up until about 13,000 years ago. Then
it was known as Lake Iroquois and when the ice dam
melted the water drained away and became its present
size, so small in comparison, a shadow of its former
self. There's a road in north Toronto called Davenport
that follows the Native trail that used to run along the
ancient shoreline. I'm sure it was called something other
than Davenport then, or maybe davenport was a word
dreamed into being by the First Nations people who
became tired of sitting on rocks and in canoes and imagined something softer, with springs. Did you know that
the various parts of the earth, the continents, are moving
closer together at the same speed that fingernails grow?
Or are they moving farther apart? Now I can't remember
but anyway it's the pace I am interested in. And its rela-
tion to grief, which you could say, in this context, passes
quickly or lasts forever.

p.p.s. Sometimes when I'm working on my book I close
my eyes and imagine that I'm in Winnipeg meeting you
at some café, maybe the Black Sheep on Ellice Avenue.
I can see you smiling now as I walk up the street. You've
got us a table by the window, there's a small pile of library
books beside you, French ones, and you've ordered me a
flat white and you're wearing a half-sexy/half-ironic mini-
skirt and billowing artist smock and you're knocking your
green marker against your teeth while you smile at me like

you've got something to tell me, something that will make me laugh. Today I'm working with my front door wide open because it's so warm. A condo is going up across the street so it's very loud. Every five minutes a guy yells heads up and then a few seconds later there's a massive crash and another dust cloud. I miss you, Elf.

It's been almost two weeks since I said goodbye to my sister in the doorway of her home in Winnipeg and promised to write letters. Now it's May, the day of Elfrieda's opening concert at the Winnipeg Symphony Orchestra. It's back on. She changed her mind again. Nic called me yesterday to say the rehearsal had gone very well and Elf seemed excited about opening night even if she looked a little drained.

My mother phoned me today while I was walking through a muddy park next to the lake. When my cellphone rang I looked at it for a second before answering.

She's done it again, said my mother.

I squatted in the mud. And said, tell me.

My mother said that she and her sister Tina had gone to Elf's place to say hi, even though Elf had asked them politely to stay away so that she could prepare herself for the concert. Elf didn't answer the door when they knocked. The door was locked but my mother had a key and let herself in. She found Elf lying on the floor in the bathroom. She had cut her wrists and she had drunk Javex. The bathroom reeked of bleach. Her breath and skin reeked of bleach. She was covered in blood.

She was conscious, alive. She held out her arms to my mother. She begged my mother to take her to the train tracks. My mother held her and Tina called 911 and they came to take Elf back to the hospital. She's in Intensive Care now on a respirator because her throat has closed from drinking the bleach. Her wrists will be okay.

I'm at the airport. I'm waiting for the plane to take me home to my sister and my mother. I bought cream at Lush to rub onto Elf's body. She has a surprisingly beautiful body for a woman in her late forties. Her legs are slim and firm. She has muscular thighs. Her smile is an event. She laughs so hard. She makes me laugh so hard. She gets surprised. Her eyes open wide, comically, she can't believe it. Her skin is pristine, smooth and pale. Her hair is so black and her eyes so green like they're saying go, go, go! She doesn't have horrible freckles and moles and facial hair like me and big bones poking out like twisted rebar at the dump. She's petite and feminine. She's glamorous and dark and jazzy like a French movie star. She loves me. She mocks sentimentality. She helps me stay calm. Her hands aren't ravaged by time and her breasts don't sag. They're small, pert, like a girl's. Her eyes are wet emeralds. Her eyelashes are too long. The snow weighs them down in the winter and she makes me cut them shorter with our mother's sewing scissors so they don't obscure her vision. I knocked over a tray of bath bombs the size of tennis balls, bright yellow, onto the floor and I couldn't figure out how to pick them up. The woman said it was okay. I can't remember now if I paid for the cream. I'm going home.

NINE

WHEN ELF WENT AWAY TO EUROPE my mother decided to
emancipate herself as well and enrolled in university classes in
the city to become a social worker and then a therapist. By this
time the church elders had washed their hands of the Von Riesen
women. When she graduated she turned the spare bedroom
into an office and a steady stream of sad and angry Mennonites
came to our house, usually in secret because therapy was seen as
lower even than bestiality because at least bestiality is somewhat
understandable in isolated farming communities. Sometimes
my mother didn't get paid by her clients with money. They

were often farmers and poor mechanics and housewives with no income of their own. So sometimes Elf and I would come home to find frozen sides of beef in the hallway or chickens in the garage and piles of eggs on the bench in the entrance. Sometimes a man would be in the driveway lying under our car and fixing the transmission or a strange woman would be mowing the lawn or watering the flowers with a gaggle of children traipsing along behind her.

Our mother found it impossible to ask her clients for payment if they couldn't afford it but the clients insisted on paying her back somehow. One day Elf and I came home from somewhere and found two large bullets on the kitchen table. We asked our mother why they were there and she said one of her clients had asked her to keep them for her so she wouldn't be tempted to fire them into her head. But how could she fire two bullets into her own head? Elf asked. The other one was for her daughter, our mother said. So she wouldn't be leaving her alone.

Elf and I went into the yard and sat on the rusty swing set. Elf explained the situation to me. Why doesn't the woman just run away with her daughter? I asked Elf. She didn't answer me. I asked again. Why doesn't the woman just run a— Elf cut me off. It doesn't work that way, she said. More people kill themselves in jail than attempt to escape. Would you kill me first before you killed yourself if we were in terrible danger? I asked her. Well, I don't know, she said, it would depend on the type of danger. Would you want me to?

When my mother and her sister Tina were kids they decided to race each other on bicycles and rather than call off the race or waste time going around a massive semi truck that was blocking their path they skidded under it and came out on the other side, unscathed and laughing.

One winter evening when Elf was sixteen and I was ten she organized a political debate of party candidates. She made lecterns out of cardboard boxes festooned with party paraphernalia and used our mother's Scrabble timer to keep our speeches under control. My father was the Conservative candidate, my mother was the Liberal candidate, Elf was the NDP candidate and I was a Communist. Although I couldn't say I was a Communist because of my parents' awful associations with Russia. Elf had once announced at dinnertime that she had a crush on Joe Zuken, the leader of the Communists in Winnipeg, and my mother had to Heimlich my father who began to choke to death on this news. After my mother had rescued him he said he wished she hadn't because if Elf was planning to marry (a crush had already led to marriage) Joe Zuken then he, my father, was finished with this tawdry life. Anyway, I had to say I was an Independent. We debated the pros and cons of women's rights and of euthanasia. Elf won, hands down. She was prepared and fervent. She had statistics to back her points and a tone that was relentlessly persuasive but always measured and respectful. She was eloquent and funny and she won.

Mind you, the judges were friends that she'd made at the music conservatory in Winnipeg and she'd paid for their efforts, secretly, with beer. She was in love with one of them, I could tell. He wore a rope belt and a paint-splattered T-shirt. He sat cross-legged and barefoot in my father's reading chair. Elf had made sure that a sliver of her blue, lacy bra was peeking out from her V-neck sweater. He couldn't stop looking at her, he shifted in his seat but his eyes never strayed, until my father cleared his throat loudly and said I say, sir, Your Honour in the green La-Z-Boy, are you hearing a word of what the others of us are saying?

The airplane lands. My mother and my aunt Tina are waiting. They're standing at the bottom of the escalator, arms linked, watching me as I float down to meet them. They look like tiny twins to me, fierce, grim-faced, getting down to the business of bearing another cross. They smile at me, murmur Plautdietsch words of endearment, and then I'm in their arms, so strong. We embrace and say nothing. I don't have a suitcase, we don't have to wait, and we walk quickly to the car.

My mother is driving fast, as usual, but this time I don't ask her to slow down. My aunt Tina is in the back seat staring out the window. I have one hand on my mother's shoulder and the other slung over the back seat, holding on to Tina's hand, so we're a human chain. Are Mennonites a depressed people or is it just us? My aunt Tina lost Leni, her daughter, my cousin, to suicide seven years ago, three years after my father killed himself. We've been here before. Everything is a repeat, another take.

Nic is at the hospital. He's on his cellphone. We wave a little and nod. Julie has shown up too. I hug her and whisper thanks in her ear and she squeezes hard. We go in by twos, no larger groups allowed. My mother and my aunt go in together. I'm talking to Will on my cell. He asks me to tell Elf something but I can't make out what it is because he's whispering. Will? I ask. Hang on, he says. I wait and it's quiet on his end. Will? I can hear him crying. Just that I love her, he finally manages to say and hangs up. When they come out my mother is calm, she won't cry now, she shrugs and shakes her head and Nic puts his arm around her shoulders and she leans into him, her head against his chest. He guides her to a chair and she sits down and stares into the middle distance, saying a few words to herself, or a prayer. I can see the marks on her arm where the dog's teeth ripped open her skin. Two holes, like a vampire bite. Aunt Tina goes to get us coffee.

Julie and I are a team and we pull up chairs to flank my sister and we hold her hands and say nothing because we have nothing to say. There is a tube in Elf's throat and a machine that breathes for her. We look at her and she looks at us and shrugs the way my mother did. How many words do we have left? She closes her eyes and then opens them again and pulls her hand out of mine so that she can tap her forehead. I don't know what she means. That she's crazy? She's forgotten something? Her head hurts? I kiss her cheek. A Neil Young song is playing over the sound system that's been set up here in the intensive care ward. He won't stop searching for a heart of gold.

Elf taps her nose, draws imaginary circles around her eyes. Julie says she wants her glasses, that's what she means. Right? Elf's chin drops slightly, a nod. I get up and look for them. I go out of the room and ask the nurse if she has Elf's glasses. She doesn't. Julie volunteers to look for them, to ask Nic or my mother if they have them. She kisses Elf on the cheek, whispers something to her that makes her eyes fill with tears, maybe she says Elf, you're the best, and leaves.

Here we are. I'm relieved that Elf wants her glasses. That there is something she wants to see. She has bright white bandages on her wrists that look like sweatbands. They're only missing the Nike swoosh. Tubes are taped to her face. I use the edge of my shirt sleeve to wipe the tear that's sliding down her cheek. I tell her I love her. One corner of her mouth is pulled to the side to accommodate the hose. I remember when she took breathing lessons, something called the Alexander Technique, and how I made fun of her. You have to learn how to breathe? She told me yes, there was a right way and a wrong way. She offered to teach me how to breathe properly using my diaphragm from deep within me but I lost interest quickly. She'd tried to be my piano teacher too, but that was a disaster. And to teach me Spanish. She told me how to say I have a little man when I should have said I'm a bit hungry.

I leave Emergency to find my mother and my aunt who are drinking black coffee in the cafeteria. My aunt Tina is older by a few years but otherwise they are almost the same person. They both have snow-white bobs, flashing cat eyes, a million wrinkles each and really strong grips. They're barely five feet tall. When they see me they both call out my name and make room between them and pull me onto a chair and put their arms around me and my aunt tells me she loves me and my mother tells me she loves me and I tell them I love them too. I can barely breathe. I'm jealous of my own mother for having her sister near her at a time like this. When my father died Tina came then also to be with my mother and my sister and me, and bought each of us a dozen pairs of white cotton panties so we wouldn't have to worry about mundane things like laundry while we were planning a funeral. When my mother had her bypass surgery Tina came then too and took me to Costco and we pushed a giant cart around an enormous warehouse buying my mother a year's supply of ketchup and toilet paper and Vaseline Intensive Care lotion, which has recently been renamed Vaseline Intensive Rescue lotion by the company to reflect the emergency atmosphere of current life on earth. During her recovery Tina bathed her sister gently, laughing, immodest, the way I helped my sister shower when she was too weak from starving herself to do it alone. My mother a Rubenesque bundle of flesh and scars, a disciple of life, and my sister a wraith. How does one give birth to the other?

Nic is talking to a doctor. I can see him through the glass wall beside the door of Elf's room. He's wearing a blue shirt with a collar, pants that are not jeans and black sneakers. One hand is on his forehead while he speaks and the other against the glass wall, his fingers splayed like a fan. I want to hear what the doctor is saying and I tell Elf that I'll be right back but when I get to where Nic and the doctor are standing the doctor has walked away and Nic is simply standing there alone propping himself up against glass. When he sees me he takes his hand off his forehead and asks me how I am. He tells me that the doctor has said Elf will probably be all right and they will know in a few hours or tomorrow morning. She has harmed her throat, he says, and may not be able to talk at all or not very well and there may be some organ damage to be determined down the line but she'll live.

When I was fourteen Elf came home for Christmas. She had just been at Juilliard on some kind of special scholarship. Amazing things were happening. She had a top agent and gigs lined up all over the world. Elf and I were sitting on the floor of the bathroom and she was crying inconsolably and I was trying to get her to stop crying and come to dinner. The table was set and all of our relatives from my father's side were seated already. We had candles, turkey, singing, the celebration of the birth of a messiah that I still believed in. Elf told me she couldn't do it, she just couldn't do it. What? I said. She couldn't stand it, the appearance of happiness, the forced enthusiasm, and everything a performance. I mean, if Jesus actually died on a cross with nails in his hands and feet to save us shouldn't we do more to express our gratitude than devour a turkey one evening in the dead of winter? She wanted me to laugh and help her to carry out some type of desperado action, to pry open the bathroom window and push her through to freedom. Let's just go have Christmas, you and me, at the pool hall, she said. I was begging her to dry her tears and wash her face and join us at the table. I told her that everyone was waiting for her. She told me she didn't care, she couldn't do it, I should tell them she wasn't joining us. I told her she had to, it's Christmas! And she laughed then sobbed, and told me I was funny but no, she wouldn't join us at the table.

I continued to beg, please, please, please get up and wash your face and put on your new Red Alert lipstick and come to the table. Our mother came to the door and knocked softly and said honey? Girls? Are you in there? We're ready to eat. Elf banged her head against the bathroom wall and it scared me. Don't do that, I whispered, and she did it again. Girls? said our mother. What's going on in there? Are you okay? I said yeah, yeah, we're fine, we'll be right there. I had Elf in a headlock and she was trying to pull out of it but I wouldn't let her. I wanted my sister to stop smashing her head against ceramic tiles and come to the dinner table. I wanted to see her weird eyes flash happiness while she told hilarious stories using the occasional French or Italian word about the city and about concert halls and all things sophisticated. I wanted my younger cousins to stare at her unabashedly with great admiration and envy, and for Elf then to put her arm around my shoulder. I wanted her to be her intoxicating, razor-sharp self and I wanted to sit next to her and feel the heat she radiated, the energy of a fearless leader, a girl who moved easily in the world, my older sister.

I waited for our mother to leave. I still had Elf in a head-lock. She kicked her legs out and made animal noises. I told her that I would kill myself if she didn't come to the table. She stopped moaning and looked at me and furrowed her brow as though we were actors and I'd deviated from the script and ruined the take.

Our father once had a plan to sell placemats to truck-stop res-taurants. He had designed these placemats himself and had thousands of them printed. The placemats were intended to educate diners on Canadian history while they chewed on their Denver sandwiches. The facts were presented in cartoon form, drawn by my father, with word bubbles, and jokes and riddles. They were meant to appeal to kids and adults alike. But most of all they were meant to educate what my father believed to be an ignorant and indifferent public. What's more interesting than our own history? he'd exclaim. It truly pained him to see his fellow Canadians drive quickly past historical plaques, dismiss Canadian content rules, fail citizen tests and screw up the words to our national anthem at hockey games. Things have happened here, he would say.

One year between Christmas and New Year's my father took the train to Ottawa to do research in the government archives and to attend Lester Pearson's funeral. He was thirty-seven years old, an elementary school teacher from a small prairie town. He stood outside the legislative building in the cold with thousands of others to pay his respects. While he was standing there he began a conversation with the man standing next to him. The man eventually invited my father to his home for a New Year's Eve party and that was the first time my father had ever been to a New Year's Eve party in his life. It was a very fancy house, said my father. In a very fancy neighbourhood called the Glebe. My father was moved by the stranger's kindness. Later, when he came home and told the story, a type of hush fell over us. I remember being afraid he would start to cry. What I took from the story was that my father had lost his leader and that he needed a friend. He had always believed that one day he'd meet his hero, Lester B. Pearson, in the flesh and that they'd have a conversation about Canada. My mother had asked him if he'd had a glass of champagne at the party and he said no, oh no Lottie, of course not. I was only seven or eight when he told us this story. Elf and my mother and I sat in awe of my father that evening when he described it all to us, a state funeral and a New Year's Eve party all in one night. But it made me feel uneasy in ways I couldn't describe at the time. I had never seen him cry before, and he didn't actually, I just knew that he wanted to, and that's the memory that always comes back to me first.

The summer when I was maybe nine years old he asked me if I wanted to go on the road with him from truck stop to truck stop all over Manitoba and Ontario while he tried to sell his placemats. I was game and away we went. I remember having only one outfit for this journey, an orange terry towel T-shirt, cut-offs and my North Star runners. I had a stack of Famous Five books. I never brushed my teeth and I ate pancakes and Oh Henry! bars for every meal. At night my father and I would stay in cheap motels and I'd fill our ice bucket and suck on chunks of ice and watch TV while my father slept and snored. When I was tired I'd put the chain lock on the door and slowly open and close it a few times to make sure it held.

He wasn't making any sales. He gave me placemats to draw on when I got bored in the car. He started to get discouraged and I sang goofy songs to cheer him up like "Pop Goes the Weasel" and "Ninety-nine Bottles of Beer on the Wall." I didn't want to go into the restaurants with him anymore because it was too embarrassing. He was so friendly, so sincere. All he wanted to do was educate people about Canada. He was willing to take very little money for a box of placemats, then he was willing to give them away for free. Even then restaurant managers and gas station owners would stare at them for a minute or two and shake their heads, no, they didn't think they wanted them.

My teeth were fuzzy and my orange T-shirt was filthy. My father was defeated and we went home. We'd been away for about a week. When we got home my mother was in the kitchen laughing with some friends of hers and Elf was practising her piano. This seemed always to be the scenario. He told my mom and her friends what had happened, but not with many words, more with his eyes and his shoulders. He went to his bedroom.

I sat down with my mom and her friends and told them a colourful story of our time on the road. I made them laugh. Elf stopped playing the piano and came to the kitchen to find out what was going on. I told her what had happened. She didn't laugh at all. She said oh no, oh no, that's awful. Is he okay?

Who? I asked her.

Dad!

She went to her bedroom too, and closed the door on us for a long time. I think it was dark before she came out because the fire station siren had sounded twice, once for kids to go inside for dinner at six o'clock and once for them to go inside for bed at nine o'clock. I'm not sure how long my dad stayed in his room.

My father forced the town hall to give him money to open up a library. They didn't want to. They thought it was a waste of money and dangerous and unmanly of my father to talk about it. He tried to convince them. It was forty degrees below zero. It was dinnertime. I asked my mom: hey, where's dad? She told me he was out knocking on people's doors to try to get them to sign the petition for a library. For weeks my father would walk the streets of East Village with his clipboard and ballpoint pens knocking on doors and begging for support. He went out at dinnertime when everyone was at home. It was dark. He went to every house in town. Sometimes my mom helped him. When he came home his glasses would fog up as soon as he stepped into the house. My mom tried to convince him to wear long johns, it was the coldest winter in history, but he refused to. She had to karate-chop his legs to get the blood circulating. Why do you hate long johns so much? she'd ask him.

Finally he had enough signatures and he brought them to the town hall and they said all right already, go start your little library. They gave him a tiny, mildewed room in an old abandoned school and enough money to get some second-hand shelves and books to fill them. He was the happiest man in the world. He hired my sister to be the librarian and she was very thorough. She made an index card for every book. She included many details. She was a teenager with long straight black hair and enormous glasses and she kept things very organized. The two of them went off to work together. They had a million plans.

I look at Elf through the glass wall of the ICU and wave. She is watching me and Nic talk about her internal organs. She's wearing an Alarm T-shirt that I gave her years ago one summer when we were both living in London, me in a dirty house full of punks and she in a pristine flat in Notting Hill with a diplomat of some sort who wasn't Italian but liked to call Venice *Venezia* and Naples *Napoli*.

So she'll live, I say to Nic. He nods and takes a deep breath and in the space of that breath is framed the question we need to ask ourselves.

I'm sitting on concrete steps outside the hospital and talking to my kids on the phone with the latest on Elf. Will has finished classes now and tells me he is willing to go back to Toronto to stay, again, with Nora whose big school dance recital is coming up while I'm in Winnipeg. But he's starting a job in Queens in a couple of weeks doing landscape work for a guy his dad knows so he can't stay forever. And he says he'll do it, but asks me: can you please just give N a pep talk about not living like an animal?

Julie has gone back to work. She left me two cigarettes wrapped in tinfoil. Just then I get a text from Dan from Borneo. *I need you.* I text him back. *What? Are you okay, Dan?* He texts me back. *Sorry, pushed send too soon. I need you to sign the divorce papers.*

I delete it and light one of the cigarettes that Julie gave me and blow smoke gently, concentrating on my breath, on soft shapes. I tell myself to think, to focus. I briefly consider texting Radek but I don't know what to say or how to say it. I get up and walk to the river for a look. The ice is gone now. The river is quieter. It's probably okay to put a canoe into it now if that's your only way home.

Now I'm sitting in the "family room" with my mother and my aunt. Nic has gone to get some food. My mother is recommending a book to my aunt. I know of the book. She is describing it as delightful. She asks me if I've heard of it and I say yeah, but I don't want to read it. My mother tells me it's a feel-good book, sometimes we need them, and I don't say anything. What are you currently reading, Yoli? asks my aunt. Céline's *Journey to the End of the Night*, I tell her. A French writer, dead, not the singer from Quebec. Where's yours? my mother asks. And I say my feel-good book? And she says no, your manuscript. Still in a plastic Safeway bag? I nod and roll my eyes. My aunt asks me how many words I have and I tell her I don't know, I can't remember how to check on my computer. I don't want to talk about it. My mother tells Tina that she doesn't like books where the protagonist is established as Sad on page one. Okay, she's sad! We get it, we know what sad is, and then the whole book is basically a description of the million and one ways in which our protagonist is sad. Gimme a break! Get on with it! Tina nods sagely and says yes and then something in Plautdietsch, probably something like heck yeah do we ever know what sad is. Sadness is what holds our bones in place. My cellphone vibrates and I look at the text. It's Nic telling me that he's in the cafeteria and that he just talked to Claudio. Claudio's dealt with everything, the venues, the insurance, and just generally calling off the tour. Tina jumps in with her own variation on the theme of sadness. I text Nic back and say *good, angry?* Nic texts back *no, concerned, helpful, stressed maybe, coming to Winnipeg from Budapest to see her.*

My mother says that when she reads my rodeo stories she gets sad thinking that I have so much sadness in me that I make all those teenage heroines so sad. Why can't they ever get the first-place ribbon? she asks. I tell her no, no, everyone has all that sadness in them, it's not just me, and the writing helps to organize it, so no big deal. I text Nic back: *When?* He texts back *immediately. Tomorrow.* Claudio's putting out a press release, saying it's exhaustion and a request for privacy. My mother says ah, okay, but still . . . I wonder about you carrying that sorrow around with you, where it came from . . . and I finally understand what she needs to hear and that she's talking about not just me but Elf too and I tell her that my sorrow was not created by her, that my childhood was a joyful thing, an island in the sun, that her mothering is impeccable, that she is not to blame.

I'm alone with Elfrieda. The sun is disappearing. The day before the day before my father killed himself he took my hand in his and said Yoli, it feels to me as though the lights are going out. We were sitting by a fountain in a park at noon.

Nic sat with Elf for hours and has gone home now. He's furious because a neighbour of theirs saw Elf being loaded into the ambulance covered in blood and told a few other neighbours and now a reporter has called Nic asking about Elf's condition. My mother and my aunt are also at home, resting. I tell Elf that we're all meeting for dinner at Colosseo and that I wish she could be there with us. The tube is still in her throat and she can't answer but if she could what would she say? I ask her if she can imagine life getting better. I ask her if her heart is broken. If life is torturing her. I tell her that I would help her if I could but I can't. I don't want to go to jail. I don't want to kill her. I put my hands over my face in the half-light of her room. I'm afraid and when I think of my fear my knees start shaking again but the sound of her breathing machine is comforting and rhythmic. I offer to sing and a corner of her mouth moves, barely. I don't know what to sing. I think for a minute and Elf looks at me as if she's saying well? What's it gonna be? I sing "I Don't Know How to Love Him" from *Jesus Christ Superstar*. I'm dying of fear. Elf and I used to belt this one out together, a passionate ballad sung by Mary Magdalene about her new crush, Jesus. She's a prostitute, jaded, and can't believe how this barefoot, bearded guy undoes her. She wants him and she tries to normalize the idea of wanting to date Jesus by claiming he's just another man, after all. I sing it quietly while the light fades and Elf disappears into the darkness of her glass room. Finally it's completely dark in the room and I've stopped singing and the only sound is the artificial breathing of the respirator. Elf picks up the pad of paper lying on her stomach and writes something on it and passes it to me. *How do you go on?* she has written. I squint at the words for a minute or two. I hold them up to the tiny red light on her respirator to get a better look. I pass the paper back to her. She shakes her head and I return the pad of paper to her stomach. We both close our eyes and time passes. Five minutes? Half an hour?

Elf, I say, are you awake? Her eyes stay closed. Elf, I say. She doesn't respond. I look at my cellphone. There are no messages. I look at the nurses through the glass. They're in their brightly lit area, talking and laughing and taking notes but I can't hear them. Elf, I say. Open your eyes. Still no reaction. I put my head gently down onto her stomach where the glass piano is. Elf, I whisper. I don't know what to do.

We are silent.

Elf, I whisper again. How do you think Nic feels? Do you know what you're doing? You're killing people.

Now Elf shifts slightly and puts her hand on my head. I sit up and look at her. Her eyes are open. For once, she looks alarmed. She shakes her head, no, no, no.

Does it make you happy to think of Nic or mom finding your dead body? I'm whispering now too. I've become her torturer and I'm so ashamed. I'm so angry and so afraid. I don't want the nurses to hear me. Elf twists my hand hard and it hurts. Her hands are strong still, from playing. I twist back and she makes a small noise that manages to escape the tube that's rammed down her throat.

A nurse comes into the room and says oh, she hadn't seen me sitting there in the dark. She's new so we introduce ourselves.

She turns the light on and sees that both Elf and I are crying and apologizes and switches it off again. I'm overwhelmed by this small act of compassion. She offers to come back in a bit.

No, no, I say, it's fine now.

I don't look at Elf. I can feel her begging me not to leave and I pick up all my stuff and say okay, well, see you later, not sure when I'll be back. I don't look at her, she can't speak, she can't protest because of the tube, and I walk out of the room.

I get as far as the parking lot and then I run back to Elf's room. I rush in and apologize and she puts her arms up to hug me. I catch my breath as she holds me. I sit up after a minute or two and she taps her heart. You love me? I say. She nods. But there's more that she wants to say. I pick up the pad of paper that has fallen to the floor and she writes that she is sorry too. She doesn't want to kill anybody but herself. I know, I say, I nod. I'm afraid of dying alone, she writes, and I nod again. Then she writes the word *Switzerland* on the paper and circles it and passes it to me. I smile and fold the paper until it's the size of a pill and put it back into my bag. Let me think, I tell her. Give me time to think.

TEN

I WAS DRIVING DOWN CORYDON AVENUE to the restaurant to meet Nic and Tina and my mom for dinner. I had forgotten where we had agreed to meet. I hoped that seeing the restaurant sign would somehow jog my memory so I drove slowly, like a parade float, peering at all the possibilities. But I was thinking about death. If I could get my hands on some barbiturates. And Seconal? There is some combination that if you take with milk . . . or not with milk. I couldn't remember the recipe for death. Years ago when I was trying to make a living as a freelance journalist I went to Portland, Oregon, to write a magazine story on assisted suicide. While I was there my cousin Leni's body was found in the Fraser River where she had pitched herself once and for all into the void. It involved a certain combination of drugs. What was it? Had I made a reservation for six p.m. or seven p.m. at Colosseo? Had I remembered to ask if we could sit on the terrace? Was it Seconal, that active ingredient? I'd have to check my Portland notes, if I still had them.

Nic worked in health science, maybe he could somehow fashion these necessary drugs from bits and pieces of whatever was lying around the office. Hey Nic, can you cobble something together that'll knock her out for good? Or somehow we could find a doctor willing to bust into a hospital stash and steal them? Or maybe it's not even stealing if a doctor takes them. Call of duty. Or a willing pharmacist? Maybe a gang. There are a thousand gangsters in Winnipeg with access to illegal drugs. Or guns.

All right, so the brain is an organ that's made to solve problems so if the problem is life and its unlivability then a rational, working brain would choose to end it. No? I didn't know what to do. It felt like someone was throwing darts at the side of my head, five seconds apart. It sounded naive to me now and selfish and fearful to say you must live, you must want to live, you have to live. That's your one imperative, the single rule of the universe. Our family had once been one of those with normal crises like a baby (okay, two babies) born out of wedlock. Our family had once been one of those typical ones that only thinks about killing each other in the abstract. Now I couldn't think or write. My fingers hated me. I was afraid that when I went to sleep I'd wake to find them wrapped around my throat.

I parked my mother's car on a side street near the restaurant and phoned Finbar on his cell and left a message: if I were to help my sister die, would I be charged with murder? I hung up. I called back and left another message: I'm not planning to kill my sister, don't get me wrong, I'm just wondering about the legal implications and all that stuff. Can you help me? I realized then that I wasn't even sure what kind of law he practised. I think it might have been entertainment law.

I closed my eyes and tried to think. What is love? How do I love her? I was gripping the steering wheel the way my father used to, like he was towing a newly discovered planet behind him, one that held the secrets to the universe.

It was Seconal, definitely! That was the drug. And one hundred pills are necessary for a lethal dose. You empty the powder into something soft like yogurt and eat it. The alternative was Nembutal which was more expensive but easier to take because it came in liquid form. All you have to do is knock back a glass of Nembutal and Bob's your uncle, as my aunt Tina would say. I wondered if my heart would give out from fear. Why are doctors so uncomfortable with helplessness. What if I'm caught and charged with murder? What will I do in jail? Where will Nora live? In Borneo? What if Elf doesn't really want to die? What would my mother say? My cell went off and I gasped, I was so startled. It was a text from Nora: *If Will's coming, tell him it's okay if Anders sleeps over.* I texted back: *It's NOT okay!* Nora again: *You said it was okay if we were rehearsing late and the subways stopped.* Me: *Fine but he'll sleep on the couch.* Nora: *Text Will and tell him not to tell Anders he has to sleep in the laundry room.* Me: *That's not a bad idea! There's an old futon in there and piles of dirty clothes to make forts with.* Nora: *Mom!* Me: *N, you're only fourteen years old.* Nora: *I'm almost fifteen. God. Remember my birthday? Are you senile now?*

———

Dinner passed like a Buñuel film. I kept an eye on my mother, on her face, her hands, expecting eyeballs to be severed, blood to flow. We were on the sunny terrace of a bustling Italian restaurant, my mother was a *Pietà*, she was Michelangelo's Mary and my thoughts were murderous. Nic was pouring sangria wearily into a thousand glasses, my mother's sister was grabbing hands and squeezing, talking fast and then asking what is Twitter?

She asked Nic about the camping expedition he made this last winter and somehow this led us to a discussion of Jack London's "To Build a Fire." We all had different theories for why Jack London has the dog abandon the dying man at the end of the story. And for some of us the word "abandon" wasn't quite accurate. My mother and my aunt hadn't read the story but they thought about it and in tandem concluded that the dog is going to get help. Nic believed that the dog understands that the man is now dying, freezing to death, and needs to be alone, the way a dog or cat prefers to be alone as it dies. So the dog leaves out of respect, giving the man his space. I didn't believe in either of these theories. It's a dog, I said, it senses that the man is dying or dead already so what can it do now? Nothing. It's over. The dog takes off. It has to find some food and shelter, first things first. Its instinct is to survive. I mean, not to . . . did Jack London commit suicide? I looked at the rest of them apologetically.

Nic had a strange smile on his face. He was crying. His hand was covering his eyes. His watch was too big for him, the strap was sliding around on his arm and he sometimes had to hold his arm still, in a certain way, to keep the watch from falling right off.

———

That evening I did many things but came no closer to making a decision about killing my sister or not. I tucked my mother and my aunt into bed with their Kathy Reichs and Raymond Chandlers. They had buried fourteen brothers and sisters. They once had a family large enough to field two entire baseball teams. It was just the two of them now, out of sixteen kids. They had buried daughters and husbands and parents. Their world view was shaped by death, littered with bodies from the jungles of Bolivia to the far reaches of Outer Mongolia. My aunt whispered something to me in Plautdietsch and I thanked her. *Schlope Schein*, the words she used to repeat to Leni and me before we fell asleep, when we were young and new to this planet and long before my cousin painted her apartment lime green and then threw herself into the ice-cold Fraser River.

I went onto the balcony and phoned Radek and left a message on his machine. I'm sorry for being such a jerk, I said. Feel free to make me a villain in your opera. I'm trying to think of that Czech word you sometimes say but I can't remember it now. So just . . . in summary . . . I'm really, really sorry. I breathed for a while wanting to say something else and then hung up.

I drove to Nic's house but didn't get out of the car. He had thin strands of rope tied to his roof and anchored to the ground with sandbags. They were taut, the strands, like strings on an upright bass. I guessed that he was using them to grow something, a beanstalk to heaven or maybe hops for his beer, if hops are things that grow vertically and wrap themselves around twine.

I drove to Julie's house and met her on her porch. I don't know what to do, I said. But she's going to be okay? said Julie. Well, yeah, I think so. Do you have any wine?

We drank the wine and talked late into the night. Her children slept. We walked half a block to the riverbank and saw things, fish maybe, jumping in and out of the water like it was really hot and had startled them. Look, I said, and pointed to the Ste. Odile Hospital, way off in the distance, its towers and wings and giant neon cross. I wonder which window is hers, I said. We walked back to Julie's house and checked the kids. They were still in their beds, still sleeping.

You can't actually do that, said Julie when we were back in our chairs on the porch. I know, I said. But can't I? No, she said. Not really. No. Because I'd be caught? Yeah, she said, but not even that. Because I'd feel guilty for the rest of my life? I don't know, she said, I'm not sure. Would you do it together with Nic and your mom?

Yeah, I guess so, I said, but . . .

So you'd all be gathered around and then she'd take the stuff and die . . .

Yeah . . .

And this is the stuff that you heard about in Portland?

Yeah . . .

And then how would you explain that to, like, the cops?

I don't know, I said. She'd do it herself, take the stuff.

Yeah, said Julie, but you wouldn't have *prevented* her from killing herself.

I know . . .

And not only that, you would have provided her with the stuff to do it.

Yeah, I know . . .

So you'd be accessories or whatever.

Hmmm, yeah, I said, I know . . . Julie poured more wine into our glasses and we sat quietly for a while.

I know, I said. Nic and my mom could say goodbye to her and then leave and then I'd give her the stuff myself so it would seem like I was the only one responsible . . . they'd be totally off the hook. I don't know . . .

But my gut instinct is that you shouldn't do it.

Yeah, but she'll do it anyway. That's *my* gut instinct.

She might not though, I mean, she might . . . there might be some change.

Maybe, yeah.

Julie went in to answer her phone. I sat on her porch and waited. I banished mental images of my father's broken body on the tracks by staring hard at the details of Julie's porch. The door, the peeling yellow paint, the torn screen, the bicycles, the roller skates, the bag of fresh soil, the tiny ceramic elephant. I wondered what a sign would be, a sign pointing in a direction. I decided that if nobody walked down the sidewalk in the next ten seconds it was probably not a good idea to take Elf to Switzerland. It was very late, however, and cold and who would walk by? I counted to ten silently. A cat walked past. Confusing. I checked my phone and saw that Dan had e-mailed me and the subject heading was Remorse. My thumb hovered over various buttons on my phone and then I pushed delete and counted again to ten but before I'd finished Julie had come back outside and poured more wine.

———

It was late. Neighbours were switching out their lights. Bottles were being smashed in the back lanes. We decided to go inside and play a song on the organ that my mother had inexplicably delivered to Julie's house in the middle of the night, that rainy night, weeks ago. David Bowie's "Memory of a Free Festival."

We both kind of sang, mumbled the lyrics, stumbled through. The sound of the organ fit with the elegiac tone of the song. We knew the song backwards and forwards, just not well. We held back, sang it comically and half-heartedly. I think that we both wanted to give ourselves up to the song, to sing it earnestly and boldly, the way it sat in our memories, but it was so late, the kids were sleeping, we were tired, and it was so late.

I was in the underground car park at the Ste. Odile Hospital screaming at a man who was standing next to his wife who was holding a young child. I had dropped my mother and my aunt off at the entrance to the intensive care ward and was attempting to park the car in a very tight space. I heard a guy saying hey, what the hell is your problem? I got out of the car and asked him what he meant. He said I was really close to his car, if I scraped his car or touched his car with my door or anything, my side-view mirror, there'd be hell to pay.

Hell to pay? I said. Did you actually just tell me there would be hell to pay if I touched your fucking car?

The guy was standing there with his wife and kid and they were all staring at me. I began to speak in a really loud voice. It wasn't a scream, but it was crazy. I told him that I was about to go upstairs to see if my sister was dead or alive and that the spaces were really small, had he noticed that, and had I actually touched his stupid car, no, I hadn't, my car was exactly between the lines, look at it, look at it, and had he ever loved a person more than a car or anyone other than himself?

I turned to his wife and asked her how she could be married to a man like this, how she could share a bed with this monster and conceive a child with him, the one she was holding in her arms, and I told her my own mother was upstairs trying to understand why her daughter wanted to die and that my aunt was also upstairs trying to understand why her daughter had wanted to die and that sometimes in life there were things we had to wonder about, things other than cars.

I was close to them. I persisted with my insane line of questioning. How can you be married to this man? Can't you all see that my car isn't touching your car?

They stared at me. The woman backed away from me with her child and said something to her husband who eventually shook his head violently to one side like he was trying to get water out of his ear and then walked away and joined his wife and kid.

I watched them leave. I crouched down beside my car, not close to his, and squatted there, trying to get my breath back. Then I went inside and got into the elevator and pushed a button, the one that would take me to Elf and the others. The man's wife was in the elevator but the man and the kid weren't there.

I'm sorry, I said to her, about all that. I waved in the direction of somewhere else. I'm sure you've got your own thing going on here. I'm really sorry, okay?

She stared at the floor numbers blinking on and off. I wanted to tell her that she had to tell me that it was okay, that she had to forgive me. That was how it worked. I told her again that I was really sorry. I'm so stressed out, I whispered. She stared at the numbers. We were going up. She got out, finally, without having said a word. I watched her walk away, down the corridor, she shifted her heavy purse from one shoulder to the other, and then the elevator doors closed.

My aunt was standing in the little vestibule next to the ICU ward in her purple track suit and her shiny white Reeboks. They were so small, like a child's. She was holding a pencil. She was doing a sudoku. When she saw me she put the newspaper on the chair and gave me a hug. She told me that my mother was with Elfrieda, that Nicolas had just been there but had to go to work to deal with a valve problem, and that Elfrieda was awake and off the respirator. She told me she was going to get a coffee, did I want one? She asked me if I was all right. I told her what I had done, that I had told an innocent woman that her child had been conceived with a monster, and other things, and she told me it was okay, it was understandable.

But I just wanted that woman to tell me that too, I said.

My aunt nodded and told me that the woman would tell me that but probably not for a while, maybe years, and then only silently, in her thoughts, so I wouldn't hear it but one day I'd be walking down some street and feel a kind of lightness come over me, like I could walk for miles, and that would be the moment when the woman from the parking lot had suddenly understood my horrible outburst, that it had nothing to do with her or her husband or her child, and that it was okay.

Forgiveness, sort of. Got that? said my aunt.

Okay, I said, so when I feel the lightness coming over me, on a street . . . I'm walking and . . .

Yes, said my aunt. Cream and no sugar, right?

She hustled off in her sportswear to find coffee and I looked at my mother and my sister through the glass wall. Elf's eyes were closed, my mother was reading aloud to her. I couldn't tell what book it was. She had a new sweater on, it had geese flying on it, she must have borrowed it from my aunt. My sister was so thin I imagined that I could see the outline of her heart. I went back to the waiting area and sat down and took my aunt's sudoku and tried to finish it. I said how the hell do these fucking things work? to myself, but loudly, and a man looked at me and flared his nostrils. I fell asleep in the chair and when I woke up my mother and my aunt were gone.

I went to see Elf and she was alone in her room, staring up at the ceiling. I sat next to her and took her hand. It was dry and I reminded myself to bring hand cream next time. It smelled like burnt hair in there. I put my head down, way down, like I was trying not to be carsick, and I didn't say anything. Elf told me that we were a painting.

You can talk! I said.

She told me that her throat was healing. She asked me if I knew of Edvard Munch's painting *The Sick Child*. No, I said, but is this it? She said yeah, that it was inspired by Munch's dying sister. I told her but you're not dying. Look at you, you're talking now. She asked me why we had to be humans. I put my head back down, way down, towards the floor.

Okay, okay, she said. Don't do that. You look so defeated.

I said well for god's sake, Elfie, how do you think I should look?

I need you to be okay, she said. I need you to—

Are you fucking kidding me? I said. You need *me* to be okay? Oh my god. Oh my god. Look at you!

Okay, said Elf. Shhhh. Please. Let's not talk. I'm sorry.

Have you ever thought about what *I* might need? I said. Has it occurred to you ever in your life that I'm the one that's colossally fucked up and could use some sisterly support every once in a while? Have you ever got on an airplane every two weeks to rush to my side when I'm feeling like shit and wanting to die? Has it ever occurred to you that I'm *not* okay, that everything in my life is embarrassing, that I got knocked up twice by two different guys and had two divorces and two affairs that were—are—not only a nightmare but also a cliché and that I'm broke and writing a shitty little book about boats that nobody wants to publish and sleeping around with men who . . . fucking ooze nicotine into their sheets from their entire bodies so they leave outlines like dead—

What? said Elf.

Has it ever occurred to you that I have also lost my father to suicide, that I also am having a hard time getting over it, and that I also am trying to find meaning in my pathetic, stupid life and that I also often think the whole thing is a ridiculous farce and that the only intelligent response to it is suicide but that I pull back from that conclusion because it creates a certain onus that is unpalatable? Like you're fucking Virginia Woolf or one of those guys, way too cool to live or too smart or too in tune with the tragedy of it all or whatever, you want to create some bullshit legacy for yourself as brilliant and doomed—

Yolandi, said Elf. I told you—

You have this amazing guy who loves your ass off, an amazing career that the whole world respects and gives you shitloads of cash for, plus you could quit any time and just be labelled mysterious and eccentric and then go live in fucking Paris in the Marais or whatever that stupid . . . fucking . . . arrondissement— No, don't try talking, don't correct me with your superior knowledge of French, you have an amazing natural fucking beauty that never seems to fade, an amazing house that magically cleans itself—

I have a cleaning lady, Yo, said Elf. You have a very low-grade understanding of despair, by the way.

An amazing cleaning lady, I said, okay? You have a mother who thinks the sun shines out of your ass.

Yoli, said Elf.

Okay, so dad died. Whatever! He loved you! You have . . . What is your major fucking problem anyway?

Plus, said Elf, I have an amazing sister. But can you . . . shhhh.

I am not! I said. I'm a total fuck-up! Can you not under-stand that? Can you not understand that I need your help! That maybe you're here for a reason which is to be a goddamn sister to me?

Yoli, she said. She sat up in her bed now and was whisper-ing hard, livid. You do not understand a fucking thing, okay? You have had my goddamn help all along. I had to be perfect so you could fuck up and you were more than happy to do it. One of us had to show some fucking empathy, do you know that word, it's a good one, you should learn it, one of us had to show some fucking empathy towards dad and all his acres of existential sadness. Who was that person? Was it you? Was it mom? No! It was me. Just so you could go waltzing around—

I don't even know what you're talking about, I said. Now you're comparing yourself to Jesus Christ? You didn't have to be anything. You chose to be on his team.

Because nobody else would be, said Elf.

That doesn't mean we didn't have empathy, I said. That means we chose life, or some semblance of it. You happen to be more *like* him than us—which is lucky for you in a million ways—but that doesn't mean we didn't fucking care.

Oh so you're saying I'm doomed.

I am not saying you're doomed! You're saying you're doomed. I'm saying you didn't *have* to be anything. And since when do you swear?

Yes, I did have to be something, said Elf. Have you ever heard of family dynamics? And don't you think I'm scared shitless?

Well then what is this all about? Why are you here? Some kind of preemptive strike? Do the thing you most fear in order to overcome your fear of doing it in the first place? I'm afraid of killing myself so I think I'll just kill myself and then I'll be able to go on living without fear . . . oh wait! This one's a little different. The logisitics are a bit—

Yoli, I'm trying to explain to you this incredible pressure I've felt to . . .

Quit then! Stop being perfect! That doesn't mean you die, you moron. Can't you just be like the rest of us, normal and sad and fucked up and alive and remorseful? Get fat and start smoking and play the piano badly. Whatever! At least you know that you will eventually get what you want most in life—

What do I want most in life?

Death!

Yoli.

So why don't you just wait for it to happen. Exercise some patience and all your dreams will come true. Guaranteed. What I want most in life is completely unattainable and everybody knows it.

What's that? Elf said. Legalized marijuana?

True love, I said. And yet I'm sticking around unreasonably and knowing it's impossible because who knows? I want to find out. I live *hopefully*.

Well, Yoli, your logic is skewed. You're contradicting yourself. You are quite certain that your dream of true love, whatever that is, will never come true but on the off-chance that it *might* come true you will stick around to find out. I *know* that my so-called dream of death *will* come true so therefore, according to your own argument, I should be free to leave. There's nothing to find out. No big surprises in the wings and nothing to hope for.

That's not what I said!

I think it is.

Listen, I said. Don't you think that mom has suffered enough with dad and all that shit and now, what, you love the perverse idea of a fucking encore?

Yoli, that's so cruel. That's beyond—

You're just dying for a curtain call, aren't you?

I'm not perfect, said Elf. I didn't mean—

Yeah, I'll say! I said. If you were perfect you'd stick around. See how life goes, how the kids do, do you ever think about Will and Nora and what this all means to—

Yolandi, shut up now, said Elf. Of course I do. I think about them all the time.

Bullshit! I said. If you thought of them, ever, just once—

Yolandi, stop it.

Stop what? I said. Stop making sense? Stop telling the truth? Sense drives you crazy?

You tell me, said Elf.

We stopped talking for a long, long time. A long time. Nurses came and went attaching and detaching things. Hundreds of thousands of babies were born while we weren't talking. The continents continued to separate at the same pace as finger-nails growing.

Yoli, look, she said finally. Can you just talk to me?

About what? I asked her.

Anything, she said.

Sure, I said, but you ask me to talk like you have some kind of hidden script you want me to follow and then when I veer from it—because I don't even know what it is in the first place—you're like no, no, don't talk. You don't want me to talk about the past because it's too painful because there were good times, there was life, and it might persuade you to change your mind and you don't want me to talk about the future because you don't see one and so what—okay, I'll talk about this second. I just inhaled. The sun moved behind a cloud. I exhaled. You're in bed. A second is passing. Another one. Oh . . . and another one! I'm inhaling again.

She put her hand up and I took it. I held it, like we were champions of something stupid but hard-won, like a whis-tling tournament, but at a World Championship level. Just then Claudio appeared at the door carrying an extravagant bouquet of flowers. Ciao! He was wearing a patterned blue scarf, folded flat into his woollen coat. His black leather shoes glistened. Yolandi, you look beautiful! (I love Claudio.) He kissed me on both cheeks. Elfrieda, my darling, and he kissed her forehead just above the new scar. Claudio, I'm so sorry, she said. He spoke to her in Italian, *ma cosa ti è successo, tesoro,* but she shook her head, no, don't, as though the language of her heart had no place here or that it reminded her of beauty and love and laughter and those things were bullets now, sharp teeth and shards of glass and cheap plastic toys you step on in the nighttime.

Elfrieda, we are together here, that's all that matters. He put the flowers on the side table and took her hand. You rescued me from Budapest, he said. He said he liked the way Budapest was beautiful and elegant and crumbling, decaying, plucky and sad, but when he spent too long there, everything started to depress him. And he said he had meetings, lunches, dinners, and he began to feel crumbling, decaying, and sad. He told us he sat in a warm hot spring that exploded from the ground, the way he had as a young man, surrounded by art nouveau architecture, it was like bathing in a cathedral. The sky was pink. The scent of lilacs filled the air. Fat Russian gangsters in tiny bathing suits played chess while their bleached blond wives hung scowling from their necks and arms festooned with gold and silver. Barbarians!

Claudio spoke English well, only a faint trace of his Italian accent. Those Russians are the descendants of the guys who slaughtered the Mennonites, I thought. Now they wear bikini trunks. Then he told us he had been standing on one of the bridges over the Danube and looking down he saw a guy sitting on the riverbank. Is it blue? I said. No, it's filthy I'm afraid, and not at all blue. Is it beautiful? I asked. Well, yes, it could be described as beautiful.

That's true, Elf said.

Well there was this tramp, or—do you call them hobos?

Do you know that *hobo* is an acronym for Homeward Bound? I said to Elf.

Yes, she said. From Woody Guthrie. I'm surprised that you know that.

I also know that there's a Hobo Museum in Britt, Ohio, I said. I love reading their newsletter, especially posts from Nowhere Man and Mad Mary. When somebody dies they say he caught the Westbound.

Elf smiled. Curious, she said.

Hm, well, Claudio pressed on, I look down at the man who is just sitting there on the riverbank staring at the water, at the sky, at the things around him. He's holding a can of beer. Then he gets up and picks up an empty bottle lying next to him and walks down one cement stair that goes right into the river, the bottom of his pants are getting wet, and he looks around as if he's making sure nobody is watching. I thought he was going to jump in and drown himself, but he didn't go any farther. He leaned over and filled the bottle with some of the river water. Then he went back and sat down again, where he was. I was so relieved. My heart was pounding while I was watching all this from the bridge. But then I thought, oh dear, he's going to drink the river water—but he doesn't. He simply sits there for a while, with his beer can and the bottle with the river water, and stares some more. Then slowly he takes the bottle and pours a little bit of it into his beer can. And then he drinks from the beer can. I was watching this and I thought, how awful, don't drink it. Of course he did, and for whatever reason it upset me deeply and I wanted to get out of Budapest.

He drank the river water? said Elf.

Yes, he added the dirty river water to his beer to make it last longer, Claudio said.

And you thought that was pathetic? said Elf.

Yes, just terribly sad.

He could have drowned himself instead, I said. Do you think that would have been better?

Of course not, but I certainly didn't want him to have to drink river water.

Well, said Elf, I guess he made—

Yeah, a choice, I said. I get it. I think that he shouldn't have had to make that choice.

I don't want to drink the river water, said Elf.

I'd rather drink the river water than drown in it, I said.

I understand that, said Elf.

So you're saying you have pride and I don't and that a person with deep character, integrity, all that, would absolutely throw himself in before he resorted to drinking river water? What about the courage you need to understand and accept that you need the beer and you have to make it last longer? What about the grace you require in order to accept the gift of life?

Claudio apologized and said he hadn't meant to upset us, it was only something he saw.

Elf said she had let everyone down.

Not at all, said Claudio. All the musicians already have other, what do you say, gigs and everyone sends you their love . . . Antanas, and Otto and Ekko and Bridget and Friedrich.

How is Friedrich?

Oh, the same, trouble with women, money . . . Claudio laughed but looked stricken.

Is everybody very upset with me?

Of course not! I'm taking care of everything, Elfrieda. You needn't give it another thought. We've got insurance for these things, as you know, it's nothing more than a small inconvenience, and one that is of no real concern in the grand scheme of things. He made a gesture. Pfft. *Non è niente*. He offered a few more reassurances and then said he had better go. He had to get back to the airport. When he leant to kiss Elfrieda on two cheeks she grabbed him for a hug.

I'll walk you out, I said.

Ciao, Claudio, Elf said, and it sounded like a sob. Ciao, ciao.

Claudio and I stood in the hallway next to a large canvas sack filled halfway with bloody sheets.

Let's walk a bit? I said. He put his arm around my shoulder briefly and asked me how I was, really.

Oh, don't ask, I said. I'll cry. But thanks. How are you? Let's go down to the main floor.

Well, considering . . . I'm so sorry, Yolandi, I'm just sick over this.

Yeah . . . She'll probably be okay, I said. I mean not for the tour but—

No, I suppose not, said Claudio. What a shame. I mean for her, for everybody.

Yeah.

Anyway, Yolandi, you needn't bother yourself with it. As you know, Elfrieda and I have been through many trials and it is to be expected. It's nothing.

Sì. Va bene.

Ah, you would like to speak Italian?

No. I mean yes, but . . .

No, no, I understand, he said.

We walked slowly past doors with numbers on them. In one doorway an old woman in a nightgown stood clutching a large round clock. She had a green handbag wedged under one arm. What time is it? she asked us.

I'm sorry? said Claudio.

What time is it? she said. She showed us her clock.

It's nearly half past four, said Claudio.

What? she said. What?

It's four-thirty, I said.

It's four-thirty? she said. It's four-thirty!

Yes.

Is this your husband? she asked me. She pointed at Claudio.

No, I said.

Your father?

No.

Your brother?

No, I said. He's my friend. Claudio introduced himself and held his hand out to shake hers but she was holding the clock tightly with both hands so couldn't follow through.

You better not be thinking of stealing my purse, she said. She backed away from us into the shadows of her room.

No, no, of course not, said Claudio. I took his arm and pulled him gently away from the woman.

My house key is in this bag! we heard her yell. She had come back into the hallway. She was still holding the clock. Claudio and I turned around, nodded and smiled, and then kept walking. A nurse told her to hush, Milly, hush.

She's never going back home, I told Claudio.

No? Why not? he said.

Because it's been sold, I said. Her nephew told me. From here she'll go to a nursing home.

But she keeps the key to her house, said Claudio.

It's the only thing in her bag, I said. She never lets go of it, or the clock, even when she's sleeping.

Yoli, said Claudio. We will find a replacement for those last concerts, there's still time. Please tell Elfrieda, again, not to worry about anything. Nothing at all. Claudio stopped walking and put his hands on my shoulders and told me he was sorry. Yolandi, he said, your sister is a rare individual. She is like no other person I've ever known. You must keep her alive. You must try everything. Everything.

I . . . yeah, I will . . . we are . . . Claudio was wiping tears from his eyes. I patted his shoulder. It's okay . . . she'll be okay, I said. I really think she'll be okay. I smiled hard.

Claudio hugged me. He said he had to run, he had a car waiting outside, but we'd meet again. His cellphone rang. *Arrivederci*, Claudio, I said. And thanks, thank you, *grazie* for the beautiful flowers.

When I came back into the room, Elf said, I know. Don't be mad. And don't preach, okay? Gift of life. You sounded like an old Mennonite, like what's his name.

I'm not mad, I said. I am an old Mennonite. So are you. You're so resentful of everything.

That's true, said Elf. That's very true.

Yeah, but of what exactly?

Elf said nothing.

Hey, I said. I had a dream that I was leaving everyone I knew, that everyone I knew and loved had gathered together on a sunny afternoon to wave goodbye to me. I didn't want to go then, when I saw them all gathered and was reminded of their love, but I had to go.

Elf asked me, Did you see me in that dream? I said yes, of course, you were there too, smiling and waving. Elf asked me if I had ever read *Lady Chatterley's Lover*. I said no. This is the first line, she said, and recited it: "Ours is essentially a tragic age, so we refuse to take it tragically."

Okay, I said, interesting. And then how does it go?

Read it yourself, she said. I can't believe you haven't read it. Maybe instead of poring over the Hobo Museum newsletter you could revisit an old classic.

I told her that it seemed like we were having some kind of *Karate Kid* conversation here, was she trying to impart wisdom or something? You're still lecturing me on what to read, I said. That's good. Elf told me her throat was sore, she couldn't talk anymore. Yeah, okay, sure, I said.

You don't believe me, she whispered.

Yeah, yeah, of course I do.

We were quiet. Elf drifted in and out of sleep or something resembling sleep. I sat on the chair next to her. I imagined running headlong through the glass walls and shattering them to smithereens. The day before my father died he dreamed that he had somersaulted boyishly through concrete walls. Over and over and over and over and out!

I had my manuscript with me, still in the plastic Safeway bag. I took it out of my bag and wrote *A Life Time of Resentment* on the cover. Then I crossed that out and wrote *A Devotion to Sadness* (which according to Chateaubriand in his *The Genius of Christianity* is "the noblest achievement of civilization" so take that Mennonite busybodies who tell me in sanctimonious sing-song and with bland pat-a-cake faces that my father's suicide was *evil*) then *Smithereens*, then *Untitled*. Then *Entitled*. Then I crossed it all out and sketched Elf in her bed.

I watched Elf sleep and I watched the nurses scurry around and laugh with each other behind their desk. I knew they couldn't stand having Elf there, a failed suicide. A nutcase. They were terse with her and no doctor ever came to talk to us. I went to the counter and asked if I could speak to Elf's psychiatrist. They told me that he had been called away to an emergency. I left the room and went downstairs to find my mother and my aunt and to text Nora in Toronto. I couldn't find them in the cafeteria and Nora wasn't texting back. I went back up to Intensive Care and there was Elf's doctor. He was standing at the nurses' desk. He was wearing a visor, like a jeweller. He was wearing ankle socks. He was the psychiatrist. I walked over to him and intro-duced myself and asked him if he had talked with Elfrieda lately.

I tried to, he said, but she wouldn't speak.

Sometimes she doesn't, that's true. But she's willing to write things down on paper.

I don't have time for reading while I'm on the job, he said. He smiled and two of the nurses giggled like they were standing next to Elvis in *Girls! Girls! Girls!*

Yeah, I said. Ha. But I mean—

Look, he said. I'm not interested in passing a notebook back and forth between us and waiting while she scribbles things down. It's ridiculous.

I know, I said. I understand. It can be laborious but I'm just, I mean, you're a shrink, right, so you must have seen this sort of thing before?

Of course I understand it, he said, I just don't have time for it. No? I ask.

Look, he says, if she wants to get better she'll have to make an attempt to communicate normally. That's all I'm saying.

I know, I said, that's . . . But she's a psych patient, right? I mean isn't she supposed to have some eccentricities? I mean doesn't she—isn't it challenging for you? I mean, like, in the field of psychotherapy. Wouldn't you welcome this opportunity to really apply all of your studies to—

Excuse me, you're who again? he said.

I told you. I'm her sister. My name's Yolandi. I honestly believe that her silence is a way of her unfitting herself for the real world, do you know what I mean? You can't take it personally. It's her way—

Of course I know what you mean, he said. I'm not sure that I agree with you but of course I understand you. I'm telling you that I don't have time for a silly game that—

Silly game? I said. Sorry, I said, but did you just call it a silly game?

He was walking away from me. Wait! I said. Wait. Wait, wait. A silly game? The shrink stopped and turned to look at me.

After just one visit with her you're refusing to help? I said. You're some kind of esteemed psychiatrist. You're just fucking dismissing her out of hand right in front of her? My sister is vulnerable. She's tortured. She's your patient! She's begging for help but wants to assert one small vestige of individual power over her life. Surely even a first-year psych student would understand the significance of that stance. Are you not . . . do you not have any professional curiosity, even? Are you alive or what the fuck?

I'll have to ask you to keep your voice down, said one of his nurses from behind her bunker. She aimed a semi-automatic machine gun at my head. The shrink spread his legs and folded his arms and stared at me while I ranted. He smiled at the nurse and shrugged and appeared to be enjoying himself, like I was a giant wave he was really looking forward to surfing later in the day after pounding back a pitcher of margaritas with his buddies.

Are you so hostile and impatient and complacent that you won't even let her communicate with you with words written down on a piece of paper? I said. Why can't you just do your job? I don't want to argue but I mean are you honestly telling me that you won't listen to her?

Listen, said the shrink. You're not the first family member to take out your frustration on me. Okay? Are you finished? I'm sorry. He walked away, down the hallway and into a room.

Because, I shouted after him, if you won't help her then who will?

I apologized to the nurses for causing a scene. I'm so angry, I said. I'm so desperate. I'm so terrified. I'm so angry. I don't know what to do. I repeated these phrases. The nurses nodded and one of them said yes, that's understandable. Your sister isn't co-operating and—

I cut her off. I said no, please. Please don't blame it on my sister. I just can't bear to hear that right now. She's not evil. I was whispering. I willed myself not to raise my voice. I can't take that right now, I said. I didn't say she was evil, said the nurse, I said she wasn't— I put my hands up around my head like I was trying on a new pair of headphones. I had lost my mind. I thanked them for their something or other and left Intensive Care.

I walked down six flights of stairs but on the second one my cell rang and I said hello. Hey Yolandi, said the voice on the other end. It's Joanna. (Somebody from the orchestra.) I just wanted to tell you how very sorry we are about Elfrieda and I'm wondering if there's anything we can do. I'd like to send something. I just don't know what. Flowers?

Imagine a psychiatrist sitting down with a broken human being saying, I am here for you, I am committed to your care, I want to make you feel better, I want to return your joy to you, I don't know how I will do it but I will find out and then I will apply one hundred percent of my abilities, my training, my compassion and my curiosity to your health—to your well-being, to your joy. I am here for you and I will work very hard to help you. I promise. If I fail it will be my failure, not yours. I am the professional. I am the expert. You are experiencing great pain right now and it is my job and my mission to cure you from your pain. I am absolutely committed to your care. (At this point I could hear Joanna saying Yolandi? Yolandi?) I know you are suffering. I know you are afraid. I love you. I want to cure you and I won't stop trying to help you. You are my patient. I am your doctor. You are my patient. Imagine a doctor phoning you at all hours of the day and night to tell you that he or she had been reading some new stuff on the subject of whatever and was really excited about how it might help you. Imagine a doctor calling you in an important meeting and saying listen, I'm so sorry to bother you but I've been thinking really hard about your problems and I'd like to try something completely new. I need to see you immediately! I'm absolutely committed to your care! I think this might help you. I won't give up on you.

Yolandi? said Joanna. Are you okay?

Sorry, I said, hi. I'm sorry. Sorry.

Are you—

Yeah, flowers. Good, thank you.

ELEVEN

I PHONED MY MOTHER ON HER CELL but there was no answer. I saw an orderly who had once been the lead singer of a local punk band. He was stacking trays and whistling next to a poster that listed the symptoms of Flesh Eating Disease.

I went outside into the sunshine and walked all the way back, along the river, to my mother's apartment. Well, I tried to walk along the river the whole way but was stopped by a group of young people piling sandbags around an apartment block. The river's flooding again, they said. It was a bit of a party for them. A day off school.

My mother and Aunt Tina weren't at the apartment but there was a note saying they had gone to East Village to visit Signora Bertolucci, whose real name was Agata Warkentine but who was always referred to, by everyone other than Elf, as Mrs. Ernst Warkentine. Even funeral announcements in East Village omitted the given first name of a woman to ensure she'd forever and ever (and ever and ever) be known only as her husband's wife. They had taken my aunt's van. Then I remembered that I had left the car in the underground parking lot and so I walked back, this time not along the river but through the dusty city streets, to the hospital.

I went up to the sixth floor to check on Elf again but Nic was there and they were staring deeply into each other's eyes and the curtain was half closed and the nurses all pretended not to notice me or were busy calling 911 to get me the hell out of there so I left again and this time went all the way down to the underground parking lot to get the car and drive it back to my mother's apartment. A part of me had been hoping that maybe the woman I screamed at would have written in the dust on my back windshield that she forgave me but she hadn't.

My mother and my aunt were still not back from visiting Signora Bertolucci. I googled things on my mom's laptop. I was trying to find out more about these drugs, Seconal and Nembutal. I scrolled down the various subject headings that Google had for helping people to die. I was worried about cops taking me in for questioning and tracking my history on this computer. I kept googling. I paused for a second when I read: *Is it possible to help someone die with magic?* And I felt good

179

about myself, proud, when I didn't click on it. Elf would congratulate me too. Let's be rational, Yolandi! The phone rang. It was my mother. She was at the hospital. I asked her how Elf was doing. She told me that Elf was having her blood tested. For what? She wasn't sure. But there was something else. My aunt had fainted.

At the hospital? I asked.

Well, no, she fainted in East Village first, at Mrs. Ernst Warkentine's, but she came to quickly and I got her to lie down for a while and then she had something to eat and after that she seemed fine again. But now . . .

You're at the hospital? I asked again.

Yes, we drove here directly to see Elf but on the way, out by Deacon's corner, Tina passed out again in the van.

What? That's so strange.

I know. And so I just drove up to Emergency here immediately and now they've admitted her. And they've put a cast on her arm. She broke it when she fainted.

Auntie Tina?

Yes, she's having some kind of pain in her chest. She's in acute cardiology, on the fifth floor.

Seriously?

Yes, so . . .

Okay, I said.

I hung up. I called right back and apologized. I meant to say okay, I'll be right there. My mother laughed. I laughed a bit too. I knew she was holding back tears. I told her again that I'd be right there and she whispered something I couldn't make out. Had she said what's the difference? My mother has been in and out of Emergency a thousand times with her own heart and breathing issues but this was the first time Tina had landed there as far as I knew.

On the way back to the hospital I thought about my crazy outburst in the parking lot. It's my past, I said out loud to nobody in the car. I had figured it out. I was Sigmund Freud. Mennonite men in church with tight collars and bulging necks accusing me of preposterous acts and damning me to some underground fire when I hadn't done a thing. I was an innocent child. Elf was an innocent child. My father was an innocent child. My cousin was an innocent child. You can't flagrantly march around the fronts of churches waving your arms in the air and scaring people with threats and accusations just because your family was slaughtered in Russia and you were forced to run and hide in a pile of manure when you were little. What you do at the pulpit would be considered lunatic behaviour on the street. You can't go around terrorizing people and making them feel small and shitty and then call them *evil* when they destroy themselves. You will never walk down a street and feel a lightness come over you. You will never fly.

A heart attack comes from the pain of remembering. That was something I'd read somewhere, maybe in the Hobo Museum newsletter, which ended each obituary with "We'll see you down the road!" So Elfrieda was reminding my aunt of her own daughter's suicide? Of the agony that precedes it and the helplessness and terror she felt trying to prevent it from happening? Or does a heart attack come from clogged arteries and fat around the waist and a two-pack-a-day habit and trans fats, not memories of pain and horror and unbearable sorrow? Because maybe one causes the other. Cardiologists and shrinks should join forces and start new hospitals. I'll get a petition going like my father did for a library and Elf did for Stevie Ray Vaughan being the world's best guitarist. I'm quite sure the continents will fuse back together before cardiology and psychiatry join forces.

My aunt's track suit and her tiny white runners were stuffed into a plastic bag that was labelled: *Property of Ste. Odile Hospital.* She and my mother were joking around in Plautdietsch, keeping their fear to themselves as usual. When I showed up they said ah, good, you're here. We're fighting about a word. Its meaning. I asked which word and they both started to laugh again.

There were already things written on Tina's plaster cast. Phone numbers. And a Bible verse. The nurse came over and did some things to my aunt with needles and tubes. I asked if she'd had a heart attack and the nurse said no but a coronary event of some sort. She showed us a sketch of my aunt's arteries. Two of them were severely blocked. My aunt said she desperately needed a Starbucks coffee from downstairs. The nurse said well, perhaps in a bit. Not now.

I told my aunt and my mother that I would go see Elf and then return to them with Starbucks coffee for everyone. They both commended my plan exuberantly, too exuberantly, as though I had just figured out how to storm the Bastille. I went to the sixth floor to tell Elf the news, that Auntie Tina was having a coronary event on the floor below her. Elf's eyes opened wide and she tapped her throat.

Can't talk? I said.

I was annoyed, crazy with misdirected rage, and not hiding it well. She shook her head. I asked where Nic was and she shook her head again.

I went out to ask the nurse why she couldn't talk. The nurse said there had been some complications but hopefully she'd regain her voice by tomorrow or the next day. Having to do with the Javex? I said. The nurse looked away, down at her clipboard. She didn't want me to say Javex. We're not sure, she said. But what else could it be? I said. A choice of hers? You'll have to talk to the doctor, she said. I'd love to, I said, but I think he's taken a restraining order out on me. The nurse refused to look at me. We were a tainted family, deranged.

I went back into Elf's room and stood at the foot of her bed. For a second I felt like her executioner come to offer her a last meal and a smoke. The world has gone a bit dark, eh? She blinked. You'd concur? I said. She blinked again.

I sat there for a while looking at my manuscript. I read a page to myself, it didn't make me happy, and then gently placed it upside down on Elf's flat stomach. Then another and another. I continued to read and place pages gently on my sister's body and she lay very still, hardly breathing, so they wouldn't fall. Finally I told her that I was going back down to the fifth floor to check on Tina and to bring them Starbucks coffee. She nodded and rolled her eyes a bit because I'd said Starbucks. It's all they have here, I said. I gathered up my pages from her stomach. Elf smiled and touched my hand. She held it for a few seconds. I realized that I'd forgotten the moisturizing cream. I knew she meant for me to tell our aunt that she loved her, that she hoped she'd be okay. I told Elf that I would tell our aunt those things and she nodded. I wanted to say: imagine mom losing her sister. How horrible, no? But it wasn't that dire, it was only an event, and I had no more energy, after taking on psychiatry, cardiology *and* Mennonite evangelism, for haranguing.

On the way to the Starbucks in the lobby I got a call from Finbar. He asked me what the hell I'd been talking about. You want to kill your sister? he said. I'm a lawyer, for god's sake. Don't tell me these things. No, I don't, I said. But I'm wondering if I should. Yolandi, he said, you're exhausted and stressed out. You can't kill your sister. You can't do anything for her other than what you're doing right now. I told him I wasn't doing anything for her right now and he said that I was there, that's what mattered. Was there something he could do for me? I asked him to drive past my apartment in Toronto and see if there were signs of life from Nora and Will and maybe he could knock on the door and ask them if they were okay and why Nora wasn't answering her phone. Although I already knew why. It was because she had poisoned Will and dragged his body into a closet and was having unprotected sex all over the house with her fifteen-year-old Swedish dancer boyfriend and she didn't have the time or the inclination to talk to her sad old disapproving mother in the midst of it all. Consider it done, he said. He promised to call later that day.

To my surprise I met a family I knew from East Village in a waiting room in the cardiology ward, where they were watching TV. They asked me what I was doing there. I told them my aunt was here, a patient. They said is that Tina Loewen? But doesn't she live in Vancouver? I said yeah, she's here visiting. She's here for an event, a coronary event. They didn't laugh.

We made some small talk. They told me that the woman's brother was having heart surgery, a valve replacement. Straightforward. He'd be doing his standard three-mile jog within a week of being discharged.

They had great faith in the doctors. They believed in rain

dances and placating the gods with human sacrifices as well. Probably. Their brother's surgeon was the best in town, they adored him. They told me that their oldest son, a guy my age, had done his PhD in economics at Oxford. Cool, wow, I said. I remembered that son, Gerhard, had teased me mercilessly when I wet my pants in grade one. He called me and Julie lezzies for holding hands at recess. He drew swastikas all over his jeans and notebooks. And now he's in London, said his mother, a policy analyst. He's basically paid to think, she said. Imagine! It seems that every time he delivers a lecture he's offered a scholarship to some university or another the very next day. It's tempting, she laughs. But of course he has to consider his wife and kids. She has a busy career of her own, curator for the Tate Modern and ambassador to Rwanda, and the kids are in good schools—rubbing shoulders with royalty, no less—that they wouldn't want to leave.

Ahhh . . . I managed to say.

You know, he saw your sister Elfrieda play with the London Philharmonic and he said it was the most amazing thing he'd ever heard. Thankfully the church has finally seen fit to allow musical instruments into the community. We were always supportive of her piano playing, by the way. Your mother and I used to bump into each other at the post office sometimes and share a giggle about the hidden piano and I always told her to keep at it, to keep paying for those lessons because Elfrieda has a real gift. God would approve even if the elders didn't. To think that somehow I contributed to her fame! I think Gerhard used to have a crush on her. Didn't he, honey? She was talking to her husband.

Hmmm? What? he said.

She rolled her eyes. And what have you been up to? she asked.

Oh, I don't know really, I said. Not much. Learning how to be a good loser.

Just then my mother came into the room looking as weary as a human being can look and not be dead. She greeted these people in a friendly, wary manner. They spoke in Plautdietsch for a while. They told her they were sorry about Tina. Thanks, my mom said, she'll be all right. (She threw down a Plautdietsch expression here that the East Villagers nodded to appreciatively.) They don't think she needs surgery, just possibly a certain type of heart medication.

Then Nic came into the room. He'd just heard about Tina. He was wearing a blue polyester-cotton blend dress shirt that had giant sweat stains under the arms. There was tomato sauce or blood on his chin. Half of his collar was turned up and he looked like a kid who'd insisted on getting ready for school all by himself.

Good grief, he said, and gave us each a hug. How is she? My mother explained again. Yikes, he said. I'm really sorry. Elf's still in ICU, said my mom. Yeah, said Nic, I was just there. Wait, said the East Village people, Elfrieda is in the ICU? What happened to her?

She cut her wrists and drank poison, said my mom. Nic and I stared at my mother. Her throat closed but she didn't die, said my mom. Not this time. She'll probably be okay too. Everyone will survive eventually. And what brings you here this evening?

Nic and I allowed for a minute or two of this gong show and then pulled the plug. C'mon, mom, let's get you home. You need to rest. I knew, as soon as the words were out of my mouth, that she'd resist. She was on the rampage, combative as hell and prepared to stamp out any ember of hope or kindness. I'm not tired, she said. But perhaps *you* need to rest. She was either being petulant or presenting a wonderful, almighty challenge.

Nic said he'd go say hi to Tina and then sit with Elf for a while longer, maybe read to her or play his guitar quietly. Any news from the doc? he said. Beats me, said my mom. I'd call him but I don't think he gets cell service at the Quarry Oaks Golf Club.

Her throat isn't right, I said. Nic said yeah, he knew that and asked me what I thought it meant. I don't know exactly, I said, but maybe there's an infection now that's making it painful for her to talk. We waved our hands around to fill the gaps. We need to phone Tina's kids, said my mom. Yeah, we'll grab some dinner first and then go home and call, I told her. She's stable, right? The nurses said? Yeah, said my mom. They'll just keep her overnight for observation. Nic said he'd call me later if there was any news on Elf. I tugged on my mother's sleeve like a four-year-old. C'mon, let's get out of here, I said. I second that emotion, she said.

I waved goodbye to the successful people and told them to say hi to their son. They called after my mom and said all the best with Tina and Elf.

She didn't really hear what they'd said and answered back I'll see ya in the funny papers!

Nora had texted me from Toronto: *A guy in a suit knocked on the door and asked me if I was all right. He said he was your friend. Are you a Jehovah's Witness now? How's Elf?*

We drove down Corydon Avenue towards my mother's apartment. How are you doing? she asked me. Fine, fine, I said. I wanted to tell her that I felt I was dying from rage and that I felt guilty about everything and that when I was a kid I woke up every morning singing, that I couldn't wait to leap out of bed and rush out of the house into the magical kingdom that was my world, that dust made visible in sunbeams gave me real authentic joy, that my sparkly golden banana-seated bike with the very high sissy bar took my breath away, the majesty of it, that it was mine, that there was no freer soul in the world than me at age nine, and that now I woke up every morning reminding myself that control is an illusion, taking deep breaths and counting to ten trying to ward off panic attacks and hoping that my own hands hadn't managed to strangle me while I slept. Nora texted: *We have carpenter ants now.* I texted back: *Good. Put them to work rebuilding the broken door.*

My mother patted my leg, don't text and drive honey, she said. I remained silent, she said something like this too shall pass and I wanted to swerve into oncoming traffic. What will you say next! I asked her. Whatever doesn't kill you makes you stronger?

Well, she laughed, I know you're ideologically opposed to clichés, but yes, that one is apt, no?

No, I said. Everything will be all right in the end and if it's not all right then it's not the end.

Is that one of those? she asked.

Yeah, it's one of those, but I don't think I said it right. And what do you mean, ideologically opposed? Being original isn't an ideology.

Okay, she said, but believing in originality is though, right?

I guess so. Do you know that people are happier when they stop trying to be happy? That's some study they did.

Well, I could have told you that, said my mom.

My phone was buzzing away, texts from men wanting divorces and children wanting me to condone underage sex and kill insects from three thousand kilometres away.

So what happens to Rhonda the Rodeo Girl this time? asked my mother. Is she still . . . what was she, fourteen?

No, this is my book book, my real book.

Oh right! Of course. What's it about again?

Oh, I don't know, I said. You don't have to make a fake effort to show interest—you're exhausted.

No, Yoli, she said, I do want to know and if anything it will help me to take my mind off things for a minute or two.

It's about a harbourmaster.

What? A what? said my mom. I thought it was about sisters.

Yeah, that too, but initially a harbourmaster. He's the guy, or woman I guess—but in my story he's a guy—who steers the big ships out of the harbour and then climbs down a little rope ladder when the ship is safely out at sea, and into a little boat that's been driving along beside the ship, and then he goes back home. But in my story the weather is too bad for him to climb down onto the little boat, the captain won't let him, the ladder is too flimsy and it's way too dangerous, they misjudged the storm that they thought was still two days away, so the harbourmaster has to go all the way to Rotterdam with the ship because that's the first port of call.

Oh, said my mom. Well, that's fascinating.

Okay, well it's not fascinating, I said. I just wanted to write a book that didn't end with a rodeo competition, you know?

Oh, but they're so exciting.

Well, not this time, mom. I've got all the excitement up front.

So then what happens once he's left the harbour?

He misses this crucial meeting he had planned for that evening and everything goes wrong.

But can't he call whomever he's supposed to meet and reschedule?

Well, I'm not sure but yeah, right, that's a bit of a credibility problem I'm having because he should be able to but then there'd be no crisis, no book.

Right, said my mom. Perhaps he's forgotten his cellphone?

Well no, because there would be an entire crew on the ship and communication technology and all that, that he could use.

Okay, but, said my mom, maybe he does call the person he's supposed to be meeting but he or she doesn't get the message on time? You know, they miss each other in some way.

Yeah, that makes more sense I think. But I just like the idea of this guy not being able to get off this ship and not being at all prepared for a journey to Rotterdam.

Right, hmmm, said my mom. And then the sisters part? Does he meet sisters on the boat?

No, I said, the sisters part is in his imagination as he sits on the deck staring at the sea.

Oh! Okay . . . memories of sisters.

Sort of, yeah, he just has thoughts— Hey, do you hear that?

What?

That clanking. Hang on.

I pulled the car into the parking lot of an "ice crematorium" called the Marble Slab (Jesus Christ!) and turned off the engine. I got out and walked around the car, staring and unsure, like I was looking at the latest Damien Hirst installation. I got back into the car and tried to start it again. Nothing. The engine wasn't turning over. That's odd, said my mom. Don't worry, I said. I thought of Anatole France angrily telling his *amour* that he would bite his fists until they bled. I tried again. And again. Nothing.

The car's dead, I said.

My mother shook her head and grinned. She started to laugh. I looked at her. I took her hand and plopped the useless key into her palm. I smiled and she kept on laughing for a while.

Oh boy, she said. Her body shook. This is getting really funny.

She suggested that we get out of the car and walk to Kristina's, the Greek restaurant next to Fresh. Yeah, I said, good idea, especially the walking part.

At the restaurant we had a surprisingly upbeat conversation about men and sex and guilt and children. Is there anything else? We drank an entire bottle of red wine. We also talked about Nic. Do you think he's okay? I asked my mom. Well, that depends on what you mean by okay, she said. He's holding up.

I guess he is, I said. I just don't know how.

How? said my mom. How are *you* holding up?

I guess, I said again. How are *you* holding up?

We laughed at ourselves, then stopped. Breath, energy, emotion, self-control, all too valuable right now to squander. My cellphone rang and my mom picked it up and said questions without answers, how may we help you? (She may have been a little drunk.) It was Jason, her mechanic at River City Auto, and he said he'd have the car towed to the garage and figure out what was wrong.

We walked back to my mom's apartment hand in hand. She taught me the military way of synchronizing our strides. It's a little skip, see? she said. She showed me. Then when we're out of sync, you do it again. She made me try it. When we got back to her apartment she talked to people on the phone about Elf and Tina (Yes, they're both in the hospital. The same hospital, yes) while I researched Nembutal online. If you "erase history" does that mean the police can't see it?

Jason called me back on my cell and said the transmission was fatally compromised and that there was no point in saving the car, it wasn't worth it. He suggested that an organization of "youth at risk" teens be allowed to pick up the car to use as a guinea pig in their classroom at a school that tried to help them pick a career other than petty criminal. They'd pay fifty bucks for the car and haul it away for good. I told him to hang on for a sec and asked my mom if she was prepared to say goodbye to her car forever. She was on the phone and nodded and shrugged yeah, whatever. I told Jason fine, let them keep the cash. He asked me to come and get the stuff that was in the car before he called up the troubled teens.

I sat on the balcony with my laptop and read that pentobarbital is Nembutal and that the brand names are Sedal-Vet, Sedalphorte and Barbithal. They're used to put animals to sleep and you have to go to Mexico to buy them but not to the border towns like Tijuana because the cops are suspicious now of these "death tourists" as they're called. You have to go deep into Mexico, into the interior, to out-of-the-way places. And then you just find the nearest pet store and go in and ask for it. I thought it was funny that some of the people writing about their efforts to purchase the drug were warning readers to avoid dangerous back streets. What's the worst that could happen? I wondered. You'd be killed?

A dose of Nembutal is about thirty bucks and you need two one-hundred-millilitre bottles to ensure speed and death with absolute certainty. And you have to take some anti-nausea pills beforehand, "travel sickness" pills, so that you don't throw up when you take the Nembutal. They're anti-emetics. You take one every hour for twelve hours before taking the Nembutal. They're sold over the counter and have brand names like Compazine or Dramamine. After you take the Nembutal you'll die in half an hour, unless you're a large person in which case it might take forty-five minutes to an hour. It will be painless. You'll fall asleep quickly and there will be no time for speeches or to finish your drink.

The problem, I read online, was not getting the drug but bringing it back over the border. So then, I thought, I had to get Elf to Mexico rather than the drug to Elf. Also, just opening the bottle for Elf would make me guilty of manslaughter. Some of the anonymous writers said that even a suggestion to the person wanting to die—all right, well how about we get that bottle now—could make you an accessory to manslaughter.

I switched off my computer and closed my eyes. I heard sirens on the Osborne bridge but I imagined a beach, a thatched roof hut, palm leaves gently undulating in a Caribbean breeze, my sister finally getting her wish, Nic, my mother (my father too, even though he's dead, because this was a fantasy and I could have dead people in it if I wanted), me, my kids, holding her, touching her, smiling, kissing, saying goodbye, saying Elfie, you, you have made an incredible difference to our lives, you have filled us up with joy and kept our secrets and made us laugh so hard and we will miss you terribly, adios, CIAO! saying it properly, together, and Elf drifting off so peacefully on a soft cloud of eternal love.

I phoned Nic but when he answered I lost my nerve entirely. I had been planning to ask him if he'd be interested in a trip to Mexico whereby we kill his wife. Instead I asked him if my mom and I could borrow his car for a few days because hers had broken down for good. He said she could keep it for as long as she needed to get to the hospital and all that, because he preferred to ride his bike. I asked him if he was still at the hospital. He said yeah.

And? I said.

Same, he said. She had some dinner. Her throat is better. And Tina's asleep in her ward. All quiet on the western front. He asked me if I was okay and suddenly I was choking. Yoli? he said. I'm okay, I said, sorry about that.

Then he told me that he was planning to go to Spain after all. I hadn't known that he'd been planning to go to Spain at all. He said he hadn't known if he should cancel or not but now he was definitely going to go—tomorrow.

Tomorrow? That's soon.

I know, he said. Elf said I should go. She said I had to go. Just for . . . you know.

Yeah, no, you should . . .

And I can't get a refund on the ticket now. I'm going with my dad, you know, he had this idea for years to go to the . . .

For how long?

Ten days.

Well, cool, okay . . .

I know, the timing is weird. But it's his dream. And she's not coming home before that, the doctor was clear on that.

Well . . .

You're planning to stay in the city for at least that long though, right, Yoli? I mean, so you'll be here—

Yes, I am. No, you should definitely go. God knows, you need a break.

You do too, everyone does, but . . .

No, go! Definitely! Definitely.

Though it just seems absurd to me to be wandering around Barcelona taking pictures of Gaudí stuff while Elf is in the hospital.

I know but everything is absurd right now and if you don't get a break soon you'll crack right up, my friend.

Well, he said. I suppose.

I mean it's not just you, it's all of us, I said. It's like how we're told to give ourselves oxygen first on planes and then give it to our kids.

I guess . . . he said.

You have to go, for the same reason we forced my mom to go on the cruise. We have to tag off periodically or we'll all end up in psych in bed with Elf.

I'd like that, said Nic. Did you see the paper today? There was a thing in the arts section about Elf bailing from her tour due to exhaustion. It said her family has asked for privacy.

We did? I said. Is anyone talking to them?

The press? said Nic. No, not as far as I know. Claudio's the only one dealing with it. He's the one who told them she was exhausted. His press release.

He had to tell them something. Nic, you really should go. Seriously. You have to go.

But that guy, Danislov or whatever, that Slovakian oboe guy who lives in Winnipeg . . . he went to the hospital yesterday to visit her.

Oh, so everyone's gonna know now, I said. Did he talk to her?

It doesn't really matter, said Nic. I mean the truth is the truth. I just want . . . I was hoping to protect her.

You have been, I said. You've been protecting her. You've always protected her. He was crying now. He was crying like a man, gulping everything back.

It's okay. I was trying not to cry too—we have to take turns breaking down or everything is lost. It's okay, I said. I drove my fists into my eyes.

It could be anywhere, he said. I don't care about Spain. I could go to Montana or something right now, just about anywhere. Sometimes I want to be four again, in Bristol, walking down the high street with my mudder.

That was how Nic said *mother*. When he said it I was lost too. We just hung up finally without saying goodbye.

TWELVE

JASON HAD SUGGESTED I COME to the garage that evening before they closed at nine p.m. I waved goodbye to my mother who was still on the phone and she blew me a kiss. I walked the three blocks to the garage and found a man peering into my mother's car. All I could see was his curved back and some thinning brown hair. I said hi and he stood up. He was wearing a T-shirt that had an old copy of Jack Kerouac's *The Subterraneans* emblazoned on the front of it. Then I realized that he was the Jason I'd known in first-year university at the University of Manitoba, the guy from my CanLit class who borrowed my notes all the time and wore yellow cords and gave me pot as payment. We called him Sad Jason then because his girlfriend had broken up with him and he couldn't concentrate on anything.

I thought it might be you when you said your name was Yolandi on the phone, he said. It's not like there's a plethora of them around.

And then all I could think of was my younger self, the person I was before I'd become all of these other selves: a soon-to-be-divorced woman in her forties who'd clumsily left her husband even if for reasons I'd thought were valid at the time, a grotesquely undiscerning lover, an adult daughter who nagged her elderly mother about the use of clichés, a sister who couldn't say the right things to save a life and thereby was flipping over to becoming homicidal, a writer who bogusly claimed to know about ocean freighters and a "death tourist." I stood there in Sad Jason's garage and wept until he awkwardly came over to where I was standing and gingerly put his greasy arms around me and said hey, it's okay, don't cry. It's just a car.

Jason was in the process of getting a divorce from his wife who had stopped seeing him in a romantic light and he was currently sort of dating a clown who worked for the Calgary Stampede luring bulls away from fallen cowboys. I told him that I'd been involved in rodeos too, in a way, and that I was also divorced, almost, living in Toronto, here to see family and things weren't going too well at the moment but you know, tomorrow and tomorrow and . . . He suggested we pick up a six of something and drive out to the floodway to catch up and to watch the river rise and the northern lights that the CBC had said were happening tonight at the edge of town. Well, they'd be happening elsewhere, he acknowledged, but we had to get away from the lights of the city in order to see them.

Jason and I had within a moment become something we hadn't foreseen back in that CanLit class a hundred years ago. We were so old. The word *no* flooded my senses and all of my better instincts and I said yeah, sounds good. In his car I asked him if he still smoked pot and he said no, not so much. Well, lately, because of the relationship thing, but otherwise not really. We drove into the darkness of southeastern Manitoba.

We parked by the floodway, under the stars, and drank beer and talked about the past. Does it all kind of kill you? he said. It does, I agreed. We tried but failed to see the northern lights. I sat back in the passenger seat and put my legs up on his dashboard and I closed my eyes. It smelled like vanilla in his car. He had a million air fresheners hanging from his rear-view mirror. He told me he was sorry about all the dog hair in the car. It was really dark. We weren't listening to music. He sat with his hands on his thighs and peered out the windshield. He rolled down the window and then asked if it was too cold. I asked him if he'd ever been to a port city like Rotterdam. He said yeah, actually, he had, good times, good times.

I apologized for being strange. He told me it was okay, it's how he remembered me. He kissed me very softly on my cheek. I kept my eyes closed and smiled. I took his hand and put it on my leg and he asked me about my boyfriend or my husband or you know. He stroked my leg. Same as you, I said, this is nothing. He stopped touching me and kissing me. I opened my eyes and apologized again for saying the wrong thing, a stupid thing. I told him it was nice to talk. He didn't say anything but he nodded and then I started kissing him and he didn't stop me. I asked him if he remembered coming over to my squalid apartment in Osborne Village with a suitcase full of knives. He said oh, was I planning to carve you up? I said no, you were cooking! Oh, yeah, he said, he remembered. We were clumsy and straightforward. I sat on his lap and then felt around for the lever on the side of the seat and pulled it up so that he fell backwards fast, horizontal now, and the moon lit up one corner of his face. Sorry, sorry, I said. I imagined that we were young and horny and very happy.

Afterwards he asked me why I'd asked him about Rotterdam. I told him that I was trying to write a book in which, at the end, one person was marooned at sea, helpless, and the other person was standing on the shore, hurt and mad. He told me that sounded really good, interesting, and I thanked him. Then, driving back into the city, he said no offence but wouldn't he be able to explain to her that he was trapped on this boat? In these times with technology and stuff? A text or whatever? I know, I said, but for some reason he can't. Okay, said Jason, but what reason? I told him that I was having structural problems and he said he told me he thought my structure was amazing and worked really well and I said ha ha, thanks, yours too. (Oh boy.)

I think the main thing, he said, is that it should really rock.

What should rock? I asked him.

The story, he said, it should just move really fast, like pedal to the metal, so it doesn't get boring. Plus, it's hard to write, right? You want to go in, get the job done, and get out. Like when I worked for Renee's septic tank cleaning.

I considered this and realized that it was the best writing advice I'd received in years. In all my life. When he dropped me off and asked if maybe we could see each other again while I was in the city, grab a coffee or something, a movie, I told him I wasn't sure how long I'd be there. I hadn't told him about Elf. Cool, he said, let's keep in touch. We kissed. I went into the lobby and waved goodbye to him through the tinted window, smiling and letting out a barely whispered monosyllabic admonishment to myself. Stop.

I took the stairs two at a time all the way up to my mom's place, repeating my incantation—stop, stop, stop—with every angry footfall and trying to remember what my friend in Toronto had told me recently: that in ten years time shame will be all the rage, talking about it, dissecting it and banishing it. We'd had a bit of an argument then because I told him that it was ludicrous to think that we could just talk our way out of shame, that shame was necessary, that it prevented us from repeating shameful actions and that it motivated us to say we were sorry and to seek forgiveness and to empathize with our fellow humans and to feel the pain of self-loathing which motivated some of us to write books as a futile attempt at atonement, and shame also helped, I told my friend, to fuck up relationships and fucked-up relationships are the life force of books and movies and theatre so sure, let's get rid of shame but then we can kiss art goodbye too. But now, as I climbed these concrete steps holding my hands and fingers to my nose to check if I reeked of sex or motor oil, I longed for a life without shame.

I found my mother playing online Scrabble with a woman from Romania whose code name was Mankiller. The games are timed and she had to make a move quickly. But Yoyo, she said as I moved past her, Nic's going to Spain tomorrow. I nodded and told her I knew that.

I went to my room and googled *purchasing Nembutal in Spain* but only found references to injectable Viagra. Then I googled *euthanasia for mentally ill* and found out that in Switzerland it's legal but hasn't been exercised that much. It's legal to help a person kill herself in Switzerland if there isn't any selfish motivation behind it. And you don't have to be a Swiss citizen to be protected under the law. Aha! Now I understood why Elf had begged me to take her there.

I weighed my options. They were heavy. Get Elf to Mexico and buy Nembutal in a pet store on a dusty side street of a sleepy, non-touristy town and then make sure she opens the bottle herself and that I don't encourage her in any way. Although the definition of *encouragement* might be cloudy under these circumstances. Get Nic and my mom to agree to this plan. Or: Take Elf to Zurich and do it all legally except that it might not work if the doctors decide that her pain is not great enough to warrant a mercy killing. Get Nic and my mom to agree to this plan. Suddenly I was feeling hopeful. But I wasn't sure if I should be hedging my bets, telling Elf that I was thinking of going with her to Switzerland or Mexico but also encouraging her to live. If I told her about the Nembutal plan she'd have only one thing on her mind, and even if there had been only tiny amoeba-sized hopes inside her, of wanting to live, they'd disappear immediately in the light of this new possibility. Also, there was nothing stopping her, when she was released from the hospital, from going to Switzerland or Mexico on her own, except that it would defeat the purpose of not being alone in her last moments of life and if Nic wasn't on board he'd notice she was gone and that money was missing from the account and he would try to stop her. What would she do?

I heard the trumpets sound the end of my mom's game with Mankiller and the slap of her laptop computer closing. Then she was there, standing in the doorway. How are you, sweetheart? she asked. What have you been up to? Having unprotected sex with your mechanic and researching ways to kill your daughter. Not much, I said, got the stuff from the car. Doing some work.

My mother talked to me about Canadian mines in Honduras, the travesty of it all, her rage against the world having found this particular nook to make itself at home in tonight. Tomorrow it would be something else, Muslim gardeners from Oshawa being held without trial in Guantanamo and languishing in solitary confinement, or any situation that was either randomly awful or awful but entirely outside the ability of an ordinary mortal to stop it from happening. The mines are destroying these villages, she said. Destroying these communities. And stripping the land of all its resources. Prime Minister Harper condones it and the wealthy owners of the mines just fly over from time to time in their helicopters laughing. I know, I said, it's unbelievable. It's horrible.

It is! she said. Our tax dollars are being spent on a sanctioned and systematic destruction of the Honduran people and nobody—

I know, I said. It's really . . . it's so awful. I could feel my right eyelid twitching. I lay down on my bed and closed my eyes. I ran through the symptoms of depression I'd read on a sign attached to the back of a city bus, part of some campaign to educate the public on mental illness. A sense of unreality, I thought. Yes.

Sorry, honey, you're tired, I know.

You are too, aren't you?

I guess I am.

I picked up the book lying next to me on the bed and flipped through it. Hey, listen to this, I said. Have you heard of this Portuguese guy called Fernando Pessoa?

Is he with the Jays?

No, he's a poet, this is his book, but he's dead now. He killed himself.

Oh brother, she said. Who hasn't.

But listen to this: "In the plausible intimacy of approaching evening, as I stand waiting for the stars to begin at the window of this fourth floor room that looks out on the infinite, my dreams move to the rhythm required by long journeys to countries as yet unknown, or to countries that are simply hypothetical or impossible."

My mother said yup, that's about the long and short of it, isn't it?

She changed the subject. She told me that Elf's smile was like my father's. It's so surprising. I forget about it sometimes and then whoah!

I know, I said. She has an amazing smile.

Yoli, said my mother.

Yeah? I answered. I put my arms around her. She was sobbing, suddenly, shaking. A keening wail I'd never heard from her before. I held her as tightly as I could and kissed her soft, white hair.

She's a human being, my mother whispered.

We held our embrace in the doorway for a long time. I agreed with her. I said yes. Finally my mother was able to catch her breath and speak. She couldn't bear to see Elf in the psych ward. That prison, she said. They do nothing. If she doesn't take the pills they won't talk to her. They wait and they badger and they badger and they wait and they badger. She began to cry again, this time quietly. She's a human being, she said again. Oh, Elfrieda, my Elfrieda.

We walked to the couch and sat down. I held her hand and struggled to come up with words of consolation. I got up and told her I was going to make us each a cup of tea. When it was finished brewing I brought two cups of camomile tea to the living room. My mom was lying on the couch with a who-dunit on her chest. Mom, I whispered, you should sleep now. The hospital again bright and early tomorrow. Isn't Auntie Tina being released? My mother opened her eyes.

It's called discharged. Yeah, she is.

I'd rather be released than discharged, I said.

True, she said, it sounds more agreeable.

I went to bed and lay there awake and thinking. I returned Nora's text about the lawyer: *He's my friend. His name is Finbar. Just checking up on you. I'm not JW.* I returned the text from my ex-husband: *Yeah, I can sign them tomorrow sometime when I'm not at the hospital. Your timing, man.* Then I texted Nora again: *And keep crumbs off the counters.* I texted Will: *If the Swede wants to spend the night, fine. The heart wants what the heart wants.* He texted back: *Are you drunk?* Eventually I heard the shower begin to spray water all over the bathroom, a shower curtain I said to myself, a shower curtain, get one, and I drifted off.

That night I had a dream that I was in a small village called Tough and I was somehow responsible for writing the soundtrack to the town. I was summoned to the home of an older couple who lived in Tough and they sat me down at their old Heintzman piano and said well, get started. I told them no, this shouldn't be me, this should be my sister. They patted my back and smiled. They brought me a jug of ice water and a glass. Hay bales surrounded the town and they were supposed to be some kind of wall or barrier. They were supposed to keep the citizens of Tough safe. When I said but they're only hay bales, the older couple, kind people who shuffled around their house purposefully, told me not to worry about it but just to focus on the score. I asked them where we were, in which country, and they pointed at the piano and reminded me of my task. There was no time for small talk.

Early, early in the morning Nic called me and asked if I could drive him to the airport and then just take his car back to my mom's for her to use. Normally he'd take the bus he said, but he was running late and still not even sure he should go and if I didn't come to take him he'd probably just go back to bed with a bag of weed and cry himself to sleep.

I picked him up and he told me that the driver's door wasn't working properly and had to remain closed all the time. To get into the driver's seat you had to slide over from the passenger side, over the gearshift and all that jazz. I told Nic I'd have it fixed because I didn't think my mom would be able to do all that manoeuvring every time. On the way to the airport he rubbed his face and asked himself out loud what he was doing.

He put his leg up on the dash and rested his elbow on his knee and his head on his hand and closed his eyes.

You'll have fun, I said. It'll be good to see your dad. Are you meeting him in Montreal?

I won't have fun, he said. But it'll be a break. No, I'm meeting him in Madrid. I wish I was going with Elf.

Exactly, I said. You need a break. You'll check e-mail, right?

Every moment, so if there's any change . . .

Yeah, I'll let you know, don't worry. What did the nurse say yesterday?

Not much, just that Elf would be there for a while. We were silent, driving, staring.

You know, I said, does she ever talk to you about Switzerland?

What do you mean? he said. No, I don't think so. Why?

Just that she'd like to go or anything like that?

No, he said. Never. She wants to go to Paris.

You mean like live there with you? I asked.

I could get work there, he said. And we both speak French . . .

I said that would be amazing. So she talks about that? About wanting to go when she's better?

Often, said Nic. I mean, I don't know when it'll happen, but we like to think about it. She just has to get through this thing. She has to get the right meds. It can take months to determine the correct dosage and combination.

Or years, I said. And providing she's even willing to take them.

Which usually she isn't, he said.

Which usually she isn't, I agreed.

He took a book out of his bag and wrote something on one of the pages.

What are you reading?

Thomas Bernhard, he said. *The Loser*.

Nic, I said, that's not even funny.

I know, but I am, you asked. Oh, can you give her these? He opened his backpack and gave me a sheaf of papers. They're e-mails from people. For Elf. Fans. Friends. Claudio sent them. Nic turned away to look out the window. We were close to the airport, following the little airplane signs, through industrial zones and windowless gentlemen's clubs and massive potholes.

Does anybody ever fix this city? I said. Nic said nothing. We got to the airport and again thanked each other for the efforts being made to help Elf. We hugged and said goodbye, au revoir and adios. All he had was a backpack and it looked half empty. I wondered if he'd bothered to pack anything at all besides his Bernhard and his favourite Chinese authors. How many days again? I called after him. He was walking through revolving doors, trying to negotiate his way through with his pack. He held up both hands like he was under arrest. Ten.

I drove back to my mom's place. I parked in visitor parking and went running up the stairs to her apartment. Ready to go? I asked her. Nic's off? she said. Yup, I said, back in ten days. The driver's door is broken but I'll try to get it fixed this afternoon. Then I remembered the divorce papers that I'd agreed to sign that afternoon. Could the signing wait one more day, I wondered, after sixteen years of marriage?

When we got to the hospital we couldn't find Elf. The nurse at the ICU desk said she'd been moved to the Palaveri Building, Psych 2 which was buildings away across the campus or whatever hospital grounds are called. We went down to the fifth floor to check on Auntie Tina and she was asleep but hooked up to more machines than before. She was pale, her mouth a gaping rictus of surprise. Maybe. The nurse said things weren't looking quite as good as they had been yesterday. There were tiny letters written on her cast, notes to herself it seemed. Cancel book club. Cancel tai chi. Cancel hair appointment. She wouldn't be going home today after all.

The nurse was wondering if Tina's kids were on their way from Vancouver and my mom said yes, my niece is coming, and Tina's husband, but what's going on?

She said Tina would need to have surgery quickly, in a day or two, to ward off a massive coronary. They were getting her ready for open-heart surgery, injecting her with some type of fluid and keeping her calm, and trying to find an available surgeon to do the operation. But the nurse seemed relaxed about the whole thing. It's like this sometimes, she said to my mom. Your sister is strong and otherwise very healthy so the operation will be very routine. She'll probably be able to drive her van back to Vancouver after a few weeks.

We left my aunt sleeping, for the time being, and went off in search of Elf. We took an elevator to the basement and walked through yet another hospital tunnel, baffled and angry. My mother was exhausted but trying to tell me more about Honduran mines. Each step was killing her but there was no place to rest, it was just a smooth empty tunnel like the large intestine of a starving person. I walked ahead of my mom, a little frantic and looking for the door that would take us up to the Psych 2 building. I called to her and my voice echoed. Mom om om om om. She stood still in the centre of the tunnel, she was tiny, an inch tall, and put her hands on her hips. Trouble lights were strung along the ceiling of the tunnel and cast an orange glow on everything. I jogged back to her and asked her how she was doing. She nodded and smiled and took big breaths.

I didn't tell you about how much water they're using, she gasped. She was referring to the mining companies.

I honestly don't know where the door is, I said. She nodded again, smiling, like a mortally injured field commander sending silent, brave messages to his men to go on without him, there was a war to fight. Like the words on Yeats's grave at the foot of Benbulben in Sligo county: *Cast a cold Eye On Life, on Death. Horseman, pass by.* All we could do was take small, slow steps towards something that might lie ahead, like a door.

We stopped and started, waiting each time for my mom to catch her breath. Soon I stopped saying things because she'd always respond a bit too enthusiastically, valiantly, and even those outbursts of air, like volleys of ammo, were tiring her out. Finally we saw a door that said Exit on it and I pushed it open and we escaped into a stairwell. We had to take several flights up, out of the basement, to the nearest elevator that would take us to the fourth floor, to the Psych 2 ward, and to Elf.

When the elevator doors opened on the fourth floor, there was Radek! His violin was strapped to his back like an underwater oxygen tank. I asked him what he was doing here and he said he'd come to see Elfrieda. I had to tell her how much her piano has meant to me, he said.

Oh, I said. I could have passed that along. But thanks.

He looked at my mom. I'm Radek, he said, and held out his hand. My mom said she was pleased to meet him and she left us there in front of the elevators. The rumour said that your sister was in the psychiatry department, he said. That it's serious, suicide.

Who told you that? I said.

I just wanted to meet her, he said, but they told me visiting hours is over. He asked me how I was and put his hand on my shoulder.

For a second I thought you were here to find me, I said. I guess I had forgotten that you'd moved on.

Wasn't it you who moved on? he said.

Are you planning to serenade her with your violin? I asked. I smiled hoping it would erase the cattiness, the jealousy embedded in the question.

I had only wanted to wish her well, to thank her.

I know, I said. I get it. I'll tell her.

But how are you? he said.

I'm fine.

Are you? he said. It must not be true then.

I have to go. I'm really sorry for . . . you know, everything. All of this. What I said.

Your time will come, he said.

What is that supposed to mean? I said. I had begun to walk away.

I mean your happiness, he said.

Oh, okay, it sounded more like a threat. But thanks, Radek. I'm sorry.

I'm sorry too.

I turned around and walked back to where he was and shook his hand. I know your libretto thing will be amazing.

And your boat book too. Or . . . rodeo?

Boat.

Ah yes, boat.

We smiled. We said goodbye.

My mom was sitting outside Elf's room, on a chair near the nurses' desk, mustering up her courage to be cheerful, an ambassador of hope, and catching her breath. I went in and sat down beside Elf on her bed and said hey, I'm here. There was nothing in this room but two single beds, one empty, and two small desks with small chairs. There was a small, high window with a cage on it and Jesus dying on a small cross over the door. Elf was motionless in her bed, also small, silent, her face to the wall. I put my hand on her bony hip like a lover in the night. She murmured hi but didn't turn to look at me. Is that you, Swivelhead? she said. I told her that Nic had left for Spain that morning, although she already knew that, that mom was sitting outside catching her breath, that Aunt Tina's condition had worsened a bit and now she needed surgery. I asked her how she was feeling. She didn't answer. I have some fan mail for you, I said. I put the pile of papers on her empty desk. She didn't answer.

Elf, I said, does Nic know you want to go to Switzerland? She slowly turned then to look at me and shook her head.

He wouldn't let me, she whispered, he wouldn't take me. Don't tell him.

Okay, but I'm so . . . I don't know what to do.

Won't you take me? she asked. Yoli, please. She was serious. Her eyes were bullets. I shook my head, no, I'm not sure about that. What about mom? Have you told her? Elf shook her head again and took hold of my arm.

Yolandi, she said, listen to me. Listen very carefully, okay? Mom and Nic can't know. They wouldn't let me go. Nic still believes in some kind of medicine that will cure me and mom believes in . . . I don't know what exactly, maybe God, or odds, I don't know, but she'll never give up. I'm begging you, Yoli, you're the only one who understands. Don't you?

Do you mean we would sneak off to Zurich? I asked. Just the two of us? That would never work.

Why not?

Because doctors there have to determine that you're sane!

I *am* sane, she said. So you've checked it out already?

I googled it.

And it makes sense, right? said Elf.

I don't know about that, I said. I couldn't look at her. Her eyes were huge. Her nails were hurting me.

Yoli, she said. I'm afraid to die alone.

Well what about not dying at all? I said.

Yoli, she said. I feel like I'm begging for my life.

Okay but Nic would obviously notice within five minutes that you were gone and he'd find you, he'd figure it out somehow, some kind of paper trail and then he'd hate me and mom would have a heart attack and it probably wouldn't even work out. It's just so improbable, Elf, it's ridiculous. You can't just sneak off to freaking Zurich in the night. It's not like a neighbour's backyard pool—

Yoli, if you love—

I DO love you! God!

I heard our mother speaking in her calm but lethal voice outside Elf's door. She was telling the nurse that Elf hadn't seen a doctor in days. The nurse told my mom the doctor was very busy. My mom told the nurse what she had told me the night before, that Elf was a human being. The nurse wasn't Janice. My mom was asking where Janice was. The nurse who was not Janice was telling my mom that she agreed with her, Elf was a human being, but that she was also a patient in the hospital and was expected to co-operate. Why? asked my mother. What does co-operation have to do with her getting well? Is co-operation even a symptom of mental health or just something you need from the patients to be able to control every last damn person here with medication and browbeating? She'll eat when she feels like eating. Like you, like me, not when we're told to eat. And if she doesn't want to talk, so what? My daughter is more intelligent than the entire psychiatric staff put—

Mom! I said. Come in here. My mom came into the room and the nurse escaped to her post.

Sweetheart, my mom said, and kissed Elf on the brow. Elf smiled and said hi and asked her if she was okay and said she was shocked to hear about Auntie Tina needing surgery.

Oh I'm absolutely fine, said my mom. And Tina will be okay. I had the exact same surgery, remember? After that safari? How are you? Elf shrugged and looked around the shitty room in a type of awe like it was one of the great cathedrals of Europe.

How does the poem go again? I asked my mom.

What? she said. What poem?

That Ezra Pound poem. Your favourite one.

Oh! "In a Station of the Metro"?

Yeah, that's it, I said. What is it about it that you like so much? I don't know, said my mom. It's short. She laughed. Why do you ask?

I don't know, I said, no reason. I was just curious. I have to sign my divorce papers this afternoon.

The Vegas wedding was legit? said Elf. She turned to our mother. You know about Pound's fascist leanings, don't you, mom?

Honey, the nurses want you to eat a little something, said my mom. I didn't know he was a fascist!

How are the kids? my sister asked.

My mother looked at me.

Good, I think, I said. Will's occupying some politician's office today in Toronto protesting a crime bill or something like that and you can watch a live feed of it online. He's staying with Nora.

What do you mean? asked my mom.

You can watch it while it's happening, I said. On your computer.

Good grief, said my mom. What channel?

Elf smiled faintly and said to say hi to him and Nora. She asked what had been happening the last time I checked out the live feed of his protest. Honey, is this a hard day for you? asked my mom. We both looked at her. They were batting balloons around and some of them were lying in sleeping bags, I said. The cops came and then left again so who knows. Will said they'll leave if the cops ask them to. What crime bill? asked my mom. Having to do with prisons and policing, I said. He's an anarchist now.

Will is? said my mom. Oh no!

No, no, I'm kidding, I said, unsure if I was or wasn't. I had forgotten about my mother's Russian association with murderous anarchists. She excused herself to use the bathroom and I whispered to Elf just let me think, okay? And you think too, like really think.

Yo, I have thought, said Elf. That's all I've been doing. Is it not obvious?

I know, I said, but can't you just think about it a bit longer? Or then stop thinking and start just observing things around you. I can't do it without Nic being there, definitely not—plus this is so crazy. It's not—

Why not? said Elf. I'm not his child. I can go with or without his permission. Obviously I want him to be there with us but he would never let it happen. We could go now while he's away.

No way.

What do you mean just observing? It's impossible not to have thoughts. Even if they're superficial that doesn't mean there isn't some form of brain activity—

I know, I said, but don't you want him to—

Hey why don't I get some lunch from the cafeteria and bring it here, said my mom. We hadn't noticed she was back from the washroom. We can have lunch in here, the three of us! And I'll check on Tina on my way back.

They won't let you, said Elf. I'm supposed to go to the cafeteria at mealtimes.

I'll hide it, said my mom. I'll smuggle it in.

Let me go, I said. You can barely breathe. They'll end up admitting you too. And I have a backpack for stashing the food.

A nurse came in with an enormous bouquet of flowers. These came for you just now, said the nurse. Aren't they beautiful?

Oh, they are! said my mother. Wow! I nodded and smiled and leaned over to smell them.

From Joanna and Ekko. Is Ekko her husband or something? I asked. Elf nodded. The nurse said she'd try to find a vase big enough for the flowers. I thanked her profusely. I was trying to get her to approve of at least one of our miscreant members.

Well these are a lovely addition to the room, don't you think, Elf, said my mom. How thoughtful of them!

Look at these blue ones, I said. How do you get blue flowers?

Honey, said my mom. Blue flowers do exist in nature. They're symbols of something, I think. In poetry.

Oh really? I said.

Of inspiration, maybe, or of the infinite, said my mother. Die blaue blume.

Can you take them out? said Elf. Can you take them away?

I flew into my aunt's room, said hi, ta-dah! I put the giant bouquet onto her bedside table and she laughed. My goodness! How delightful! she said. They're from Elf, I said.

I told her I was sorry about the latest developments, that Elf and my mom and I were going to have a quick lunch and then my mom and I would both come back here, to her ward, and visit properly. She waved off any urgency, meh, relax, if your mother can do it I can do it, and laughed again. She was talking about the surgery. She held up her arm, the one with the plaster cast, and said it was really bugging her. Did I want to write something on it? I wrote *I love you, Auntie Tina!* She looked at it and told me she loved me too. She asked me to get her a pen or a stir stick or something that she could stick into her cast so she could scratch her arm. It was driving her nuts. What are these numbers? I asked her. She told me she had written down Sheila's and Esther's cellphone numbers on her cast. Sheila and Esther were her daughters, my cousins. They were older than me and Leni, their sister who died, and often babysat us by giving us giant bags of red Twizzlers as hush money and sneaking out with their boyfriends. Leni and I would wait for them to leave and then go out and wander around town by ourselves until we'd eaten all the Twizzlers and the bedtime siren had gone off at the fire hall. Tina asked me to bring her a Starbucks coffee—but don't tell the nurses. Just sneak it in. Small black. I told her I was a mule already, no problem, she could count on me.

I went over to the nurses' desk and asked if they knew when she'd have her surgery. Tomorrow morning at six, they told me. With Dr. Kevorkian. At least that's what it sounded like to me. I went back to my aunt's bed. So, tomorrow! I said. I sounded hysterical to myself.

Yup, said my aunt. Going under the knife. They've been drawing on my body, mapping it all out. Cut along the dotted line. What a hoot.

I asked her about my cousins, her kids, were they both coming.

Sheila called, she said, and she and Frank are getting here this afternoon.

I quickly e-mailed Sheila from my BlackBerry and told her to send me her flight info and I'd pick them up at the airport. Frank was my uncle, Tina's stalwart and jokey husband. He could barely walk from diabetes but he was game to travel here to be by Tina's side. I kissed my aunt and she held me tightly, incredible strength for a pre-op heart patient, and looked me in the eye. Yolandi, she said, give my love to Elfrieda. Tell her I love her and tell her that I know she loves me too. She needs to hear that.

I promised I would and turned to go.

Also! called my aunt from her bed. We are Loewens! (That was their maiden name—my mother's and Tina's.) That means lions!

I smiled and nodded—and I murmured to the nurse passing me that my aunt was the king of the jungle so please handle her with care. The nurse laughed and squeezed my arm. Nurses in cardio are far more playful and friendly than they are in psych.

If you have to end up in the hospital, try to focus all your pain in your heart rather than your head.

THIRTEEN

AIRPORT, CAR DOOR, BUY A SHOWER CURTAIN, get divorced. I spoke aloud to myself. I stood in the elevator and pounded on the letter *M* until the damn thing lit up and we were on our way down to the main floor. Airport, car door, get divorced. There was something else I'd forgotten. I texted Julie and asked if she could meet me at the Corydon Bar and Grill in one hour, we'd have tequila shooters because an ancient *Chatelaine* magazine in the cardio waiting room had said that it's important to celebrate a divorce rather than feel shame and guilt and remorse, and then come with me on my errand run. She texted back that she was at the Legion with posties, at a meat raffle, drunk already, but that I could pick her up any time.

I bought a couple of egg salad sandwiches, a ham sandwich, a couple of apples and a bag of chips—none of us ate chips—and a giant bottle of water and one small black Starbucks coffee. Took the elevator back up to cardio and thought, while I was standing there leaning against the wall with my face against its cool shiny steel, that I should try to find Benito Zetina Morelos and ask him what he thought about killing my sister. I needed someone to tell me what to do.

Benito Zetina Morelos was my old philosophy professor. I was in his medical bioethics class at the same time I was giving my notes to Jason the mechanic in CanLit. Benito Zetina Morelos was the expert on this stuff, he was on CBC panels all the time, talking about euthanasia, about all sorts of things having to do with the right to die, basically. He'd gone to Oxford. Once, in his class, he started talking about a Mennonite Rhodes scholar who was studying with him at Oxford and who couldn't handle the freedom, this was the sixties or seventies, and got wildly involved with drugs and ended up dead. This was actually my cousin, one of my four thousand cousins, and my mother had told me about his misadventures when I was a kid, and there was Benito Zetina Morelos using him to illustrate how hard it is to go from one extreme to another. We were pretty certain he'd died of a drug overdose, but nobody knew for sure because his parents were so heartbroken they didn't want an autopsy, they just wanted his body to come home where it belonged and be buried in the plain cemetery of our tiny, country Mennonite church. Now I desperately needed Benito Zetina Morelos's advice. Since taking his course I had bumped into him a few times in Winnipeg, walking his dog and reading at the same time. If he didn't have his dog with him he'd walk around the Kelvin High School track, around and around, always reading, often with a pen in his mouth. All right, airport, car door, divorce papers, Benito Zetina Morelos. Shower curtain!

I arrived at my aunt's floor, gave her the coffee, kissed her again and high-fived, we made some jokes about the unpredictability of life and how hilarious it all can be from a certain angle—or any angle. She made a reference to Isosceles: what if he had laughed at every one of them, every angle. And I took off for Psych 2.

We had our secret lunch in Elf's room. My mother sat calmly. I paced while I ate and Elf had maybe three tiny bites of her sandwich, firing at me with her eyes while she chewed, her brow furrowed and hair a wild nest. A pastor from my parents' old Mennonite church in East Village had come to the hospital to visit Elf while my mother and I were away. Somehow he had managed to talk his way in past the nurses' desk. He had heard, probably from the successful family in the waiting room, that Elf was in the hospital. He told her that if she would give her life to God she wouldn't have any pain. She would want to live. And to deny that was to sin egregiously. Could they pray together for her soul?

Oh my god! I said. Holy fuck!

Elf is livid, said my mother, looking directly at my sister. Aren't you? My mother sat directly in the path of a shaft of sunlight breaking through the caged window, an areola of gold surrounding her, radiating heat. She wanted Elf to show her rage, to use her prodigious verbal skills to tear this little creep to ribbons, even now that he had left.

What did you do? I asked Elf. I hope you told him to go fuck himself. You should have screamed rape.

Yoli, said my mom.

Seriously, I said.

I recited a poem, said Elf.

What? I said. A poem? You should have strangled him with your panties!

Philip Larkin, she said. I don't have any panties. They've taken them away from me.

Can you recite it for us now? asked my mom. Elf groaned and shook her head.

C'mon, Elf, I said. I wanna hear it. Did he know it was Larkin?

Are you crazy? asked my mom.

C'mon, Elf, just say the poem.

"What are days for?" asked Elf.

What do you mean? I said.

"Days are where we live."

What? I said.

Yoli, said my mom, shhh, that's the poem. Let her say it already.

"They come, they wake us
Time and time over.
They are to be happy in:
Where can we live but days?"

That's cool, Elf, I said. I like that.

Yoli, said my mom, for Pete's sake, there's a second verse. Listen. Elf, go on.

"Ah, solving that question
Brings the priest and the doctor
In their long coats
Running over the fields."

Hmm, I said. Well, there you go. What did he say to that?

Nothing, said Elf.

Tell her why nothing, said my mom. She shook like old times. She covered her mouth.

Because by the end of it I had taken off all my clothes, said Elf.

He left pretty quickly, said my mom.

That's so crazy! I said. Oh my god, that's fucking amazing!

I was trying to be like you, she said. It was all I had.

Get out, I said, that's all you. You're unbelievable. Fucking amazing!

Yoli, said my mom. Enough already, good grief, with the swearing. Now I see where Will and Nora get it from.

A striptease to a Larkin poem, I said. Fucking brilliant!

Eventually my mom told me I should go and do the things I needed to do—oh yeah, my divorce!—and she'd stay for a while and take a cab home. On my way out I spoke to Elf's nurse.

Please don't let anybody other than family in to see Elf, I said. And you won't let her go any time soon, will you?

No, of course not! she said. She'll be here for a while, considering everything that's happened. And by the way, that was an anomaly, that guy. He said he was her pastor and sailed right on by. I'm sorry.

Oh my god, I thought, the nurse actually apologized. No

problem, I said, Elf dealt with it. But please don't let her go.

We won't, said the nurse, don't worry, okay? Her eyes were kind and deeply set. I could have stared at them all afternoon, for the rest of my life.

Okay, thank you, I said, because there's nobody at her place. Her husband is in Spain and there's nobody there.

This was a refrain in my family. We were a Greek chorus. How many times would I beg hospitals not to let my people go? Elf and I begged and begged and begged the hospital in East Village not to let our father go but they let him go anyway and then he was gone for good. We are only family. And the doctors are busy packing as many appointments into a day as they can to pay for the next cycling holiday in the Pyrenees. The nurse reassured me. Nicolas, she said, had already talked to her, she knew he had gone to Spain, and she promised that Elfrieda wasn't going anywhere any time soon. I struggled to stop myself from throwing my arms around her and telling her I loved her.

On the way out of the hospital I checked the messages on my phone. Dan was furious with Nora. Apparently she had somehow broken into his e-mail and put out a mass letter to all of his contacts declaring that he was gay and that it felt so good to finally tell the truth and that he hoped everyone would understand and let nothing change between them. Somehow, my ex implied in his message to me, it was my fault that our daughter had got a bit drunk with her friends and made a "bad choice."

Those were ALL my contacts, he wrote. *Work too. Everyone. And she's just laughing about it and won't apologize. Like mother, like daughter.*

I texted him back and said *but are you gay, really?*

He texted back: *Are you thirteen years old, really?*

I texted back: *Also, what work?*

He texted back: *It has nothing to do with rodeos so perhaps it's beyond your realm of comprehension.*

I texted back: *Maybe she's angry with you for always being in Borneo. How's the surf?* And then quickly turned off my cell.

I googled: *can writing a novel kill you?* And found nothing useful. I sped to my hippie lawyer's office—he had a pierced ear and a goatee and lived in Wolseley, the same neighbourhood as Julie—and failed to get out of the car through the driver's side, swore, slid across and ran inside and said I had four minutes to sign the papers and that nothing in the world would give me more joy than to scrawl my stupid name in triplicate on this particular document. I whipped out my Visa card and said let's pay for this right now and seal the deal. I guess this is the cost of freedom! My lawyer's secretary laughed but I could tell she pitied me. I was going insane. I ran back to my car, again failed to open the driver's door, banged on the window and swore quietly into the wind which was turning into something other than a gentle breeze, maybe into a mistral, the wind that can make you crazy, so that in France you can be acquitted if you kill someone while it's blowing. I ran around and slid in through the passenger side and sped to Jason the mechanic, my last night's boyfriend. I drove directly into the garage, threw it into park and once again forgot about the door that never opens and slumped in my seat, defeated.

Jason emerged from under the hood of an SUV and opened the passenger door for me and said come here. I slid out headfirst like a newborn and he hugged me, and I told him about the driver's door and that I had to be at the airport in twelve minutes to pick up my cousin Sheila and my uncle Frank who were flying in to be with my aunt, their mom and wife, who suddenly had to have heart surgery, and that I'd just officially gotten divorced. Jason rubbed my back. He told me that divorce was one of life's top stressors—that and a death in the family— because it's like a death, and that it was okay with him if I cried. He gave me a loaner to pick up my relatives and said he'd have the door fixed later in the afternoon, no worries, no charge.

I had forgotten about Julie. I sped to the Legion on Notre Dame. Horrible music was playing on the loaner car radio but I couldn't figure out how to turn it off. She was sitting on the curb waiting for me, inebriated and holding on to a bunch of frozen steaks. She got in and I told her I was divorced. I know that, she said. No, but now—I just signed the papers—it's a done deal. Congrassulations, she said. She tried to turn the radio off.

How does it feel?

To be officially divorced? I asked.

Officially divorced, she said. Those are two awful words. They shouldn't even be words.

Last night I dreamt I heard a man telling me that a petroglyph dog equals eternal love.

I've heard that too, she said. How's Elf?

Same, I said.

Are you still thinking of killing her? said Julie.

It's not killing her. It's helping her.

I know, said Julie, but are you?

Don't tell anyone, I said. Elf hasn't mentioned it to Nic or my mom. She just wants me to take her to Switzerland, the two of us.

Oh geez, said Julie, will you? Hey, what's wrong with your eyes?

I told her I had to track down my one-time philosophy professor, Benito Zetina Morelos.

That sounds like a Bolaño novel, she said. Do you have his e-mail or his phone number? She took my hand and held it. I shook my head and told her I had to go to Kelvin High School and find him at the track, maybe. Tonight, she said, you should stay at my place and let me make a steak for you. I have wine. I think you really need protein. I can't, I said, I have to get my mom and my cousin and my uncle to the hospital for six a.m., that's when my aunt is having her surgery. And they're all staying at my mom's. Okay then tomorrow night, she said. I don't think you should do the Switzerland thing. I don't know, I said. Just because something's legal doesn't make it right, she said. Yeah, yeah, I said, but the core of the argument for it is maximizing individual autonomy and minimizing human suffering. Doesn't that sound right? Are you hot? she said. She held a frozen steak to my forehead.

We drove to the airport and Julie stayed in the car right out front and snoozed with her arms full of meat while I went in to get my cousin and my uncle.

In the airport we hugged each other all at once, a team huddle but with nothing but a Hail Mary left in our playbook. We'd been through all of this before. We loved each other. We fought for each other. When worlds collapsed we were buried in the rubble together and when we were dug out of the rubble and rescued we all celebrated together. There wasn't much to say about Elf and Tina. We were going directly to the hospital. We all talked at the same time in the car. Sheila about mountains and inoculations because she was both a mountain climber and a public health nurse and my uncle Frank about the toonie-sized hole in his leg and hyperbaric chambers because he was a diabetic and Julie about how she won her meat and me about car rallies in Morocco. I had a plan to join one that was for women only—we would drive from Dakar to somewhere else and sleep in the desert with camels and Bedouin guides. It might take us two months. Julie would be my partner. I hadn't told her yet. What? she said. We sleep with Bedouin guides? She'd navigate, I said, and I'd drive. We'd take a mechanics course from Jason before we went and we'd be sponsored by Canada Post. This was my plan. My uncle said that considering how I was driving right now I probably had an excellent chance of winning the race and that it wouldn't take me two months.

I dropped them off at the hospital, told them that my mom was in the psych wing with Elf and Tina was in cardio waiting for them. I'd call my mom on her cellphone in a couple of hours and then come and pick everyone up again and we'd go somewhere and have dinner.

Righto, boss, said my uncle Frank hobbling off to see his wife, while Sheila, like her mother, grabbed me hard and told me we'd get through all of it, we'd fight our way through. I have fifty-six first cousins alone on this side, most of them male, not to mention all of their various spouses and kids, but Sheila is the toughest of them all. She could easily saw off your arm in the wilderness if it was caught in a trap and that was your only way to escape. She fell off a mountain once and lay there with a crushed left leg for an entire day and night until the rescue helicopter figured out how to drop his ladder into the tiny crevice where she had fallen. She told the pilot that she fought off unconsciousness by alphabetizing the first names of every one of her cousins and then going through each one in her mind and describing them to an imaginary audience. She told me she had put me in the *S* category, for Swivelhead. Sheila's family and my family are part of the Poor Cousin contingent. We have Rich Cousins who are extremely rich because they are the sons of the sons (our uncles, all dead) who inherited the lucrative family business from our grandfather, the father of Tina and my mother. In the Menno cosmology that's how it goes down. The sons inherit the wealth and pass it on to their sons and to their sons and to their sons and the daughters get sweet fuck all. We Poor Cousins don't care at all though, except for when we're on welfare, broke, starving, unable to buy cool high-tops for our children or pay for their university tuition or purchase massive fourth homes on private islands with helicopter landing pads. But whatever, we descendants of the Girl Line may not have wealth and proper windows in our drafty homes but at least we have rage and we will build *empires* with that, gentlemen.

Julie came with me to the track at Kelvin High but we couldn't see Benito Zetina Morelos there, just students sitting on the track smoking pot and acting cool. When do you have to pick up your kids? I asked Julie. I don't, she said. Mike has them today which is why I allowed myself the smallest of pleasures at the Legion this afternoon.

Let's go to Garbage Hill, I told her.

Garbage Hill used to be a garbage dump until they planted grass on it and now it's a place where you can hang out in the summer and toboggan in the winter even though there are giant signs saying No Tobogganing! It had been given some pretty name but nobody remembered it and the sign had been graffitied over. Everyone called it Garbage Hill, even the mayor who wasn't much of a mayor but more of an auctioneer selling off bits and pieces of the city to the highest bidder. It's not very high, not much of a hill really, but it's the highest point in Winnipeg and I thought I needed to get as close to God as I could though for what I wasn't sure, either to pray to him for mercy or to crush his skull. Or to thank him. This last piece was advice given to me by my aunt Tina when my father died. She told me that even if I didn't wholeheartedly believe in the existence of God it felt good to close your eyes and make a mental list of all the things you were grateful for.

Julie and I sat cross-legged on the top of the hill in the prickly brown grass and reminisced about a photo shoot she'd done there four hundred years ago when we were triumphant high-schoolers.

Are you tired? she asked.

I'm making a list in my head, I told her.

Of what?

Things I'm thankful for.

Am I on it?

Are you on it! I said.

She closed her eyes and made her own list.

Can it be something as small as discovering that your bread isn't mouldy after all so there'll be toast for the kids for breakfast? she asked.

Yes, I said. My eyes were still closed. Right now I'm thanking God for twist-offs.

Oh, good one, she said. And prehensile thumbs.

Are you still drunk? I asked her.

No, she said.

So, I googled it and it'll cost me—

What did you google?

The Swiss clinic in Zurich.

Oh! Okay.

I googled it and it'll cost five thousand two hundred and sixty-three dollars and sixteen cents for the treatment and another nine thousand two hundred and ten dollars and fifty-three cents for related costs.

What are related costs? she said.

Medical costs and official fees and a funeral.

But you wouldn't have the funeral there, would you?

No, that's true, I'd bring her body back.

But cremated? she asked.

Yeah, definitely. So that costs too, I imagine.

How much does it cost? she said.

I have no idea.

I still don't think you should do it, she said. I think it's only for people who are dying anyway.

No, I said, it's for mentally ill people too—it's called "weariness of life" and they have the same rights as anybody else who wants to die according to Swiss law. You can argue that she is dying. She's weary of life, that's for sure.

We looked at the city, the sky, ourselves. Julie smiled and said my name. I said hers. I don't know, she said.

I don't want her to die, I said, but she's begging me. She's literally begging me. What do I do?

Julie shook her head and said she didn't know. Then she

suggested that I wait a bit, see if the treatment or pills would work for her this time, just wait it out. I could do that, I agreed, but was afraid they'd let her go and that would be it, she'd be gone.

But this whole Zurich thing seems so improbable, said Julie.

I know, I said, but it's not, it's possible, and I could do it for her. I should do it for her.

Well, not necessarily, said Julie. Just wait a bit, see what happens.

Twenty-one percent of the patients at the Swiss clinic are patients who aren't physically terminally ill but who are weary of life.

Do you think you could live with yourself if you did it? she asked.

Or if I didn't? I said.

Either way, she said.

I had to get back to the hospital to pick up the crew and forage for food somewhere because we had to eat after all, again, eating—it seemed so embarrassing and ridiculous at this point—and Julie was going to see her Jungian therapist. Don't tell him about this conversation, I said. Don't worry, said Julie, everything is confidential. No but seriously, I said, they can report things to the cops if they think there's the possibility of a crime or whatever. She hugged me. She promised not to tell anyone about our conversation, including her therapist. You're trembling, she said. I can feel your heart banging away at your rib cage. We heard voices in the distance. A woman saying okay, you know what, seriously? Fuck you. And a guy saying oh, okay, seriously, you know what? Fuck *you*. Then the woman: Do you know how much money I spent? And the guy: Do you know how much money *I* spent?

Wow, said Julie. You'd really want that guy on your debating team. Amazing rebuttals, dude.

Just then a Frisbee came sailing past our heads, missing Julie by a hair.

Oh my god, she said, do you realize that the word *dude* could have been the last word I spoke on earth? Would you promise to tell people it was something different, for my sake?

I would, I said. You can count on me. Like what word would you like?

Oh, I don't know, she said. Like *presto* or something.

You mean like as in now you see me, now you don't?

Yeah, she said.

Okay, I said. I'll tell your kids and parents and everyone that your last word was *presto*.

Thank you.

We had dinner in a tiny café on Provencher Boulevard close to the hospital and then we all went back to my mom's place and played our Mennonite-sanctioned Dutch Blitz card game, screaming the word *blitz* when we won. My mom and my uncle Frank swore in Plautdietsch and everyone hollered and shrieked and cards flew, and my mom had to stop to catch her breath and use her nitro spray and my uncle had to shoot up with insulin. Afterwards I found enough clean linen and blankets to make up beds for Sheila and my uncle—I'd sleep on an air mattress— and I bid them all good night, we'd rally in the morning at five. Before she went to sleep Sheila and I sat on her bed and talked about our sisters, Leni and Elf, and their unfathomable sadness, and about our mothers, Lottie and Tina, and their perpetual optimism. What's holding your leg together now? I asked her. Nuts and bolts and scrap metal and baling wire, she said. She showed me the scars that ran up and down the entire length of her crushed leg. She brought out a box of chocolates and we each had two. I'm sure your mom will be okay, I told her. She's unbelievably tenacious. That's true, said Sheila. She's the Iggy Pop of old Mennonite ladies. We ate two more chocolates each. And then I zipped back to the hospital to see Elf.

I took my dad's old bike, which my mom kept in her storage cage in the basement, and sped along the path that ran next to the exploding river. At the hospital I didn't even bother locking it up, just flung it onto the grass next to the front doors of the Palaveri ward like I was a kid all over again and running late for the six p.m. start of *The Wonderful World of Disney*. The nurse at the desk said it was too late but I told her that I had some very important news that couldn't wait. She didn't believe me, that was obvious, but told me to go ahead anyway, she had no backup staff for fighting and was deep into the final chapters of *The Da Vinci Code*.

Elf was asleep on her side, her face to the wall, and I lifted the blanket and crawled in next to her. She had her back to me but her hand was resting there on her shoulder, like she'd been hugging herself as she fell asleep, and I touched it. I squeezed it softly and held it. I thought how strange it was that this limp, bony piece of flesh could produce such powerful music. I timed my breathing to hers, slow and steady. I closed my eyes and slept with her for a while, I think it was an hour or two or maybe only twenty minutes.

When Elf was a kid she walked and talked in her sleep all the time. My parents had to rig up booby traps by the doors so she wouldn't leave the house altogether. I hummed a song about ducks swimming in the sea, a little song she had taught me when I was a kid. A song about bravery, about being a freak. She didn't wake up. I don't think she woke up. I didn't want to leave but I knew I had to. When I left the nurse asked me to please respect the visiting hours in the future and I told her yes, I will. In the future I will respect everything. My dad's bike was still there, damp in the dewy grass, and I picked it up, it seemed lighter than it had been and I looked to make sure it was the same bike, a faded red CCM three-speed, and it was the same one—how could there be two? it wasn't a parade—and I hopped on and rode off into the rest of the night.

Everyone was asleep in my mom's apartment waiting through dreams for tomorrow. I lay on an air mattress on the living room floor. There was a small blue bookshelf beside me. There was the obligatory collection of my Rhonda books (all inscribed with love and gratitude) on one of the shelves, stiff and quirkily CanLitty with their signature spines, and a slew of whodun-its crammed in there next to them, well read and better loved. Some of them, the fatter ones, were cut in half or even threes and held together with rubber bands because my mom didn't like to haul entire giant books around with her all over tarna-tion and she didn't go anywhere without a book, or a partial book, in her big brown bag. Next to the whodunits were a few books written by other people she knew, sons and daughters of friends, people in her church, old classics and a book of poetry by Coleridge, Elf's ex-boyfriend. I took it from the shelf and read a few poems, including this one:

In fancy (well I know)
From business wand'ring far and local cares,
Thou creepest round a dear-lov'd Sister's bed
With noiseless step, and watchest the faint look,
Soothing each pang with fond solicitude,
And tenderest tones medicinal of love.
I too a SISTER had, an only Sister—
She lov'd me dearly, and I doted on her!
To her I pour'd forth all my puny sorrows
(As a sick Patient in his Nurse's arms)
And of the heart those hidden maladies
That shrink asham'd from even Friendship's eye.
O! I have woke at midnight, and have wept,
Because SHE WAS NOT! . . .

I had found Elf's Coleridge poem! The one she'd taken her signature AMPS from. All my puny sorrows. I lay on the air mattress. I fell asleep, but not fully. It wasn't a deep sleep and somewhere in the spaces between sleep and lucid dreaming and full consciousness I had an idea. An idea came to me. I would invite Elf to Toronto to stay with me for a while when she was released from the hospital. I'd be there to take her home with me for a visit. We could walk and talk and rest and there would be no pressure and I would be at home, working, sort of, so she wouldn't be alone. And Nora would be there too. Then we could really examine this Zurich thing at length and if she still wanted to go it would be so easy to leave from Toronto instead of Winnipeg. Nobody else would have to know until it was over and then I'd figure out how to deal with all of that then.

In the morning we all crawled out of our beds and clustered like baby birds at the dining room table, poking at our food, hopping up and down for jam and salt and cream, goading one another on with fake enthusiasm. Piled into the car—Jason had dropped it off in visitor parking with the keys under the mat, the driver's door opened now—and took off for our new clubhouse, the Ste. Odile Hospital. It was too early to see Elf but we all gathered around my aunt's bed and hugged her and kissed her and told her this surgery thing would be a snap, a breeze, a walk in the park. Yeah, yeah, she knew that, good grief, enough of these morbid pep talks, let's get the show on the road. Sheila gently massaged Tina's arms and legs. My mother held her hand. My uncle Frank promised he'd have her Starbucks coffee ready and waiting for her after the surgery and she told us to go somewhere and relax for Pete's sake. The anaesthetic was beginning to take effect. Tina's eyes were glassy. Her words came more slowly. She had a mysterious expression on her face. They wheeled her into the operating room and we stood together under a fluorescent light, praying maybe, or maybe not, and not moving one way or another.

At a certain time—when Tina was still being operated on, having veins taken out of her leg and put into her chest, and the word from the doc was that everything was going very well—my mom and I and my cousin Sheila and my uncle Frank trekked over to psych to say good morning to Elf. We'd managed to find a wheelchair for my uncle—he hadn't wanted to use it but we insisted and he tried to do a couple of wheelies down the hall. We filed past the nurses' desk in psych like some pathetic army's last line of defence and one of them said oh, um, how many of you are there? And my mother said there's one of each of us. But, said the nurse, you can't all go in at the same time. We know that, said my mom, and kept walking. We all fell in behind our field commander and marched (and wheeled) onward, ever onward.

Elf was sitting on her bed writing. I looked at her notebook and saw the word *pain* written at least fifty times. I picked it up. Shopping list? I said. I flipped it over so the others wouldn't see it and we sent silent messages to each other with our eyes. We all had a conversation then about god knows what. Sheila told us about a young mom she was treating for tuberculosis. She was so young when she had her kids, said Sheila, that when they caught the chicken pox she did too. She was so young that on the day she finally married the father of her kids she also lost a twelve-year-old molar.

Elf picked up her notebook and tore out a blank page and wrote a short letter, folded it and gave it to our uncle to give to Tina after her surgery. He put his arm around her and said blessings on you, girl, and she told him she was sorry that he had to visit her here. He said no. We don't apologize for being sick, for being human, for being weary (Uncle Frank has obviously never been a woman). Elf said but still, she was. Elf was an atheist normally but these days she didn't seem to mind people promoting comfort in His name. My mom and Sheila and I talked louder about nothing much so that Elf and my uncle could think they were having a private conversation about sadness and giving up and strength.

We talked about the Blue Jays spring training for a while. Starters and Closers. Then we were all holding hands. My uncle then initiated a prayer session. And my mother softly began to sing *du* again, you, you, you are always in my thoughts, you, you, you give me much pain, you, you, you don't know how much I love you. My mother and my uncle sang it out in Plautdietsch, they knew the words by heart, and Sheila, Elf and I certainly knew the *du, du, du* part which we sang resolutely. Then we sang a hymn, "From Whom All Blessings Flow." Mennonites like to sing in tense situations. It's one option if you're not allowed to scream or go nuts emptying a magazine into a crowded plaza. I began to cry and couldn't stop no matter how hard I tried. When the others left Elf's room to go back to see how Tina was doing I lingered behind and whispered to my sister it's time to fight now. Yolandi, she said, I've been fighting for thirty years. So you're leaving me to fight alone? I asked her. She didn't answer me.

I took her hand and said Elf, I have a plan.

FOURTEEN

MY AUNT'S SURGERY IS OVER. So is her life. At first every-thing was going well, very well, and then even after the surgery everything was looking good. The doctor came out to meet us all and pulled off his mask and smiled and shook our hands and said he was happy with the way things had gone in there. But then her organs started to fail one by one and even though the doctors and nurses attempted to save her they failed too and in the end we lost Tina.

We sat on chairs in the waiting room, our heads in our hands, we were in a row, staring at the floor. We'd thought it was a slam dunk. We cried quietly. We whispered. Our platoon had taken another unexpected hit and Uncle Frank couldn't speak at all. We forgot about his insulin shot. Sheila told us that lately Tina had been calling him while she was in Winnipeg to remind him. My mother had lost her last sibling, her closest sister. She stood up and left the room and I stepped into the hallway after her and saw her lean her forehead against the concrete wall.

The nurses in Cardiology gave Sheila a plastic bag that said *Property of Ste. Odile Hospital* on it. Aunt Tina's fuzzy slippers and sudoku book and Kathy Reichs' novel and glasses and toothbrush and moisturizer and purple fleecy track suit and slinky black camisole and high-top white Reeboks were in the bag.

We had a family meeting right there on the spot. Sheila would take her dad home to my mom's apartment in a cab to make phone calls and to figure out how to get Tina's body back to Vancouver. I would go tell Elf what had happened and then go get more groceries and especially more coffee, something very bold from the Black Pearl my mother specified, no more of this Starbucks stuff. My mom would take Nic's car and go to the funeral home way down on Main Street to talk to her pal Hermann, another Mennonite, and see what he could do for them in terms of an urn and cremation.

I sat on a bench by the Assiniboine River and e-mailed Nic from my BlackBerry. I told him that in five or six days my mom and I would be going to Vancouver for Tina's funeral and could he make arrangements to come home from Spain earlier so Elf wouldn't be alone. I phoned my kids and told them what had happened and they were silent on the phone, incredulous. I could hear their non-stop music playing in the background. I waited for them to be able to speak. And then we said goodbye.

Suddenly the skies became dark purple with flashes of light and the wind picked up and made waves on the river. It was a typical prairie storm, angry with the dryness it had been forced to endure, and everyone around me ran to take cover from the hail. I crawled under the bench and lay there, very still, and listened to the giant balls of ice pummel the wood above me. I saw gum and graffiti, even there, on the underside of the bench. Initials and hearts and curses. I thought about my aunt and my mother sliding unscathed under that massive semi truck on their bikes, coming up on the other side laughing and breathless. It must have felt amazing.

Now I'm learning something. Go into hard things quickly, eagerly, then retreat. It's the same for thinking, writing and life. It's true what Jason said about cleaning a septic tank. My aunt came to Winnipeg to be with my mom, to help her, except then she died. My mother sat in moonlight on her balcony writing a eulogy for her sister. The city was spread out in the soft darkness, calm after the big thunder and hail storm, still moist and warm like a woman very satisfied in love. My mother was often asked to write eulogies because she had a breezy style that was playful, good with details and totally knife-in-the-heart devastating. I made food, a big pot of pasta, and then after dinner I went for a walk with Sheila and we sat on the curb outside my mom's apartment block together while she talked on the phone with her sister who was back in Vancouver waiting for the sad delivery of her mother's ashes. What can I say? said Sheila on the phone. What can I say? We finally went back inside and my mother listened to Sheila talking about Tina for quite a long time and then at midnight Sheila went into her bedroom. I knocked on her door and offered her some more of the chocolates. She took them and I hugged her and said good night, *schlope schein*, the way her mother used to do and she hugged me and we both cried and I brought her more Kleenex from the other bedroom. I found my mother out on her balcony and suggested she go to sleep. She said no, she needed to write a few things down. She wouldn't mind being alone for a while.

Is this almost too much? I asked her. Almost, she smiled. I left her alone to write the eulogy.

I went back inside and found my uncle Frank sitting by himself on the couch in the living room in the dark. I hadn't seen Uncle Frank cry before. He told me Tina was older than he was in years but much younger in her soul.

Is that true? I asked him. You married an older woman?

Well, I had to, he said. Before I could get him to explain what he meant by that he told me that Tina died fast the way she did everything and we both agreed that that's the way we wanted to go too. Lingering is the worst, said Uncle Frank. Your grandfather, Tina and Lottie's father, lay in a bed for nine years. Before that he was the most rip-roaring chap I'd ever known. He was his own man. Then he had that stroke. He lay in bed so long that his arm fused onto the side of his torso. The skin grew together, it didn't know what else to do, and he was stuck that way.

Really?

Really! he said. Thankfully your mother pulled the plug when she did. Well, not literally pulled the plug, but one day she just decided to let him die.

What?

We were all taking turns suctioning him—his lungs, I mean. Your mom, Tina, all the kids and their various spouses. It was the end. He was finally dying. His lungs were filling up and we were all doing shifts, suctioning. Do you know what that is?

Well, not really. But I can imagine.

Nine years in bed and before that oh, the energy of that man, the life in him. *Yoma!* (Plautdietsch expression loosely translated to "Damn!") It was your mom's turn to be with him and it was just the two of them. It was late. He said Helena, Helena, that was his dead wife's name, your grandmother, I'm coming, I'm coming—

Wait—what? He thought he saw grandma?

Yes. Not thought. He did see her! So your mom made an executive decision, that's like her eh? These Loewen girls are spark plugs. She didn't suction him. She was a nurse then, she'd been trained. She could have done it of course but she decided not to. His lungs filled up with fluid and she held his hand and said the things we say in times like that and let him go. Best thing she could have done for him. Hard, Yoli (he said something in Plautdietsch looking up at the ceiling, a reverie, a memory), but still.

My uncle was such a big guy. He sat on my mom's flowered couch and cried for his tiny lion-hearted Tina, his spark plug, and I sat next to him with my hand on his leg.

My mother and I were on a plane. Before we left I talked with Elf. She didn't talk at all. I told her things would be okay, truly, that I needed her, that I understood her, that I loved her, that I'd miss her, that I'd be back for her, that being together in Toronto for a while would be amazing, that Nora was really looking forward to it too, that I understood that just because she didn't want to live didn't mean that she necessarily wanted to die it's just that that's sort of how that one goes, that she wanted to die the way she'd lived, with grace and dignity, that I needed her to be patient, to fight a little longer, to hold on, to know she was loved, to know I wanted to help her, that I would help her, that I needed to do some stuff, that mom and I had to go to Aunt Tina's funeral in Vancouver, that I'd be back, that she'd stay with me in Toronto for a while, a total break, that Nic was here now, back in Winnipeg, that he'd see her every day, that I had to go, that I had to know she'd be okay while I was gone, that I would bow down before her suffering with compassion, that she could control her life, that I understood that pain is sometimes psychic, not only physical, that she wanted nothing more than to end it and to sleep forever, that for her life was over but that for me it was still ongoing and that an aspect of it was trying to save her, that the notion of saving her was one that we didn't agree on, that I was willing to do whatever she wanted me to do but only if it was absolutely true that there were no other doors to find, to push against or storm because if there were I'd break every bone in my body running up against that fucking door repeatedly, over and over and over and over. Will you eat something? I asked. Will you talk?

She put her arms up like a baby waking up from nap time and wanting to be held and I fell into them and bawled.

On the way out of the psych ward I stopped at the nurses' desk. I put my hands on the counter, palms up like I was ready to have them nailed to the Formica. Then I begged. Please, I said, don't let her go. The nurses, two of them in sky-blue uniforms and ponytails, swivelled around from their computers and looked at me. Please don't let her go, I said again.

Sorry, said the nurse closer to me. Let who go?

My sister, I said. Elfrieda Von Riesen.

Why would we let her go? said the nurse. Is she due to be discharged?

No, I said. She's not. I'm asking you please don't believe her if she tells you she's fine because she'll be very convincing and you'll think okay, let's free up a bed, let's let this one go, but I'm asking you to please not do that.

Sorry, said the nurse. You are?

I'm her sister!

Oh right, said the nurse. You mentioned that. She looked at her files. The other nurse didn't look away from her computer screen. Why would we let her go? said the nurse again. Did her doctor tell her she'd be leaving?

No, I said. I was gripping the counter like the guy on the cliff in *Deliverance*. No, he didn't. I'm just trying to get reassurance. I'm worried that you will let her go because she will ask to be let go and she will seem very normal, very sane.

I guess that's for the doctor to decide, said the nurse.

Okay, I said, but the thing is she wants to die and if you let her go I'm afraid she'll kill herself even if she tells you in a very convincing way that she won't kill herself. I could feel my heart throbbing. I was mumbling now, looking down, dribbling words onto the front of my shirt, nobody could really hear me and they strained to make out what I was saying.

Sorry, I beg your pardon? said the nurse. I think the doctor will be the one to determine whether she's okay to leave.

Just then Janice came around the corner from the rec room and our eyes met and I said oh, Janice! Janice! I'm just asking for Elf not to be let go while I'm gone. I'll be back to take her home with me to Toronto for a few weeks or months and I'm just asking that—

I was coughing, I couldn't speak. Janice was holding a guitar. She laid it on the counter and came to where I was standing. She put her hand on one of mine. She looked me squarely in the eye.

Don't worry, she said, the way she is, and considering what she's been through, there's no way we're letting her go home any time soon and certainly not without a plan in place. We don't know what that will be yet, a long-term facility or ongoing out-patient visits to psychiatry, but we promise we won't let her go home until we have follow-up care in place.

Okay, I said. Okay. I touched the guitar, its smooth golden surface.

Yoli, she said, I think it's a great idea for Elf to go to Toronto for a while. I thanked her and she let go of my hand and it wasn't completely like falling from a high ledge.

I fell asleep and woke up flying through blue skies past soft white clouds, my mother's head on my shoulder, my bag open and spilling its contents all over my lap. I felt my forehead, a thin layer of sweat. Everything was oozing out of my body now, blood, sweat and tears, like a fire sale, everything had to go, even all the junk in my bag was bursting out like nothing I had or was could contain another thing. My mom woke up and for a while stared straight ahead. Then she said huh, and turned to look at me for a second like she was trying to remember where she was and who I was. And I thought, oh stay this way, don't remember. Stay this way. But she snapped out of her post-nap fogginess and said hey Yoli, sometimes we just have to be brave, that's it. One time when my mother was a social worker for Children's Aid she had to apprehend a baby from its meth-head sixteen-year-old mother. The girl attacked my mom in her office and broke my mom's glasses so they left a deep cut on the bridge of her nose and the jagged scar still shines white against her summer tan. I stroked the little scar and my mother took my hand away from her nose and held it in her own.

I agree, mom. But how brave, exactly? I asked.

Well, said my mom, at least as brave as Aleksandr Solzhenitsyn.

So mom . . .

Yes, Yolandi? She smiled and put her head closer to mine so she could hear me speak.

I think it would be really great if Elf came to stay with me in Toronto for a while when she gets out of the hospital.

Oh! said my mom. Well!

I'll be at home all the time and Nora will be there a lot. It'll be a different scene for her. No pressure. It's worth a try, right? I could rent a piano for her if she wants to play and we could even get a boat or something.

A boat? said my mom.

Because I live by the lake. We could get a small rowboat and go out on the lake if we wanted to.

We were quiet for a while thinking and listening to two teenage girls in the row behind us having a conversation about school and their volleyball team and boys and rashes and then we heard another voice, an older woman who sounded drunk, saying: listen, I will give you two kids one hundred dollars . . .

each . . . if you can finish this flight without ever saying the word *like* again. The girls stopped talking and the woman said deal? The girls said, like, each of us? And all of us within earshot of this smiled at each other. Then a man in the aisle began to complain that somebody's kid had bit him in the ass when he'd stood up to get something from the overhead bin. It was true, I'd seen it, a three-year-old was marching up and down the aisles, bored out of her mind, and suddenly came face to ass with the guy and just opened her mouth wide, chomp, and the guy screamed, he hadn't known what had hit/bit him and the little girl stood there with her arms folded across her chest while her mother apologized profusely in a posh British accent, ordering the kid to say she was sorry. I won't, insisted the little girl, also with a lovely accent, and the mother said you will and the girl said I won't, you will, I won't. Finally the guy whom she'd bitten said it really wasn't a big deal, just a big surprise that's all, and let's be done with it. But the mother was relentless, kept insisting that her kid apologize, you will, you absolutely will, until a whole bunch of people from seats 14A to 26C all yelled out she won't!

That sounds wonderful, Yoli, my mom was saying. What does Elf think about it?

She wants to do it, I said. I'm going to get Nora's room ready for her. Nora's totally fine sleeping on the futon in the living room. I'll be at home anyway trying to finish this book. We'll walk and eat and sleep. We'll do whatever Elf wants to do. It's worth a try, right?

I like the idea of the boat, said my mother. And Nicolas? You've talked to him about it?

Not yet but I'm sure he'll be okay with it, I said. I mean he'll miss her, obviously, but it won't be forever.

But are you sure you're up to it? said my mom. We don't know what Elfie will do. Ever.

I know, I said, but what difference does that make? Either way, if she's here or in Toronto with me, we'll worry anyway. So maybe a change will be the best thing? The tour is off now so she doesn't have to think about it. Or anything.

Well. My mom sounded unsure. It could be a good thing, couldn't it?

After the funeral we all sat around in the big dining room of the church, eating ham and cheese sandwiches and reminiscing about Tina. Uncle Frank sat hunched over, his face very close to whoever was talking, intense, nodding, not wanting to miss a word. If he could absorb every single sentence uttered about his beloved mercurial wife, store every word and syllable somewhere deep within his body, then maybe he could keep her for a little longer. I loved the way he listened as though his life depended on it.

The funeral had been held in a Mennonite church so the usual squad of perpetual disapprovers (they don't take breaks, not even for funerals) stood huddled in one corner, occasionally firing glances at the rest of us but we were used to their negative juju and tried never to let their gaze meet ours. As we entered the sanctuary before the funeral service my mother sighed and breathed oh Lord to the backs of a hundred black-suited men who were already seated on their side and I knew what she meant. Don't engage, I whispered in her ear, and she squeezed my hand as we walked to the front of the women's side with our family. Violence is eternal. It changes shape and gets in like water.

What's a pacifist supposed to do with eternal violence if it can't be volleyed back *directly* at the enemy? We sang hymns in four-part harmony. Uncle Frank was in the front pew on the men's side and while we were singing "What a Friend We Have in Jesus" he swung around and gave my mother and me two thumbs up, which we returned.

After the funeral, in the dining room, I overheard snippets of a conversation my mother was having with my cousin Hans: she came to Winnipeg to help me and then she died! Earlier, before the funeral, some of my cousins and I went to Leni's grave. It said *Safe In The Arms Of Jesus* on her tombstone. My aunt's ashes would be buried just a bit down the hill and slightly to the north of Leni. The cemetery is small and green and old and reminds me of the cemetery in East Village where my grandparents, Helena and Cornelius, are buried, and behind them, in a neat row, the little graves of six of their babies. Of the sixteen kids that Helena gave birth to only ten made it to adulthood. I wondered how that worked, Helena's grief. If, at the end of the day, after all her chores were done and the evening was softening things a bit and she had a minute or two to cry or think, I wondered if she knew exactly who or what she was crying or thinking about, and if it even mattered. I wondered if my grandmother had ever said to my grandfather, honey, no, not tonight, we already have fourteen or maybe fifteen, I've lost track, and of those fourteen or fifteen, sweetheart, I have buried six and I'm more tired than all the world. And now her Tina's gone as well and her Lottie is the last one standing, and fighting off armies of her own. So it goes.

After the funeral, people took turns going up onto the little stage and telling stories and recounting memories of Tina, a

Mennonite tradition called *freiwilligis*. I saw relatives I hadn't seen in years. Sheila was the convivial emcee of the event. Her husband Gordon had to say a few words off the cuff to kill time while Sheila tried to stop herself from crying long enough to do her thing at the microphone. Gordon thanked us all for coming and said what a shame that Tina, being the party animal she was, couldn't be here to take part. Then Sheila rolled her eyes, somewhat more composed now, and took the microphone from Gordon. She said well, folks, in all her life my mother's heart has never failed her . . . until now. She said a few more things and then opened up the mic for others. There was a table beside her covered with photographs of Tina in the various stages of her life. My favourite one was of her hanging out the window of her dad's Oldsmobile when she was seventeen and waving goodbye, a giant grin on her face. See ya later, pioneers! I'm going to the city!

On the floor next to the microphone was a beautiful wooden urn, like a small wishing well, that held Tina's ashes. One of my fifty-six cousins' wives was up there talking about the way Tina sped around town in her van with the flame on the side and knew how to evade cops at every turn and while this woman was talking her little toddler son crawled up onto the stage and over to the wooden urn. He sat next to it and banged on it for a while and then, while his mother, oblivious, kept talking about Tina and all her charming qualities, her boldness, her tenderness, her zest for life, the little kid somehow managed to take the lid off the urn. We all watched, open-mouthed, as he started to sift through the ashes of Tina and then fling them around up there, having a heyday playing with his great-grandma's remains, and his little white-shirt-and-shorts outfit grew black from the dust and so did his face. And then he started putting the ashes into his mouth with his little dusty hands and by this time everyone had noticed, and his father was up on the stage picking him up, a lot of people were laughing now (except for the perpetual disapprovers who looked on in stern horror) and his mom stopped talking at the microphone and turned around and she saw that the boy's father now had everything under control and he brushed the ashes off the boy's clothes and wiped his face and put the lid back on Tina's urn and brought the child back to the table and the mother, my cousin's wife, turned calmly back to the microphone and finished her story about Tina and her van and I learned another thing, which is that just because someone is eating the ashes of your protagonist doesn't mean you stop telling the story.

I stood in the foyer of the church and spoke quietly to Nora on my cellphone. She thought she had broken her toe doing something weird on her friend's mom's treadmill and was distraught because she was sure she wouldn't be able to dance in her final recital which was in a week. And Will had to get back to New York to start his summer job and her dad was still in Borneo. She was crying. Can you stay at Zoe's place for a few days until I get back? I asked her. No, she said, Zoe's parents were taking her to Churchill to see the polar bears, or something like that. What about with Anders? I asked. He's stayed at our place enough times. That would be weird, she said, can't you just come home?

FIFTEEN

WHEN I GOT BACK TO TORONTO I sat in my big brown chair
for three hours staring at the wall. Nora's toe wasn't broken
after all, only sprained, so she could do the final recital. She
soaked her feet in warm water. She was always standing on one
leg, the other one stretched into some unimaginable distorted
pose. She asked me when Dan was coming home from Borneo.
I don't know, sweetheart, I said, and watched her wilt a bit, her
shoulders slump and her eyes go dark. Do you think he'll be
back for the recital? she asked.

The ants were gone. Will had cleaned up the house and

the three of us had Chinese takeout and watched some of the World Cup on TV before Nora went off somewhere with Anders and I drove Will back to the airport. I hugged him for a long time, overly long probably, in his opinion, but he didn't try to break away. Are you okay? he mumbled, and I said yes, more or less. I love you, he said, you're a good mother. Oh my god, I said, thank you! My eyes filled with tears instantly. You're a good son! We stopped hugging and stood apart, smiling. And you're a good sister, he said. The tears fell, it was hopeless. I apologized and Will waved it off. He took my hand and held it for a few seconds. And you're a good brother! I added. Okay, mom, he said. I have to go. I'll see you in a month or so. I'll call tonight. I watched him amble through security, say a few casual words to the guy behind the conveyor belt, hand over his boarding pass for inspection, take off his belt and put it in a bin, all these gestures made with such precision, such calm. Total control. Or it seemed so. Was he a man now?

Nic and my mother were spending most of their time at the hospital with Elf. Our conversations were brief, like pit stops. Updates. We're all alive? We're all alive. Any changes? No changes. We were all in a bit of a stupor, a state of suspension. I spent hours on my computer researching our Swiss option and trying to figure out what I should do. I didn't talk about it with anybody in Toronto. I went to the bank and asked a man in a small room if I could get a loan for twenty thousand dollars. I figured that would be more than enough to get us there and me back and pay for the "treatment" and a hotel, and even the cost of cremation and an urn. I put a pile of Rodeo Rhonda books on the desk. He asked me if I had collateral and I said no, I have nothing. I told him I hoped to get an advance on my next Rodeo book soon and I'd be able to pay them back then. He said I should come back and talk to another person next week with a copy of my book contract. I told him I didn't have it yet, that my agent was working on it. I told him that I also had another book in the works (except I said boat accidentally, I have another boat in the works) but that I hadn't finished it, and the guy said well, without a contract showing that I had funds coming in—from books or boats—there was no way that he could give me a loan.

Elf had money but it was in a joint account with Nic and he'd notice if such a large chunk of it went missing. I phoned him and asked him if Elf had mentioned the idea of her coming to Toronto. No, he said, but if she wants to, why not? His voice was quieter than usual. He didn't ask for details. He just said yeah, why not? Why not? I told him about the boat. I was obsessed with the boat. He said as far as he knew Elf wasn't really into boating but maybe, why not?

I sent an e-mail to my publisher and told him Rodeo Rhonda number ten would be on his desk in less than a month. I wrote like crazy. I had a bit of money left from an arts grant I'd received for the harbourmaster book and a really tiny amount left from the sale of our house in Winnipeg. Every day I called Nic and my mom for updates. Nic went to the hospital, usually twice a day, and said as usual not much had changed, Elf's psychiatrist is never available to talk, and my mom had stopped going quite as often because she just couldn't bear it, there was no change, the staff berated Elf continuously for not following the programme and lectured my mother on tough love and threatened to electrify my sister's brain with shock therapy— and I called the nurses' desk to beg them and to be reassured that they wouldn't let her go. The truth was, though, that she was dying in the hospital. The nurses told me they wouldn't let her go. They told me to make myself some tea and calm down. I asked if I could speak to Elf and they said only if she comes out of her room and answers the phone herself in the rec area. Sometimes I would call the nurses' desk late at night and ask if Elfrieda was there. One time they told me yes, she's here, you need to go to bed. I was trying to tell the nurse over the phone don't tell me I need to go to bed but somehow managed to stop at don't—and then apologized.

I made arrangements with Nic to call me from his cell when he was visiting Elf, and he put the phone to her ear and I talked about our plan, that I was still figuring things out, what to do, that either way I'd see her soon, I had a bit more work to do and then I'd be back in Winnipeg. While I talked she breathed, I think, but didn't speak. Then one time I called and she spoke, suddenly. Her voice was clear and strong.

When are you coming to get me, Yoli? she said.

I lay in bed a lot during the days trying to work on my Rhonda book. I wondered if maybe Mexico would be a better option, a better place to die. It would be cheaper to get there. I imagined a hammock swaying gently like a cradle, a return to infancy, to the void, and then to nothing. Mexico was more about death than Switzerland was, in my mind. It was an earthier place, more chaotic and mysterious. It was a country that celebrated the Day of the Dead by partying in cemeteries. Switzerland was about sharp pocket knives, marking time and remaining neutral. Nora made us smoothies and we ate paleo meals, her new fad diet, a lot of meat and nuts, like cavemen. Her recital was sweet and elegant and moving. On the way home afterwards she and Anders spilled Slurpees and dropped things and groped at each other awkwardly in the back seat of the car. If Will had now "reached the shores of manhood" as my father would have said, Nora was still riding that gloriously messy wave of adolescence out there on the open sea, the shoreline only barely visible to the naked eye. It was spectacularly hot in our apartment and the branches from the cutaway trees were beginning to grow back and engulf us once again in green. We were moving backwards in time, into the darkness.

I called the hospital relentlessly at all hours of the day and night. She's there? She's here. She's there? She's here. You won't let her go? We won't let her go.

SIXTEEN

I CALLED ELF AND TOLD HER over the phone that soon I'd have the money to go to Zurich. I'd use credit cards. But the next morning my mother called to say they were giving her a day pass. They were letting her go home to celebrate her birthday, a concept I found curious in these circumstances. Or maybe Elf hadn't regretted being born, necessarily.

I was so obsessed with making sure she stayed in the hospital until I had scraped together the money I needed to take her to Zurich that I'd completely forgotten about her birthday. My mother said that Nic was on his way to the hospital to pick her up and she was going to order a birthday cake to be delivered and buy some champagne and some flowers she could take over to their house, and it was going to be good. She said this emphatically, as though she were an oracle. It was a decision. I got off the phone with my mother and sat down in the palm of a moulded plastic hand-shaped chair that Nora had found in somebody's garbage and said well, then she's gone.

Nora came home later in the morning and I told her that Elf was going home for the day to celebrate her birthday. That's so nice, said Nora. It'll be hard for her to go back to the hospital though. I agreed. Very hard. I phoned Nic on his cellphone but there was no answer. I phoned my mother's apartment but there was no answer. Nora asked me if I wanted to play tennis with her so we roamed around the apartment looking for balls and rackets and put on our ratty shorts and T-shirts and headed off to the court with the droopy net a few blocks down the street. We played many games, running far too much, missing almost everything, apologizing like girls and gasping for air. We had played four or five games and were almost done, sitting on the sidelines sharing an ice cream we'd bought off a truck, "It's a Small World" blasting from its rooftop speaker. I had been trying to remember the words. It's a world of what and a world of what? My cellphone rang and it was Dan. Oh no, I thought, not now. I answered it and he asked me if I was okay, where I was, what I was doing, and I answered all his questions accurately. Aren't you in Borneo? I asked him. He said yes, he was. But Nic had called him in a panic when he hadn't been able to reach me. Yoli, he said, I'm calling with bad news.

I asked him if my mother knew and he said no, Nic had tried calling her at home and on her cell but there was no answer.

She's out looking for a cake, I said.

Ah, said Dan, okay. And he said that Nic had tried calling me but there was no answer.

Yeah, because of tennis . . .

Yoyo, he said. I handed my phone to Nora.

Please hold this, I said. I don't want it.

Nora and I walked back to our apartment. She carried both rackets and the balls and I held her other hand, the free one. I thought it was strange that I could hear the subway rumbling there beneath the ground and then realized it was only my thoughts smashing against one another and attempting to rearrange themselves into something new.

The hospital called me several times. I didn't answer at first because I was busy booking a flight to Winnipeg and calling my mom every minute with no success. Finally I answered the hospital's call. It was somebody I'd never met. She called herself the executive director of something. She asked me if I'd received the news and I said yes. She told me she was very sorry. I hung up. She called back and asked if she could talk to me, if she could explain what had happened. I told her I knew what had happened. She spoke in a soft voice, very professional, no pauses, no openings, no debate. I watched Nora move around the apartment getting our things ready for the trip to Winnipeg. The woman asked me if I was alone and I said no. I told her I was sorry but I had to go, I had arrangements to make and I still hadn't managed to get a hold of my mother. She told me that she understood but that she needed to explain some things.

How shall I frame this? she said.

I asked her: why did you let her go when every day and every night you promised that you wouldn't? Were we playing a game? Was I not supposed to believe you? She asked me if I would hold for one tiny second, she had a call coming in from the police relating to my sister's situation. Situation? I said. I sat on the floor and waited and waited and heard Lionel Richie's "Three Times a Lady," the same song being played over and over so that I had lost track of how many times a lady she was, and then eventually realized that I didn't have to hold, that I didn't have to do anything that the executive director asked me to do. That was the situation. I pushed the end button on my phone and stood up and went to help Nora with the packing.

I phoned Will but he didn't answer his cell. I phoned his dad in Manhattan and explained what had happened. Would he please try to get a hold of Will and buy him a ticket to Winnipeg immediately. I'd pay him back. He told me he was sorry, that he'd pay for the ticket, that he'd leave work now and go and find Will who was probably at his landscaping job in Queens. He and I hadn't really spoken in years. He'd known Elf, of course, way back. Now he was crying on the phone. I waited. I'm sorry, he said again. She was an iconoclast, he said. She was kind to me. She was so *into everything*. I thanked him. We said goodbye. I phoned Julie and told her what had happened and asked her to go to my mom's apartment and wait for her there. I phoned two

of my mom's friends and told them what had happened and
to go to my mom's apartment and to wait for her there. I still
couldn't get Nic on his cell. I tried my mother again. She was at
her apartment. It was too soon.

Are there lots of people there? I asked her.

No, why? she said. I'm here alone.

They're on their way, I said. She asked me what happened.

Tell me, she said.

SEVENTEEN

LATE IN THE EVENING we were all together in Nic and Elf's living room. Nora and I were still wearing the clothes we'd played tennis in. Do we have other clothes? I asked Nora. Yes, she said, we have dresses for the funeral and underwear. Will had arrived in a cab from the airport. Now he was in the bathroom. He was there a long time, crying by himself, the way young men and old women prefer to do it.

Nic told us that he had picked Elf up at the hospital and they went home and then she asked him to go to the library for her. Let's have lunch first, he said, and she agreed. He said the lunch was wonderful. It was normal. It was nice. Just sitting across from her at the table like old times. Then he went to the library to get the books that she'd requested, it would only take twenty minutes, the library was nearby, and when he came back the house was empty.

What books did she want? Will asked. He'd come out of the bathroom now. Nic said books from her past, the ones she remembered had changed her life in some way or had given her . . . that made her feel alive, I don't know . . . His voice trailed off. Will said like which ones? Nic said like D. H. Lawrence, Shelley, Wordsworth . . . I don't know. They're over there.

He waved at a sloping tower of books beside the computer table. We all eyed them, briefly, then looked away. They had failed. We couldn't look at them. We sat in the silent, yellow living room, my son and daughter on either side of their grandma, close, like sentries. They had their arms hooked through hers as if to keep her from floating upwards and disappearing like a helium balloon.

My mother was saying one thing a lot. Ain't that the truth, she said, when Will said she should sit. Ain't that the truth, she said, when Nora hugged her and said Elf was out of pain. Ain't that the truth, she said, when Nic thanked her for giving birth to Elf, his one and only. Ain't that the truth, she said, when all of us answered, quite in unison, with the word *breathe* after she had posed the question what now?

It was a beautiful house. I looked at Elf's piano books piled neatly on top of the piano. I looked at the pieces of glass she'd collected over the years arranged neatly on top of one bookcase. Well, Elf, I thought, you're so clever. Getting him to leave you alone on the pretext of getting books. Of going to the library. Of course he'd do it. Books are what save us. Books are what don't save us. The library. Of course. Elfie, you're unbelievable! I almost laughed then. What had she said about libraries and civilization? Because you make a promise, she'd said. You promise to return the book. You promise to come back. What other institution operates in such good faith, Yo?

The doorbell rang. None of us moved. It rang again, twice. Oh, said Nic. Wait, I said, I'll go. It was the guy from Tall Grass Bakery with the birthday cake my mom had ordered for Elf's party. I thanked him and brought it into the living room and showed it to the gang. It was a delicate white cake, moist and light at the same time. There was a message for Elf written in icing, an emphatic wish for happiness. We all had a piece. Nic cut the slices carefully and served them to us on Elf's plain white china and we ate the cake and watched the evening sun sparkle and refract on the blue glass bowls.

At the end of the evening when there was no more cake or sunlight, we left. Nic saw us all out and stood on the front step in his khaki shorts and old punk T-shirt, his weekend clothes, meant for relaxation and comfort. My mother asked him if he'd be all right and he opened his arms to her, his head bent very low to rest on her shoulder. Will asked him if he should stay, sleep over. Nic said no, no, waved it off, but thanked him. His parents, his brother, his friends from other places, all would be arriving in the next couple of days. Tonight he was alone.

Later at my mother's apartment I opened up the package that Nic had given me as I left. It was a copy of a story Elf had written. I had no idea she'd been writing a book. She called it

Italy in August. I peeked at a random page and read a short paragraph in which the protagonist expresses her all-consuming passion for Italy, that she wants to go there because it's where her "fictional sisters" went. Then she listed some of these fictional sisters and the books they appear in, and how each one of them protected her in a way, pulled her up and out of life's quicksand moments, the bullshit, the agony of being alive. Ah, so Elf had other sisters! For a second I felt jealous. They had helped her and I hadn't. She loved these books and they loved her back. The jealousy passed. I had a strange feeling then, as though my grief could be diluted a bit, spread out amongst all of us women, us sisters, even though only one of us was real. I flipped through the manuscript to the end and read the very last paragraph.

> Though it isn't customary to say goodbye to the reader at the end of a book, I feel that I can't end this account without also saying goodbye to you. It has turned out to be a book of goodbyes. I can only suppose I needed to say those goodbyes at length, to analyze the reasons for them and to understand them a little better. As you have been my companion on this journey, indeed my audience, the very reason for this exercise, I find myself suddenly bereft at the thought of parting ways with you too. As you have the advantage over me, in knowing more about my life than I will ever know about yours, I can only write in generalities when I wish you good fortune in all things in the future. As well as from the bottom of my heart, to bid you *auf Wiedersehen* and *adieu*. If there are tears in my eyes as I write this, they are for you. *Arrivederci.*

Will slept on the couch in the living room and Nora, my mother and I slept together that night in my mother's giant bed. She swept all the things that were on it, whodunits, clothing, glasses, agenda, her laptop, onto the carpet, but we didn't get much sleep. We talked late into the night and early into the next morning, about Elf, her inimitable style, about the past, about anything. Except the future, that was mortal combat territory. It was June and the sun rose early. For the last six weeks I'd been flying back and forth, back and forth, from the west to the east to the west to the east.

This is the strangest slumber party I've ever attended, said Nora.

Ain't that the truth, said my mom.

We watched some World Cup soccer on TV, it was an endless tournament it seemed, on for months. We wept with the losers, we looked to them for guidance, how to deal, and turned away from the winners, they didn't interest us in the least, and then Nora thought we should exchange shirts the way the players did after the game and my mom ended up wearing a tiny sweaty (still from tennis) T-shirt that said *Norwegian Wood by Haruki Murakami* and Nora in my old sweaty T-shirt that said *Inland Concrete* on it and me in my mother's soft worn-out nightie from another era, a gift from my father. I imagined him choosing it for her at the Hudson's Bay store on the corner of Portage and Memorial Boulevard. It was a tradition for my father to buy my mother a nightgown for Christmas. And almost always a lamp. Things needed to gird yourself against the night. Or one to help you sleep and one to help you stay awake, like pills. Sometimes Elf and I would help him pick out the nightgowns. Sometimes they were sweet, modest and flannel. Sometimes

269

they were short and flimsy. I hadn't really ever spent much time wondering about my dad's frame of mind when he chose these nightgowns. Or maybe the influence Elf and I wielded over the process shifted over the years as we became women ourselves.

I lay in bed counting in my mind the number of times Elf had used the word *goodbye* in that short paragraph. Four times, plus another three times in different languages. Goodbye times seven. All right, Elf, all right. In the very early morning light I saw Nora and my mother sleeping, finally, on their sides and face to face, holding hands, all four hands entwined like a skein of wool, like a mating ball of garter snakes, so that whatever was inside them would be very well protected.

One evening when I was a child and Elf was a teenager and we were all together as a family in our little Mennonite town getting ready to eat our supper Elf went over to the dining room table and snorted through her nose and said hey, excuse me, but who's the Mickey Mouse that set this table? It had been my father, put to work by our exasperated mother, who just before that had been reminding him of the year we were living in, how it had contained some groundbreaking denouement on the rights of women and other types of people. Our father rarely got angry at anyone but himself but this time he got a little huffy, saying how he'd gone and tried to be a modern man, by setting the table, only to be met with snide derision so why should he bother? Anyway, the thing about it is my memory of how Elf said who's the Mickey Mouse that set this table? Those were the exact words that came to my mind when I saw her smashed-up face, after my mother insisted on seeing her body before it was cremated. It was a train, the thing that had smashed her face, just like the one that killed our father. She hadn't waited for it long, apparently, her timing was good. Where does the violence go, if not directly back into our blood and bones? Nic and I walked my mother up the aisle in the empty funeral home sanctuary and stood on either side of her with our arms linked tight as though we were about to perform a Russian folk dance. The funeral director had suggested to my mother that if she wanted to see my sister's body then she should perhaps just look at her hand. He could have her up there in the wooden box entirely covered except for one slim, pale hand made visible. My mother disagreed with him. I will see my daughter's face, she said. So there she was, the hole in her head sewn up like a homemade baseball and that's when I thought who's the Mickey Mouse that stitched up my sister's face? And then, after about a minute of staring at her, hoping that she would blink or open her eyes and laugh at this absurd spectacle, I changed my mind and I felt a powerful, oceanic feeling of gratitude towards the funeral director who had tried so hard to restore my sister's beauty for one last look from her mother.

Elfie left me her life insurance. She also left me, à la Virginia Woolf, a monthly sum of two thousand dollars for the next two years so that I can stay at home, in a room of my own, and write. So get to it, Swiv, she wrote in a little note she'd left just for me. Everything else, except for trust funds she'd set up for my kids and money for my mom so she could travel comfortably and buy herself powerful hearing aids and a spiffy new car, went to Nic. I'm going to use the life insurance money to buy a dilapidated fixer-upper house in Toronto. I think Elf would be pleased with my decision. Was she calling my bluff? Had she ever intended to come to Toronto? Had I ever intended to take her to Zurich?

My mother is moving to Toronto to live with me and Nora.

Can I? she asked on the phone.

Please do, I said.

There was no debate, no discussion. It was time to circle our wagons. We've lost half our men and supplies are dwindling and winter is coming. We three ladies will live in this old wrecked house, the one that I just bought thanks to Elf.

EIGHTEEN

I'M LYING ON AN AIR MATTRESS in an empty house in the middle of the night half listening to Nelson tell me about his babies, the ones here, the ones in Jamaica, and the grief that the baby mamas are giving him, which is why he has to work all night as well as all day. Nelson is standing on the top rung of a stepladder straining to reach the ceiling with his paintbrush. I'm not sleeping with Nelson. I've hired him to paint. I'm drifting in and out of consciousness trying to remember how a conversation went, one I had with Elf years ago. It was something like:

Hey, what's that in your ear?

My ear? Nothing.

Yeah, there's something in your ear, Yoli. Like semen or something . . .

I don't have semen in my ear.

Yeah, it is! I'm pretty sure. Yeah, you've got semen in your ear!

It's shampoo.

It's not shampoo, come here.

Stop it!

Seriously, come here, let me check.

No.

Then what is it? Taste it.

It's shampoo. I just had a shower.

How can you tell? Taste it.

Elfrieda, I don't have to taste whatever is in my ear, which is shampoo, to know that it's not semen because I haven't been in any type of situation—

Ha! God, you're a liar . . . Relax. I love that you have semen in your ear.

I am listening to Nelson tell me about his life while he paints fresh white over battered walls. My new house is falling apart but has good bones, according to my real estate agent. I'm afraid she means it literally. Yesterday I found a book in the kitchen cupboard, left behind by the previous creepy owner, called *Serial Killers A to Z*. My real estate agent hadn't wanted to show me this house at all, it made her grimace and feel dirty, but I told her time is running out. My mother is coming.

The house is close to a polluted lake, wedged in between a funeral home, a mental hospital and a slaughterhouse. Something for each of us, said my mother over the phone when I'd described it to her. The walls are cracked, or missing or crumbling, the floors are wrecked, the stairs, every set of them, are broken, the bricks are disintegrating into red powder that floats around the house like volcanic ash and gets into your eyes and mouth, the roof needs replacing, the foundation is full of holes, the yard is overrun with weeds, and skunks live under the deck. Late one night I came upon a hooker (Will, since starting his second year of university, says to call them sex trade workers) and her client having a meeting and using my back fence for purchase. I said oh brother, the way my father would have if he'd ever encountered a lady of the night. On the tip of the prostitute's nose was a red dime-sized scab as though she had originally decided to leave the house as a clown but then changed her mind back to prostitute. Every morning I pick up the used condoms and needles with a long stick and put them into a blue pail near the back gate, a gate that opens the wrong way and smashes me in the face several times a day. When the pail is full I'll . . . I'm not sure. The so-called yard around the house is only dirt and garbage and the ground is saturated with poisonous lead from the surrounding factories.

I have four weeks before my mother arrives with her United Allied moving company monster truck to whip this sinkhole into shape. Nora will live on the top floor, in the attic with the squirrels, me on the second with the mice, and my mom on the main floor, close to the skunks. We will all be able to step out of our broken back screen doors, on different levels, and break into song like they do in *La Bohème*. This is where we've come to heal. As they say. There's an abandoned cinder-block motor parts factory across the lane, behind the house. It blocks a lot of the western sky except if we go to the third floor roof, and then we can see almost all the way back to Winnipeg.

There's a moat of sludge around the cinder-block factory and people throw garbage into it, cribs, broken tennis rackets, computers, soiled underwear, alarm clocks. Late at night two mysterious wordless men in hip waders stand in the sludge and vacuum it out of the moat so that it runs brown and toxic down the back lane south towards Adelaide, and on to King Street and finally to Lake Ontario where it will find its own. I've hired someone to attach a bedroom to the back of the house, one that is large and bright and warm and that will one day have a beautiful view onto a flower-strewn yard topped with blue skies and soaring hopes and dreams. For my mother.

One of the guys I've hired to repair the house has invited me out on a date sort of, to his support group for adult children of alcoholics. When I told him that my parents weren't alcoholics he said it didn't matter, we've all got our shit. Another one, who used to be a philosophy professor in Bucharest, has begun to urinate off the front steps and is encouraging all the other guys to do it too. He claims the smell of human urine will drive away the skunks. At night, after hot, humid days of negotiating various prices, always in cash with various men doing various things in, on top of and outside the house, I lie on this air mattress in our empty home and listen to Nelson tell me stories in the dulcet tones of his Jamaican birthplace of babies and women and work.

———

My right eye has exploded because it's August. It has puffed out and gone dark around the border. I have an allergy to autumn, to shorter days and longer nights, to death. I had an argument today with a friend. She lured me out of my house on the pretence that I needed some fresh air, a change of scenery. That I had to move on. Baby steps.

It was a mistake.

We sat in a café called Saving Grace on Dundas and ordered eggs. She told me that she's been worrying about me so much, it must be awful, everything I've been going through, and that in her opinion "to die by one's own hand" is always a sin. Always. Because of the suffering it causes the survivors. I asked her what about all the people who suffer because of assholes who are alive? Is it a sin for the assholes to keep on living?

Okay, she said, but we're here on this earth, and even if we didn't choose to be, we inherit all kinds of duties, to the people who raise us and to the people who love us. I mean, everyone has personal agonies, sure, but to die by one's own hand, ironically enough, even though it's an act of self-annihilation, seems to me the ultimate act of vanity. It's just so incredibly selfish.

Can you please stop saying to die by one's own hand? I asked.

Well, what should I say? she said.

Suicide! When someone's murdered do you explain it as, oh, he died by the hand of another? This isn't the freaking *Count of Monte Cristo*.

I just thought it was more delicate, she said.

And also, I said, selfish? How could it be selfish? Unless you've seen the agony first-hand you can't really pass judgment.

Okay, she said, but if your sister had been thinking of how it would affect you when she—

AFFECT ME? I said. I'm sorry. People were looking at me. Listen, I said, I don't think you understand. I don't want to be presumptuous, but really how could you understand what another person's suicide means? My friend asked the waitress for more coffee. I said that actually, now, I'd begun to measure a person's character and integrity by their ability to kill themselves.

What do you mean? she said. Look, I don't think—

Jeremy Irons, for example. I bet he'd be able to, I said. Vladimir Putin? No way. I said the names of a few people we knew and said yes or no after each name. Then I said my friend's name and paused. I stared at her with one exploding eye and she told me we shouldn't talk about suicide anymore because it might rupture our friendship. I told her that we would talk about it forever. I told her that if she didn't want her plane to crash she should go over all the ways that it could crash in her mind. She told me I might be having buried-anger issues and I told her oh, mind reader, do you fucking think so?

I tried to apologize, to ease the tension. I didn't know what to say. I quoted Goethe the way my mother did from *Aus meinem Leben: Dichtung und Wahrheit* . . . "suicide is an event of human nature which, whatever may be said and done with respect to it, demands the sympathy of every man, and in every epoch must be discussed anew" . . . but while I was saying the words my friend was checking her cellphone, calculatedly not listening to me. I had offended her. I didn't blame her. I wanted to get back on track. Somewhere I had read that animals are an excellent neutral subject. I asked her if she had pets. She said I knew that she didn't. I told her about Lefty. She was a border collie, right, I said to my friend. And you know when my kids were little they'd have all their friends over and they'd all be playing in the backyard and I'd check on them every once in a while, and then one time I looked through the window at them and they were all squeezed into one corner of the yard—but it was like they were oblivious to it and they just kept on playing—and do you know why? Because Lefty was a border collie. And border collies are herding dogs. It was in her nature to herd, so my kids and their friends eventually all became squished into the corner of the yard and Lefty had done what she was meant to do. She had no control over it. She had to herd. So do you understand why I'm fucking mad?

Afterwards I got drunk on Revolucion tequila. There are two crossed pistols on the bottle pointing towards the sky, to God, and I phoned my friend and whispered another apology into her machine. I was about to tell her that I did think she had what it took to kill herself but stopped myself mid-sentence and switched it to I think you have what it takes to endure.

I phoned Julie but her son told me she was at a movie with Judson and their grandma was babysitting. Tell her I love her, I said. And I love you too, and your sister. And your grandma. I love you all.

NINETEEN

MY MOTHER IS HERE NOW IN TORONTO and the three of us, my mother, my daughter and I, are living in the house. The first time my mother saw the house was a few weeks ago late at night in the middle of an electrical storm. It was raining hard, horizontally, little pellets, and the night was a deep purple with lightning flashing like knives stabbing at the earth. I had parked the car in the driveway. Nora was in the back seat with a couple of her friends from school. My mother got out of the car and tried to open her umbrella but the wind was whipping it around and so she struggled for a bit while the rest of us stared at her through the car windows as though she was a mime doing a performance of some kind and then she finally gave up, to hell with it, and tossed the umbrella up into the air and let the wind have it altogether. We watched the umbrella fly up quickly like the Challenger and then down again, straight down, and then just seconds before it hit the ground it zoomed directly at my mother's head but she dodged it and it hit the car. We were all getting out of the car by now, already drenched from one second in the rain, and then my mother managed to grab the umbrella and she walked it over to the moat beside the lane, the disgusting toxic garbage-filled moat surrounding the cinder-block car parts factory, and threw the umbrella in there. What phony baloney, she said. As if to say what fools we are to think we can escape the wrath of atmospheric disturbances. We stood laughing in the storm and watched the useless umbrella sink into the sludge. At some point, but not tonight, I'll suggest to my mother that we put our garbage into the blue bin rather than the cesspool out back. Oh, right, I forgot that you believe in recycling, she'll say. You know all that stuff goes to the same place. Recycling is just a government conspiracy meant to make us believe that we're saving the earth so they can go about making nasty deals with mining companies to make an extra buck or two. Finally we made it into the house and found Nelson there high up on his ladder putting the final touches to my mom's ceilings, rap music cranked and the intoxicating smell of weed.

My mother inspected every inch of the house slowly, carefully, grinning, drops of rain falling from the tip of her nose, sighing, running her hands down banisters, over walls, nodding at some feature, pointing silently at another, remembering a detail from her childhood, standing back and staring like she was at the Louvre and concluding that it had style, an odd charm, a warm vibe, that she saw us living here happily. Bravo! she said to me and we all, Nora and her school friends and even Nelson who had come down from his ladder to tag along with us for the house tour, high-fived and hugged.

I had put four bottles of beer in my fridge and my mom and Nelson and I toasted to our future or to the improbability of the moment, or just to its passing, or to private memories, or simply to the broader theme of shelter. The rain stopped for a few minutes and we all went out onto the second floor deck— the old, creaky one with broken Christmas lights hanging from it—to look at the sky and Nelson told us riddles about hurricanes and their eyes and the girls laughed and laughed, they thought he was hot, and my mother, with her back to us and her hands grasping the railing, was quiet and looking westward. Then, quite suddenly, she turned around and recited her favourite Wordsworth poem. I'd heard her do it before, but this time it ripped at my heart.

> It is a beauteous evening, calm and free,
> The holy time is quiet as a Nun
> Breathless with adoration; the broad sun
> Is sinking down in its tranquility;
> The gentleness of heaven broods o'er the Sea:
> Listen! the mighty Being is awake,
> And doth with his eternal motion make
> A sound like thunder—everlastingly.
> Dear Child! dear Girl! that walkest with me here,
> If thou appear untouched by solemn thought,
> Thy nature is not therefore less divine:

Thou liest in Abraham's bosom all the year;
And worshipp'st at the Temple's inner shrine,
God being with thee when we know it not.

Whoah, said Nelson. You hear that? He was looking at the girls. You hear what grandma threw down? Shit! The girls clapped and asked her if it was a song or what and I held my bottle aloft and made a new toast, to the lees of life, I said, a callback to another poem my mother sometimes pulled from her hat but also to the Alfred Lord–referenced inscription in my mother's old high school yearbook, the one beneath her photo: *Lottie drinks life to its lees!* She winked at me.

To the what? said Nora.

The girls had to pee and I suggested they do it into a cup and throw it under the front steps to keep the skunks away, like the renovation crew guys had recommended. Don't worry about my mother, Nora told her friends, she's a hippie. When she was a girl she had nothing to play with but the wind. You don't have to pee into a cup. We have a washroom.

Nelson and my mother chatted briefly about poetry and the power of seas, their riptides and undercurrents, all of their invisible strength, and the girls eventually wandered off into the night. I went downstairs and had another look around my mother's part of the house. She had insisted that all the bars come off the windows. My renovation crew had balked at this, they worried about her safety on the main floor. I won't live in a prison, she said. They're coming off. I wandered back into her living room. I took a pencil from my backpack and climbed up Nelson's ladder, to the top, and wrote on a part of the ceiling that he would be painting over very soon, maybe even later that night.

AMPS. I climbed down and then hollered up to my mother that we should go and get some sleep. Tomorrow morning the truck with my mother's belongings would be arriving from Winnipeg and she and I would supervise the move, instructing the movers where, in which room, to put what and how to assemble certain pieces and then we would stay here in this place and live.

My mother is wearing a patch over one eye. She's sitting in a room full of old people who are all wearing a patch over one eye. I've come to pick her up. One man welcomes me to the pirates' convention. It's the left eye, for every one of them, that is patched over. We're in a room at St. Joseph's Health Centre in Toronto. I find my mother deep in conversation with a couple in matching windbreakers and she waves me over to make introductions. She explains that the cataract doctor does all left eyes one week and then all right eyes the next. She has been given six tiny bottles of eye drops with instructions for use.

For the next couple of weeks Nora and I take turns administering the drops. Our days are punctuated with these drops sessions. In between drops we have to wait a few minutes for my mother to absorb the hit. While we wait we play mad duets on the piano to pass the time. We play really fast. Sometimes we play my mother's favourite hymns like "Children of the Heavenly Father" but at breakneck speed, which makes her laugh. Nora can play "Somewhere Over the Rainbow" in less than ten seconds and an even faster version of Handel's Sarabande.

Six different types of drops, two or four or six drops from each bottle, three minutes in between drops, four times a day! We come at my mother with tiny bottles and she obediently removes her glasses and puts her head way back and pushes her soft white hair away from her eyes. When it's over she sits at her computer playing online Scrabble with tears, real and manufactured, pouring down her face.

Invincible calm, I tell her.

Invincible calm, she repeats.

You will triumph, I say.

You will triumph, she answers.

A couple of days ago my mother came home from a walk around the neighbourhood with news that put her in a jubilant mood.

I've found something out, she said. I went into the funeral home on the corner and found out that I can be cremated for fourteen hundred bucks. That's everything included. And they've got a door-to-door policy. They'll pick up my body and return it in a can.

She showed me her new shoes, a quality pair of black leather slip-ons that she'd bought at a trendy Queen West boutique. My mother is not a hipster or a style maven. She's a short, fat seventy-six-year-old Mennonite prairie woman who has lived most of her life in one of the country's most conservative small towns, who has been tossed repeatedly through life's wringer, and who has rather suddenly moved to the trendy heart of the nation's largest city to begin, as they say, a new chapter in her life. She doesn't know anybody in Toronto but she loves the Blue Jays, which bonds her to strangers of all kinds. She is the absolute embodiment of resilience and good sportsmanship.

I've started making a shit list of shops and cafés on Queen West here in the "art and fashion district" who treat her with less respect and professional friendliness than they treat their younger and more glamorous clients. My mother doesn't even notice, she's jovial and curious and delighted and oblivious to snottiness. She's a bit loud because of her mild deafness and she laughs a lot and has questions about everything and no embarrassment in asking. In her mind there is no reason why she and a group of beautiful film students hanging out at the Communist's Daughter could not party together every night of the week. She is the antithesis of what the Queen West crowd would like themselves to be. She's comfortable in her XXL pink cotton shorts and the T-shirt she won at a Scrabble tournament in Rhode Island. She would like to engage these pale, thin retail workers in conversation, she'd like to get their story, she'd like to know where the products come from, how they are chosen, how does one wear this, how does it wash, she's trying to learn more about her new home and to become acquainted with her world, which makes their cold bony shoulder treatment of her that much more heartbreaking. And then I boycott them forever. So does Nora, even though it pains her a bit because she is young and fabulous and ultra-fashionable and would like to go into these shops occasionally but whatever, we smite you, snobs.

My mom's already pals with the dry cleaner guy on King who knows me only as Lottie's daughter and she chats every morning with Straight Up Cliff, the waving guy across the street. She even offered to give him, or his sons, my couch. Three large men, one with a fresh cut on his nose, came to our door this morning and told me that Lottie had told them I had a couch for them. No, I said. I don't. A misunderstanding.

Can you not give my things away? I asked her later.

A guy wearing a shirt, tie, jacket, socks, shoes, hat and no pants, none, no underwear either, walked past our house and my mother saw him and ran to her bedroom for a pair of her sweats to give him. He thanked her and then wrapped them around his neck like a fluffy scarf and she told him well, that would work too. When I asked her if she wouldn't miss those comfy sweats she told me that she'd stop giving my things away but that she'd do whatever she wanted with her things.

She's joined a church, too, a Mennonite one on the Danforth, and they've asked her to become an elder. Is that some official thing? I asked her. Aren't you one already? You're quite old. She explained to me that there are only three elders in the church and that she is very honoured to have been asked. Back in our little hometown of East Village a woman would never have been asked to be an elder in the church. A woman wouldn't have been asked (told) anything except to close her mouth and open her legs. She'll think about it for a while. She zips around town on the TTC visiting cranky shut-ins from her church, singing hymns with them, helping them to prepare meals, making them laugh, making herself useful. The church people have come around and planted things in our hideous front yard. Flowers, shrubs, perennials, some decorative rocks. And Alexander, our next-door neighbour, has spread wood chips all around the yard too, so now our house has become a beautiful sort of community project.

We don't talk about Switzerland or whether I should have taken my sister to Switzerland to help her die. I'm pretty sure Elf never mentioned Switzerland to my mother and I don't dare ask her about it. In the evening, when her Samaritan work is done, my mother pours herself a honking big glass of red wine and watches her beloved Blue Jays get creamed again. Nora and I can hear her from the second and third floors shouting at her television on the main floor. Send him home! Hustle, man! We don't flinch. We're used to it. She's been a Jays fan forever and knows the stats and the stories behind all the players. All right, that guy's blown his rotator cuff, that guy's throwing garbage, that guy tested positive for some hoohaw. The CL they just signed? Well, he's on the DL with a pulled groin! They're calling them up from Triple A!

My mother had something like a date a few weeks ago. She told the old fellow, as she called him (I think he's ten years younger than she is), that what she'd like to do is get a glass of wine somewhere—this wine habit is something she's quickly picked up in Toronto, she's been buying a Merlot lately with a label that says DARE!—and then go to a Jays game. She invited me along and the whole time I chatted with the guy who was not that interested in baseball but, I found out, smokes two joints a day for his advanced arthritis. You're dating a pothead, I told her. Meanwhile my mom watched the game like a scout, hunched over and beady-eyed, and recorded everything, hits and misses and runs and errors, into her programme. When the guy tried to talk to her, to ask her if she'd like a hot dog or something, she said C'MON UMP! WAKE UP! WHAT ARE YOU DOING, SNIDER? TWO MEN OUT AND THE BASES LOADED! After the game, after we'd dropped off her date somewhere in the east end of the city, I asked her what kinds of things he did and she said she didn't really know, he'd just got himself a phone though, so he wouldn't have to call her from a pay phone anymore. He goes to the University of Toronto, she said. Cool, I said, what for? To shower, she said.

Late last night I went downstairs to say hi and she wasn't there. There was a note on the table. Yoli, she'd written, I've gone to a lecture on Eritrea. There's schaubel zup and schmooa kumpst in the fridge. I called her on her cellphone and when she finally answered I heard raucous voices and whooping in the background. Where are you? I asked her. It's after eleven. She said hang on, hey guys, where am I? I heard a guy answer her and she told me she was at the Motorcycle Café on Queen Street and somewhere having a burger and watching the game. Extra innings. By yourself? I said and she told me no, no, there's a huge gang of people here and then there was more laughing and yelling and eventually I couldn't hear her at all.

I'm sitting on my couch, the one my mother tried to give away to the neighbours, and my tears are beginning to sting my eyes. A low point is when you can't even depend on your tears not to hurt you. I've been next door, at the other neighbour's. Her name is Amy. She's a new mom, I see her almost every day, taking her baby for a walk. A month ago she found a fallen starling on the sidewalk and took it home to nurse it back to health. She built a little house for it in her back bedroom, with a branch and a Frisbee full of water, and put live earthworms in a bowl of dirt and she fed him baby food and apple sauce on the end of a tiny Popsicle stick and she played starling songs to him so he could learn how to sing in his language. After about three weeks of taking care of him she decided that the bird could be on his own now and should leave the nest she'd made for him and she opened the door of her back bedroom and the starling hopped onto her shoulder and then the two of them walked along the upstairs hallway, down the stairs, along the downstairs hallway towards the open back door and then suddenly the bird saw his chance, the rectangle of light from the open door, and he flew off. Amy passed her iPhone to me and said you want to see the bird flying away? My husband filmed it. The bird was a small dark blur flying through the air and out into the light and up, gone. He moved so fast. As I watched this short video something inside of me smashed, it was so startling and irreversible that starling's departure, and I was crying but trying not to, but it felt like I'd been tear-gassed.

———

Now I'm looking at a box of cards sent from Elf over the years. Every occasion remembered, all of them written in her trademark coloured felt markers. Look at all these exclamation points, I think. All these occasions—birthdays, Christmases, graduations—marked with emphatic endings. And then again. We reconfigure and we start again and we start again. We huddle in a field with our arms around each other, our helmets knocking, and we rework our strategy and then we run another play. When I was a kid I told Elf (or had I only told myself?) that I would keep her heart safe. I would keep it preserved forever in a silk bag like Mary Shelley did with the heart of her drowned poet husband or in my gym bag or in the top drawer of my dresser or tucked into that hole in that ancient tree in Barkman Park in our faraway hometown next to where I stashed my Sweet Caps. Now I'm crashing around my house searching for those felt-tipped markers. If I can find the pink one and the green one I'll be okay until the morning. I search and then I give up searching.

———

Living with my mother is like living with Winnie the Pooh. She has many adventures, getting herself into and out of trouble guilelessly, and all of these adventures are accompanied by a few lines of gentle philosophy. There's always a little bit more to learn every time you get your head stuck in a honey pot if you're my mother.

She was out all night last night. This morning she showed up at the front door—she'd forgotten her keys—with her hair sticking up all over the place and her nightgown tucked into her pants. Oh good, you're up! she said. I forgot my key!

She had just returned from the sleep clinic where she spent the night with electrodes on her head, dreaming. The sleep technician got angry with her because she was reading her book. She told my mom she was there to sleep not to read, and my mom told her she couldn't sleep without reading first. The sleep technician asked my mom to hand over her book—it's a Raymond Chandler—and my mom laughed and said you have got to be kidding me, hand over my book. Not a chance. Then the sleep technician was a bit rough with her, yanking the sticky round electrodes off her head in the morning and not saying goodbye when my mom left. It drives my mom crazy when people don't say hello and goodbye. It's old school, she says. It's the end of civilization when people don't say hello or goodbye.

Apparently, said my mom, my heart stops beating ninety times an hour while I'm sleeping. You've got sleep apnea, I told her. Clearly, she said. She looked at herself in the mirror and laughed at her reflection.

She showed me the apparatus that she'll have to sleep with now, a giant plastic mask with a hose, which she'll strap to her face and then breathe in moisture from a contraption that the face mask is attached to. We have to get jugs of distilled water and keep the thing filled. She put the mask over her face and walked heavily towards me like Darth Vader. If somebody breaks into my bedroom while I'm wearing this thing, she said in a muffled voice, they won't stick around for long. Then she breathed hard from behind the plastic and it filled up with condensation. She yanked it off. Too bad I'm not still wearing my patch, she said. I'd be a force to reckon with, wouldn't I?

She opened her laptop for a quick game of online Scrabble. The last guy she played with was from France and he offered to show her a picture of his penis. She wrote him back *No merci. Do you have photographs of Paris?*

I have just realized something. It's not me who's survived, who's picked up and gone on, who's saved my mother by bringing her to Toronto, it's my mother . . . and she's taken me with her.

So, I said, you dreamed at the sleep clinic?

Boy! she said. Did I ever. I had an epiphany.

Yeah? I said.

Well, you know how I hate cooking so much?

Yeah.

Well, I've been wondering about that. I've been wondering what I should do about that. So I had this dream last night and it came to me. Frozen food! Just a voice telling me that. So I figured out, from my dream, that I should go to the freezer aisles and get a lot of frozen food, pizzas, meatballs, perogies, chicken fingers, whatever, and stock my freezer and that'll be the end of it. I won't have to worry about cooking but I'll still have food to eat. It just came to me like that, like a billboard: frozen food!

That sounds pretty good, I said. My mother was dreaming of survival. She was having survival dreams. She was having dreams that were telling her how to keep being alive. I wouldn't tell her that frozen foods are full of sulphates, who cares, when she was deep into the cure.

I had a dream of my own. It wasn't a Switzerland-scenario dream. Elfrieda and I were in her yellow kitchen next to the giant picture window talking and laughing about nothing. We were just pleasantly lost in a maze of words that didn't mean much, telling stories and making each other laugh. We were there but then, in my dream, I wanted to tell Elf something more urgent, something about my work, about my fear of finishing my book and of how it would be received and then there was a pause in our chatter and Elf was yawning, and I thought now I will tell her this urgent thing but she put her hand up to stop me so I kept my mouth shut. She took my hand and she looked hard at me, she put her face closer to mine so I would really get what she was about to say, that she meant it, her eyelashes a black fringe, she was being serious, and I thought oh thank god, she'll say something to make me feel better, braver, and then she said Yoyo, you're on your own now. And my feeling in the dream was the feeling I had when I watched my neighbour's video about her bird. The suddenness of it, something lost in a second forever. My sister was a dark blur moving towards a rectangle of light. But now after hearing my mom's survival dream I think maybe this is *my* survival dream and it's not a nightmare. It's the beginning of my own cure. Because to survive something we first need to know what it is we're surviving.

On Fridays we have family meetings. Sometimes Nora doesn't come to the family meetings because she has better things to do—there is Anders, there are parties, she's young. We give her the minutes from the meetings. I'm not sleeping around anymore. I'm embarrassed about it and Elf isn't around anymore to remind me that I'm not a slut and that *there's no such thing okay Yoli, have I taught you nothing, please stop equating morality with outdated self-serving patriarchal notions of women's sexuality.*

Finbar called to ask if I had killed my sister and needed legal counsel and I told him no, she saved me the trouble. He apologized. He hadn't known it was that serious. He said he was sorry. I thanked him. He said but we had something, right? I liked the way he put that. It might have been a hallucination but it was something. I said yes, and I thanked him again. We said goodbye forever, behaving like grown-ups. I live with my mother and my daughter. We stand outside on our various perches, on all three floors, and shout things at each other like the smoking women in *Balconville*. I don't have time to sleep around. I have raccoons and dreams and water guns and grief and toxic moats and guilt and used condoms to pick up from the driveway.

My mother said I couldn't tie off grief like a used condom and toss it in the garbage. I asked her what she knew of condoms and she told me she had been a social worker for a long time which is what she always says after surprising us with information we didn't think she had. Yesterday I was walking through

Trinity Bellwoods Park and discovered my mother lying on a bench, sleeping. I sat beside her for a while and read the paper. After ten or fifteen minutes I gently nudged her and said mom, it's time to go home. She told me she loved sleeping outdoors. Is that true, I said, or were you out walking and suddenly overcome with exhaustion?

My sister gave me an emergency ladder once. It was the kind of ladder that you hook onto your upstairs window ledge and then climb down it if there's a fire in your house. For years I stored it in the basement but now I'm beginning to understand the wisdom of keeping it on the second floor.

I phoned the hospital in Winnipeg and asked if I could please speak to the patient named Elfrieda Von Riesen. They told me she was not a patient there. I told the hospital well that's strange because she definitely had been a patient there and the last thing I'd heard was that she wasn't going to be leaving the hospital any time soon. They said well, they had no information regarding that. I told them I was tired of all their fripperies. They were sorry about that. I hung up.

And then it was almost Christmas already. Nic was going to join us. He was on the phone from Winnipeg. He had an idea for the headstone: *And sleep as I in childhood sweetly slept, Untroubling and untroubled where I lie, The grass below; above, the vaulted sky.*

What's that? I said.

You don't know? he said.

I don't know every poem, I said.

It's John Clare.

Did Elf like him?

Very much. It's called "I Am!" He wrote it in a mental asylum.

No way, I said.

Pardon me?

Let's not have everything tied up to lunacy, I said.

You mean for the inscription?

For everything.

Well, do you have suggestions?

When I got back to Toronto after Elf died I had wanted to take some of her ashes with me and keep them here but Nic didn't like the idea of divvying her up so they're all buried under an enormous tree in the Elmwood Cemetery in Winnipeg. My mother had suggested that she be buried with our dad out in East Village and the cemetery guy had said sure, there was room for three if they were urns and not coffins (suggesting that my mom would eventually go in there too) but Nic said no way, Elf had said expressly that she did not want to be buried in East Village. That would be like giving the body of Louis Riel back to the Canadian government as a souvenir. What about your backyard? I asked Nic. After all, she was a homebody. He said very funny and that there were legal issues with a backyard burial. She wasn't a cat. That's true, I told him. He told me that I had done everything I could and that no one was to blame. I wasn't sure about that. What about Zurich, I wondered. She would have died peacefully and not alone. That's all she wanted. I had failed. We didn't talk about that. I told him he had done everything possible too.

She was the one who got the pass, I said. You know how she would have been. She could talk her way out of the ward.

But I should have fought harder to have them keep her, he said.

You couldn't have fought harder.

So no John Clare poem?

Maybe. But I don't like the asylum connotations. Plus, if it's a poet it should be a woman.

But most of the really great woman poets killed themselves so that has connotations too.

I know and that's the thing we're trying to avoid here, right, is labelling her even after death.

Yeah, true, so then we just have a blank stone?

Maybe, yeah, just her name and the dates.

Maybe.

So then the original idea of the poem still holds, though, in a way . . . let me lie. Just let me lie.

Beneath the grass and vaulted sky.

Do you ever have dreams about her? he said to me over the phone.

Yeah. Do you?

Yeah, indirectly. Like it's summertime but the coldest summer on record, colder even than any winter has ever been. What are yours?

Well, the other night I dreamt that I was in a fishing village, some outport in Newfoundland or something, and I had to go to the grocery store to buy some meat and when I got there it was a dirt floor and there were lambs lying around everywhere.

They weren't small and white like in the Bible, they were dark grey and as big as a greyhound dog. But they were lambs. Some of them were dead, some were just barely alive. There was a guy with a knife. He was butchering them but he didn't really know how to. He'd hack a hoof off or a tail or maybe a snout. He didn't know what to do. I just stood there looking around at the lambs and then he said he'd had it. And then he made one more cut. And then he said no, it was the knife that had had it, like it was something almost living or just that it wasn't sharp anymore and couldn't cut properly, I wasn't sure.

What does it mean? said Nic.

I don't know, Carl Jung, I said.

But I did know. It was about Zurich.

You know what? Nic asked. I've got an idea. Why don't we put a line of music on her headstone and no words at all?

Nic and I talked on the phone for a long time about the line of music we could engrave on the stone, and the whole time I wanted to bring up Switzerland but didn't know how to because if I told him Elf had asked me to take her to Switzerland that would be like telling him that she didn't trust him to do it, or that he didn't understand her, and I didn't want him to feel those things. He was a man alone already. And besides, what was the point in bringing up Switzerland? I had to work it out for myself whether I was the lamb or the butcher or just the knife.

When Elfie was twelve she was finally chosen to play Mary in our church nativity pageant. She was very proud and nervous. She had been lobbying for the Mary role for years. C'mon, this part was made for me! I'm not sure our Sunday school teacher was finally convinced of that—a twenty-something virgin who didn't talk much?—or just really tired of being harassed by Elf. But she gave her the part and said just please no strange surprises. Elf was well aware of her responsibilities, of being demure and tender and mild even though she'd been unconventionally impregnated by an invisible force and was now expected to raise the Messiah and all on a carpenter's salary. I was six. I was supposed to be a shepherd, relegated to some back row where all us younger kids would stand with dishtowels on our heads or angel wings gaffered to our backs. I told my mother I refused to be a shepherd. I would be Mary's sister, the baby's aunt. My mother told me that the baby Jesus didn't have an aunt in the nativity scene, that it didn't make sense. But I am her sister, I said. I know, said my mother, but only in real life. I paused. But, I argued, Jesus had "wise men" and camels at his birth but no relatives? How much sense does that make? I know, said my mother, but the Bible says . . . Just this time, I told her. Elfie needs me. She's got a new baby. I'm her sister, I'm going.

My mother didn't bother to fight with me. I put together my sister/aunt costume, a flowered sheet, and trudged off to rehearsals with Elf who was a bit embarrassed by me but she'd gotten used to that a long time ago and only sighed wearily once. The pageant director phoned my mom a few times to complain. She told my mother she couldn't convince me to budge from Elfie's side, that I had just wedged myself in there between her and Joseph and wasn't moving, and the boy playing Joseph was getting really annoyed by it. Jesus doesn't have a pushy aunt in this thing, he said. It's not in the Bible. My mother told the pageant director she had no advice for her. I got to play my sister's sister and everybody tried hard to ignore me but I knew I'd been there and more importantly so did Elf who was a fantastically demure Mary, just sitting there placidly and holy, while I bustled around a bit making sure the kid was breathing, the cradle was secure, the straw was fluffed, Joseph wasn't swearing out loud, all the things a good aunt would do when her sister has a baby.

We had to get a Christmas tree. Nora and I went to the No Frills parking lot across the street from the Runnymede Library on Bloor Street West and bought the biggest, most beautiful tree in the lot. The tree had plastic straps around it, keeping it skinny and portable, but the guy who sold it to us said it would puff out when we took them off. He tied it to the roof of our car. He called it the Everest of trees. We drove home with the tree and lugged it into the house through my mother's back door. It took up the whole living room. As we took off the straps it kept getting bigger and bigger. Needles were everywhere. It was much too big but we loved it. My mom sat knitting me a black boat-necked sweater in her easy chair while Nora and I tried to put up the tree. Nora played the new Kanye West record on her laptop. My mother asked her what it was. *My Beautiful Dark Twisted Fantasy*, said Nora. She sang some of the lyrics along with Kanye. Honey, said my mom, you're not a monster. I know, Grandma, said Nora. Thanks. My mother sat in her easy chair knitting and nodding in time to Kanye.

We were trying to get the tree to stand in the stand without falling over. Nora was balanced on the arm of the couch wearing leather mittens and holding the top of the tree. She had strands of Christmas lights around her neck all ready to go. I was lying on the floor trying to get those metal screws to go into the stump of the tree. My mother was sitting in her chair saying to the left, to the right, now the left, no the right. Kanye West was rapping about what he needed badly. We couldn't get it straight. Then we thought we had it.

Nora, let go, I said. I let go too. The tree started to fall over to the left and Nora grabbed it before it crashed onto the piano. My mother laughed. There was flour on her forehead and chin. She had been baking tarts earlier on. I got back down on the floor and swore and Nora held the top with her mittened hand and my mother said hey, the tree wanted to lean, we should let it.

What, I said, just let it lean against the piano and have it like that?

No, said Nora, do you see people just leaning their trees against stuff? No, you don't.

We kept trying. Then we thought maybe we should get a rope and tie the tree to the curtain rod. We could disguise the rope to make it look more Christmassy.

Ah, the Christmas Rope, said Nora. A beautiful new Von Riesen family tradition.

It's really a big tree, isn't it, said my mother.

One more time, I said. We worked and worked to make it stand straight and on its own without a rope. Back away now, I told Nora. We both moved slowly away from the tree and it was standing alone, there it was. O happy day. We had succeeded in doing something normal. The ceiling was very high but the top of the tree was touching it. We breathed. We eyed it for a while. Okay, I think it's good, I said. Let's have some wine, said my mother.

I opened a bottle and we went to the dining room table and sat there and toasted to our success. We lifted our glasses high, even Nora had a bit of wine, and said things about Christmas, about ourselves, like here's to us. Our shoulders dropped. We were proud. We were covered in pine needles and the room smelled so good. My mother gazed towards the tree. Nora and I had turned our backs on it. We were sipping our wine. Then my mother shouted and Nora and I turned around in slo-mo, Kanye got loud again, and we watched the tree fall. It fell slowly at first, discreetly, like it was having a heart attack in public and it didn't want this to be happening but it was happening. Then it picked up speed and as it crashed to the floor it took things with it, a painting of two boys playing in puddles, the television, the books on top of the piano, a sculpture of a girl in a dress being shy, an almost empty coffee cup and a large plant. It finished falling and lay still on the floor.

Hoo boy, said my mother. Head count, said Nora. We toasted to ourselves again and laughed hard. My mother just couldn't stop. Then Nora and I went back to help our fallen comrade and finally, finally made him stand alone for good in the living room without a rope.

Claudio stopped by for a visit. He stood on the front porch, snow on his shoulders and cap, cradling gifts, perfectly wrapped. I thought I would see Elf behind him, shaking off her boots, big green eyes sparkling. He pulled a bottle of Italian wine out of his coat. We sat in my mother's living room next to the piano. My mother plays hymns on it. A lot of Elf's old piano books from her early years are piled on top.

Claudio put the gifts under the tree and handed my mother a bag. These are letters of condolence from a few of Elf's colleagues, he said. And from fans. Wow, that's quite a tree.

You might want to keep your distance, Nora said. She was setting the table. We tasted Claudio's Italian wine and we toasted to Christmas, to the birth of a tiny Saviour (we're waiting), to family, to Elfrieda.

Okay, let's sit down, said my mom. Claudio asked us how we were doing and we told him we were okay. How was he doing? He was still in shock, he said. He had honestly thought music would save her life. Well, said my mother, it probably did, for as long as she was alive.

He told us that a guy named Jaap Zeldenthuis had filled in for Elf on the tour.

He's not Elfrieda Von Riesen but I think he did pretty well given the short notice, said Claudio. Critics noticed a few rhythmic vagaries in his playing, a certain waywardness. But it's all right, Jaap was performing with jet lag. I was pleased with Elfrieda's obituary in the *Guardian*. I liked it because it's about what is special about her playing, its colour and warmth, and not just the usual stuff about her rigour and discipline. *Der Spiegel* was good too, very beautiful, and *Le Monde*. It bothers me that the other papers made a big problem of her health issues, an obituary must not read like another sensational headline story. Did you see them?

My mother made a dismissive noise. Pffft. No, I didn't, she said. I used to read those things but not anymore.

I read them, I said, and you're right.

There was a heavy silence in the room. We stared at the tree for a while and then Claudio said I must tell you that in the gifts there is a video recording of Elfrieda's last rehearsal. He told us that Elfrieda had given the best performance of her life that day, that she had played beyond herself, as if there was no physical barrier between herself and the piano and she could express her emotions at will, and when she was finished the orchestra stood and applauded her for five minutes. Elfrieda buried her face in her hands and wept, and then half of the musicians also wept, and now Claudio was crying too as he told us this. We thanked him for telling us the story, and for the video, and we promised we'd watch it. We all hugged him at the front door and he held on to the banister. He wouldn't leave.

I'm sorry, he said. All those years.

We brought him Kleenex. He stopped crying and then started again. Finally he let go of the banister and we said goodbye. I had the feeling that we would never see him again. I remembered the story of him discovering Elf, sitting outside in the back lane behind the concert in her long black dress and army jacket, smoking, crushing her cigarette into the asphalt, only seventeen.

Let's not have forced gaiety this Christmas, said Nora, like it was a dish. We'll have a tiny bit of it, I said. I remembered Elf bashing her head against the bathroom wall that Christmas Day when we were young. I can't do it, she'd said.

Nic arrived late on a Thursday night. He looked thin. We were having our Christmas early so that Will and his new girlfriend Zoe could spend time with her family at a resort in Mexico and so that Nic could be with his family in Montreal.

Zoe travelled everywhere with her accordion. She had played us some sad but hilarious songs. The accordion is the best instrument for mournful occasions because it is melancholy and beautiful and cumbersome and ridiculous at the same time. She had a new tattoo which reminded me of the one I was trying to erase. I had forgotten about it and now it was only a bluish smudge on my shoulder like a mild bruise. Over dinner we talked about secrets. I told everyone how Elf had kept my secrets. She was a crypt. Then everyone looked at me as if to say oh yeah, like what secrets?

Over dessert, my mother told us a story. She said she had a secret too, and she might as well tell it. We were all intrigued. Me especially.

Are you going to tell me who my real father is? I asked.

Yeah right, she said. No, it's about a book. When my sister Tina was nineteen she was reading *For Whom the Bell Tolls*. One day I picked it up to have a look and she said oh no, you can't read that book, it's not for you. So I put it down.

How old were you? asked Nora.

Fifteen, same as you, said my mother. So one day, for some cockamamie reason, I was mad at Tina. Spitting mad, I don't know why. She wasn't at home that day and I saw her book lying on her bed and I took it and read the whole darn thing in one shot.

Wow, said Will, you really showed her.

I never told her, said my mother, but boy did that feel good. And wicked!

So what did you think of the book? asked Nic.

Oh, said my mother, I loved it! But I thought the sex was plain stupid.

Well, I said, you were only fifteen. (I glanced at Nora who made a face.)

We smiled. We ate our dessert.

Do you wish you'd told her? I asked.

Ha, said my mother. I wonder.

TWENTY

WILL AND ZOE HAD LEFT EARLY that morning for Mexico City and Nic for Montreal. Nora was Skyping with Anders who was back in Stockholm for the holidays. I was reading in my mother's living room, a book that Will had given me for Christmas called *Prison Notebooks*. I put it on the floor and got up to make a call to Julie in Winnipeg. My mother was making odd noises. She lay on the couch close to the tree. Her breathing was different. It was shallow and she blew out of her mouth like an athlete after working out. She was dying. I called an ambulance and away we went to the hospital. Eventually they saved her life again by pounding on her chest and shooting her up with nitroglycerine and other strong chemicals that would blast through her recalcitrant veins and ease her overworked heart.

Wow! she said. That's enough to jar your mother's preserves, she told the paramedics, and one of them made her repeat it twice so he could tell his friends.

It was all familiar to me, the gurneys in Emergency, but hers was a cardio case not a head case so there were no lectures from the staff, no righteous psych nurse demanding of her: why won't you behave? Nora came to the hospital. We sat on either side of my mother. She was lying behind a brown curtain, hooked up to machines and drips, sleeping. When she woke up she said, well this is a fine how do you do. Christmas Eve yet! She told us she had dreamt of Amelia Earhart.

The pilot? What about her? asked Nora. Did you solve the mystery of her disappearance in your dream? Then we'd be famous.

My mother said that in her dream a man had told her that Amelia Earhart was his favourite missing person. She cried just for a few seconds. She whispered that she was sorry, being here on Christmas, just like Elf had apologized to my uncle for being there in psych. We held her hands and told her meh, who cares, who cares. Nora told her we'd celebrate with the Ukrainians instead sometime in January.

Amy, our next-door neighbour, came by with a basket of food, wine, cloth napkins and beautiful china dishes and silver cutlery. We had our Christmas Eve dinner in Emergency with everything laid out on my mother's stomach. She was our table. She had always been our table. Nora carefully removed my mother's oxygen mask for a second so she could have a sip of her drink. The nurse had said one sip, because it's Christmas, but my mother had two sips. Big ones. We drank champagne out of plastic sample cups and toasted once again to a straying notion of ourselves and to the lenient nurse who came around and smiled and to Elf and to my father and to my aunt Tina and to my cousin Leni. We sang "I Wonder as I Wander," my mother's favourite Christmas song.

Nora and I stayed late until my mother had fallen asleep for the night and then we went home. I stood on the second floor balcony in the night and watched it snow into the moat.

The next day I went to see my mother at the hospital. She had made friends already, she had been spooling out amusing anecdotes from behind her brown curtain for the benefit of her fellow patients, and Santa Claus apparently had made his rounds too. My mother was always dying, at least once a year. She's worked a lot of emergency rooms like a stand-up comedian on tour, from Puerto Vallarta to Cairo to Winnipeg to Tucson to Toronto.

Move all the stuff off that chair, she said, and sit beside me. She laid her whodunit on her chest carefully face down and open so she wouldn't lose her place. There's something I want to tell you, she said. She held my hand. Her hand was warm, her grip was strong, like Tina's.

I already know, I said. That you love me, that I bring you so much joy.

No, she said, I want to tell you something else.

It was Christmas Day. I phoned Julie. Merry Christmas, I said.

Merry Christmas to you too, she said.

It was the first time in both of our lives that we were alone on Christmas Day. We said really? Is that true? It was true. Her kids were with her ex, their father, and Will was with his girl-friend's family in Mexico and Nora was at Dan's place. He had finally returned from Borneo. And my mother was in the hospi-tal. Should we drink together over the phone? she asked.

And suffer its deleterious effects? I said. I was quoting our old Sunday school teacher, Mrs. Skull. She had prayed, espe-cially for Julie and me, that we would come to our senses and stop partying in the bushes with French boys. We couldn't stop. It was too good. We wouldn't stop! Our old Sunday school teacher told us that she loved us but that God loved us more. We told her to try harder. She told us that sinful women adorn their bodies and not their souls. Should we go naked? Julie had asked. When she left the room for Kleenex, Julie and I escaped out the fire exit. The last step on the ladder was still two storeys up from the ground and we had to jump the rest of the way down. We loved the way our soles hurt afterwards.

We sat in our living rooms drinking Scotch and talking and listening. Here's to something, this panoply, I said. Yes, said Julie, this cock-eyed carousel. We lifted our glasses and tapped them against our phones. You're the strongest person I know, I said. I didn't tell her that I thought she had the right stuff to kill herself. I was trying to retrain my beliefs and change my template for success.

Is everything unbearable? she asked.

Nope, I said. What are we doing right now?

Well, that's true, she said.

Whose birthday is it again? I asked.

That hippie kid, she said.

Looks like we weren't invited to his party this year, I said. We agreed we wouldn't have gone anyway. We should become Jewish.

Remember that guy outside the 7-Eleven on Corydon? she asked me.

Allan, I said. (Allan was a brilliant cellist once, on the verge of becoming a prodigy and going to Juilliard, and then he smashed his head on the dash of his car when it hit a cement truck on black ice and now he stands alone outside the 7-Eleven on Corydon asking people really politely for change. He's still handsome. He seems sort of hollowed out but his eyes are really bright, the whites really white and the blues really blue, like Greek islands. He mumbles words and sometimes it seems like he's laughing at everything like he's just been thrown a surprise party. We don't know who takes care of him.)

I dreamt I slept with him, said Julie. And I offered to be his girlfriend, she said. And take him home with me and take care of him but he didn't want to. He was really sweet and was trying not to hurt my feelings. He showed me his blisters from the cello strings that would never go away. He asked me if he could borrow a pair of warm mittens though, that was all he wanted.

Did you feel rejected? I asked.

Yeah, she said, a bit. I wanted to comb his hair for him too, it was so tangled. And wash him.

Julie and I talked for hours and hours through the night until Boxing Day. We were really happy when Christmas was over. Then we really had something to toast.

———

May 3rd, 2011

Dear Elf,

Auntie Tina once told me that I'd be walking down the street one day and suddenly feel a lightness come over me, a feeling like I could walk forever, some magical strength, and that would mean I was being forgiven. I wish I had taken you to Zurich. I'm sorry. Auntie Tina said one day I'd be flying and not even know it.

Did I tell you about the hospital stuff with mom? I think I already did. She's fine now, again, for a while. I had an embarrassing moment in the hospital that I haven't told anybody about. At one point in Emergency mom grabbed my hand—you know the way she does, how it's actually almost painful like she's a Mafia don pretending to be nice—and said she had something to tell me. I figured for sure it would be what she always tells us when she's dying in Emergency, that she loves me, that I've brought her so much happiness and all that, but instead she whispered to me that I had to stop getting drunk and phoning the hospital in Winnipeg. She told me that she had tracked my activities—it's all her years and years of reading whodunits finally paying off—and she realized I was going out in the early evening to Wino Town, or whatever the liquor stores are called here, and buying myself a bag of booze and coming home and drinking alone and listening to Neil Young songs that remind me of you and working myself into a parox-ysm of grief and rage and then pranking the hospital in Winnipeg by calling them and asking if I can speak to you and then acting all incredulous when they tell me that you're not there.

She held my hand really tightly the whole time and she locked her eyes to mine so I couldn't escape, and I felt so ashamed and weak and stupid and crazy. And I started crying and nodding and saying I know, I have to stop, I'm so sorry. And I cried and cried. She didn't actually know what I had said to the hospital just that she knew I was calling them on a regular basis because she was opening the phone bills and looking at all the Manitoba numbers—this is the problem of living with your mother, Elf, another problem you will never encounter—and then she just put all the pieces together. She asked me if I was trying to haunt the hospital which I thought was an interesting way of putting it, and I told her I didn't know what I was doing, that it didn't matter, that I was sorry, that I would stop. Then even though she was the one dying and all hooked up to different cables and power cords and things she pulled me into her massive bear hug and rocked me like a baby from her horizontal position in her little white bed and I was kind of hunched over her sobbing while my bag kept falling off my shoulder. She had her arms around me. I pretended she was you and dad and Leni and even Dan, all the people I've lost along the way, and then she whispered things to me, all about love, about kindness, and optimism and strength. And about you. About our family.

How we can all fight really hard, but how we can also acknowledge defeat and stop fighting and call a spade a spade. I asked her what we do when a spade isn't a spade and she told me that sometimes there are things like that in life, spades that aren't spades, and that we can leave them that way. I told her but I'm a writer, it's hard for me to leave those spades so undefined, and she said she understood, she liked mysteries to be solved too, God knows, and words to be attached to feelings. She tapped her whodunit, the one lying on her chest, the one protecting her heart, that somehow with all this hugging hadn't moved an inch. She told me that the brain is built to forget things as we continue to live, that memories are meant to fade and disintegrate, that skin, so protective in the beginning because it has to be to protect our organs, sags eventually—because the organs aren't so hot anymore either—and sharp edges become blunt, that the pain of letting go of grief is just as painful or even more painful than the grief itself. It means goodbye, it means going to Rotterdam when you weren't expecting to and having no way of telling anyone you won't be back for a while.

Well, I've stopped pranking the hospital, you'll be relieved to know. Remember that time I thought it would be a real kick-ass idea to go to school with some of mom's pantyhose pulled over my face and you quietly whispered into my ear on your way out of the house: Swivelhead, attempt to be cool. You have no idea how often I evoke those words. Essentially, it's what mom was trying to tell me in the hospital.

So she recovered, as she does, and to celebrate she and Nora and I took a trip to NYC to see Will and Zoe. They took us to MOMA, to a show where everyone was naked and in pain. It was the Marina Abramović

show. It was the talk of the town. All of us gallery-goers
huddled in one room wondering how we'd get to the
next one. There was only a narrow doorway that we had
to pass through, but there were two suffering, naked
people standing face to face in the doorway so we would
all have to take turns squishing up against them as we
went through. Nobody made a move to go through the
doorway. The kids and I had lost track of mom when she
was wandering around looking at things. We were whispering about certain celebrities we saw in the room. Nora
knew them all, they were fashion designers and actors, but
the rest of us were clueless. All the people were clustered
together getting restless, and murmuring and wanting to
move to the next room but wondering how to get through
the door. Then Will said hey, there's grandma, and we
looked towards the narrow doorway where the naked man
and woman stood facing each other. Nobody had gone
through it yet. Then we saw mom in her purple cords
and windbreaker standing at the doorway with her hands
on her hips. Oh my god, said Nora, she's going through.
She went sideways through the doorway and her stomach
grazed the man's penis. Then she stopped in the middle,
right there between the man and the woman, she didn't
hurry through at all, she was savouring it. She looked up at
the naked man's face, into his eyes, he was expressionless,
and she smiled at him and nodded. She was greeting him,
politely. Then she somehow turned around in that tight
space to face the woman and she looked into her eyes too
and smiled and nodded and then she smiled back at all of
us huddled in the first room as if to say all right, people,

let's go, follow me, and she stepped through and one by one the rest of us followed her.

On our last day in NYC mom took us all out for a giant steak at a place in Brooklyn, close to where Will and Zoe live. It was late and dark when we left the steakhouse. We walked along the streets singing. We tried to remember all the things the mother is going to do for her crying baby in the mockingbird song. We finally remembered them all. Nora and mom and I linked arms and Nora sang a Weepies song called "Somebody Loved." Will carried Zoe on his back and zoomed around on the sidewalk and she laughed and bounced up and down and lost one of her flip-flops so we had to go back and retrace our steps in the dark which I suppose is the meaning of life.

Sometimes train whistles break through the silence of the day. Those dissonant chords that remind me of your mournful pounding on the keys when I screwed up my page-turning duties. Wait for the last measure, Dodo Brain! There are tracks close to our house. Sometimes I can hear the wheels rumbling on the rails. Sometimes I can feel the ground shake. It's comforting. It's a greeting or a proper goodbye. Mom would approve. You know how she is about hello and goodbye.

Remember our neighbour Mrs. Steingart (the one you renamed Signora Giovanna) standing in the middle of our living room with her hands on her hips, glaring at mom for not being a good-enough housekeeper and dad for not being enough of a man and us for not being normal-enough children and how we were all lying, sitting, slumping with books in our hands, utterly oblivious to her admonishments, and she stomped off home saying we were only word people, we were a word family, one day we'd have to open our eyes. To what? A messy house? Now I remember her parting shot. Words won't feed the admiral's cat! It did give me pause, I may have looked up from my book, but only because of the words she'd used to compose her threat and not the threat itself.

Remember the way mom used to swim beyond the wake and bob along to god knows where, the deep and choppy sea, until someone noticed and came to her rescue? What do words mean, Elf? Everything or nothing? They can't just mean *something*. By the way, I finally checked out your beloved D. H. Lawrence. Remember when you expressed incredulity at my not having read *Lady Chatterley's Lover*? God, you're a snob sometimes. Well, I read it. And yeah, the sex was hot. I'd find time in my busy schedule of needlepoint and flower arranging to visit that guy in the woods too. I wonder if Frieda wrote those parts for D. H. and then just had to keep her mouth shut while he racked up the fame and lived in fancy hotels in France with hippie girls. Anyway, you're right about the first paragraph. I want someone to project it on the front of my house in giant letters made of light and shadows. And if they flickered a bit, that would be the best. And of course they'd disappear in the sunshine because everything does. And that would be perfect.

"Ours is essentially a tragic age, so we refuse to take it tragically. The cataclysm has happened, we are among the ruins, we start to build up new little habitats, to have new little hopes. It is rather hard work: there is now no smooth road into the future: but we go round, or scramble over the obstacles. We've got to live, no matter how many skies have fallen."

And thanks for keeping all my secrets. Remember that midnight cavalcade I led through the wilderness to get to the boys' camp? You are now the official keeper of my secrets.

You knew I didn't have the guts to take you to Zurich, didn't you? And you knew you weren't coming to Toronto.

I love you, Elf, I have to go. I have to trim the bushes that are engulfing our backyard. It's so overgrown now that to get to the back lane we have to slither through this jungle on our stomachs with our rifles held high above our heads and this is not an easy thing for mom to do every day before she makes her rounds on Queen West.

Arrivederci, Bella Elf!

p.s. I've met a guy. We walk around and around the city talking and having late night Ping-Pong games and the first thing he told me about himself was how he'd been caught suddenly in crossfire in New Jersey. He'd been shot, wrong place at the wrong time, and he died in the ambulance and came back to life in the hospital, then died again, then finally came back to life for good but had to remain naked in an ice pack for two weeks until his heart was ready to start again. He walks me home every Wednesday night and kisses me on the cheek twice

before he says good night because he used to live in Paris.
Sometimes when we play tennis he jumps over the net
and runs to kiss me, too. He has tinnitus which means his
head is always humming. He also has an enlarged aorta.
He writes his dreams down on his laptop first thing in the
morning with a pillow over his head. It's springtime now,
I guess. Mom is at the stove stirring rib sauce and reading
Raymond Chandler's *The Long Goodbye*. Julie called and
I put her on speaker so mom could hear her too. How
are things? I asked her. She told us that Winnipeg was so
green now, the entire province. All of Manitoba just unbelievably green. Do you remember? And do you remember
the light? And the warmth? And I told her yeah, I could
almost picture that. Almost? she said. No, I said, I can.
I see it. How it's so green? she said. I had to think for a
second or two. I closed my eyes. Yeah, I said, I know. It's
an amazing green. I remember now.

Elf and I were on a plane. We were choosing chicken or beef, we'd
forgotten to pre-order a vegetarian meal for Elf, and we were
drinking wine out of little bottles and reading our horoscopes to
each other from an old issue of *People*. She was wearing a striped
raincoat, I think it was a Marc Jacobs, and high black boots. I
wore Converse high-tops and a new short poncho. When I put
the poncho on to show Elf she said farewell to arms. Well, we'd
taken our jackets and ponchos off for the flight and put them
in the overhead bin. Elf wore jeans that were oxblood, so the
label said, a really dark red. And mine were ordinary blue and a
little bit faded. Elf was tired and put her head on my shoulder

and slept for most of the flight and I read. I didn't really read but I tried to. It felt good to have Elf's head on my shoulder. It was heavy. Her hair smelled like a grapefruit. The book I was reading or trying to read was a self-published genealogy of a Russian family from the Odessa region. When the plane landed we were in Zurich.

Elf woke up and smiled sleepily and I said we're here. She asked me how the book had been and I said well, detailed and full of names that only she would know how to pronounce. We took a cab to our hotel and put our stuff into the room and then walked a few blocks to a really nice restaurant that the woman at the front desk of the hotel had recommended. Before we went into the restaurant we took pictures of each other standing on a bridge. We asked a man walking past if he would take one of us together and he took three or four just to make sure we'd have a good one. He asked us if we were there on a holiday. We told him we were sisters.

At dinner Elf told me stories about her trips to Europe, when she was a young prodigy. I told her some of mine. At first we laughed a lot, sort of nervously, but eventually we both relaxed and only laughed when things were funny. I ate a lot. I kept ordering new dishes. Elf didn't eat as much but she liked the warm bread they kept bringing to us in a wooden basket. I remember apologizing to her for having dirty fingernails and she said it was no problem and besides I'd been working really hard lately. When she said that I cried a bit and she came around from her side of the table and gave me a hug. Some people in the restaurant looked at us hugging and smiled.

I ordered another dessert and coffee. Eventually they told us the restaurant was closing. We walked slowly back to the hotel arm in arm like old-fashioned girls and lay down together in the huge white bed.

Remember when we watched that solar eclipse? I asked her. You came to my school and dragged me out of Gunner's English class to watch it with you.

Yes, she said. It was so cold.

Well, it was winter and we were lying in snow. In a field.

Wearing welding helmets, she said, weren't we?

Yeah. Where did you get them from?

I can't remember. I guess some guy I knew in town.

Wasn't it amazing? I asked her.

The eclipse? It really was, she said. The path of totality.

What? I said. Is that what it's called?

Yeah, remember what dad said? She dropped her voice. The path of totality passed over Manitoba in the early afternoon.

Oh right, you mean when he said it in that super serious tone? It was so funny. She laughed.

The next one's not supposed to be for another fifteen hundred years or something like that, I said.

Then I guess I'll miss it, said Elf.

Yeah, I guess I will too.

Maybe not, said Elf. Who knows?

There was a skylight over our bed and we could see stars. Elfie took my hand. She put it on her heart and I felt its strong and steady beat. We had an early appointment the next morning. Elf said it was like getting married or writing an exam.

It's torture to have to wait all day, she said. Let's just get up, shower, and go.

END

ACKNOWLEDGEMENTS

With regards to the writing of *AMPS*, I'm deeply grateful to my agent, Sarah Chalfant, and to my editor, Louise Dennys: serious pros. Whoah. To my oldest friends, Carol Loewen and Jacque Baskier, who continue to save my life and who will find this "acknowledgement" ridiculous. (And to Winnipeg, city of my dreams.) To my Toronto friends for rolling out the welcome mat. To the Rutherfords for their collective embrace! To my kids (you all know who you are—there aren't any others, don't worry, ha) who simply will not stop calling me on my bullshit. To my mother, Elvira Toews, Life Force! To Erik Rutherford for his sharp pencil, countless readings, and especially for his blind love. And finally, to my beautiful sister, Marjorie Anne Toews: comic genius, badly missed.

Miriam Toews is the author of six bestselling novels: *Summer of My Amazing Luck*, *A Boy of Good Breeding*, *A Complicated Kindness* (Canada Reads 2006, Canada Reads Canadian Bestseller of the Decade 2010), *The Flying Troutmans*, *Irma Voth* and *All My Puny Sorrows*, and one work of non-fiction, *Swing Low: A Life*. She is a winner of the Governor General's Literary Award for Fiction, the CBA Libris Award for Fiction Book of the Year, the Rogers Writers' Trust Fiction Prize and the Writers' Trust Marian Engel/Timothy Findley Award. She lives in Toronto.